NOTHING DO

SCARLETT FINN

ISBN: 9781914517648

www.scarlettfinn.com

Also by Scarlett Finn

GO NOVELS
GO WITH IT
GO IT ALONE
GO ALL OUT
GO ALL IN
GO FULL CIRCLE

EXILE
HIDE & SEEK
KISS CHASE

WRECK & RUIN
RUIN ME
RUIN HIM

THE BRANDED SERIES
BRANDED
SCARRED
MARKED

FORBIDDEN PREQUEL DUET
ALL. ONLY.
ONLY YOURS

THE FORBIDDEN NOVELS
FORBIDDEN DESIRE
FORBIDDEN WANT
FORBIDDEN WISH
FORBIDDEN NEED
FORBIDDEN BOND

BOMBSHELLS & BILLIONAIRES (ROXIVERSE)
NOTHING TO HIDE
NOTHING TO LOSE
NOTHING IN BETWEEN: ONE
NOTHING TO DECLARE
NOTHING TO US
NOTHING IN BETWEEN: TWO
NOTHING TO SAY
NOTHING TO GAIN
NOTHING IN BETWEEN: THREE
NOTHING TO YOU
NOTHING TO THIS PREQUEL: ONE WILD NIGHT
NOTHING TO THIS
NOTHING IN BETWEEN: FOUR
NOTHING TO DO
NOTHING TO NO ONE
NOTHING TO FEAR
NOTHING TO DENY
NOTHING TO BEAT
NOTHING TO THE WEDDING
NOTHING TO TELL
NOTHING TO IT
NOTHING TO SEE
NOTHING TO WIN
NOTHING TO OFFER
NOTHING TO PROVE

LOVE AGAINST THE ODDS STANDALONE COLLECTION
SWEET SEAS
HEIR'S AFFAIR
RESCUED
MAESTRO'S MUSE
GETTING TRICKY
THIRTEEN
REMEMBER WHEN...
RELUCTANT SUSPICION
XY FACTOR

KINDRED SERIES
RAVEN
SWALLOW
CUCKOO
SWIFT
FALCON
FINCH

MISTAKE DUET
MISTAKE ME NOT
SLEIGHT MISTAKE

LOST & FOUND
LOST
FOUND

THE EXPLICIT SERIES
EXPLICIT INSTRUCTION
EXPLICIT DETAIL
EXPLICIT MEMORY

TO DIE FOR...
TO DIE FOR TRUTH
TO DIE FOR HONOR
TO DIE FOR VIRTUE
TO DIE FOR DUTY
TO DIE FOR LOVE

RISQUÉ & HARROW INTERTWINED
TAKE A RISK
FIGHTING FATE
RISK IT ALL
FIGHTING BACK
GAME OF RISK

ONE

THE WARMTH OF THE Pacific sun, sea salt in the air, yep, vacation was upon them. Okay, so it hadn't been high on her agenda that year, or, well, ever, but she and her sister had arrived.

"A tropical paradise!" Alessia exclaimed. "I told you. Didn't I, Thea? Didn't I tell you?"

Right on the beach, the first-floor deck ran the length of the hotel. Ten rooms, maybe twelve, side-by-side with only a strip of green and a few palm trees framing the sand and sea on their doorstep.

The Florin sisters weren't used to the vast blue ocean or breathing such fragrant air. Her eyes closed. Seduced by the beauty and atmosphere, her imagination couldn't help but get carried away.

"Thea!" Alessia grabbed her arm to shake her. "I told you!"

She smiled. "Yes, you did."

In many ways, she and her sister were complete opposites. The vacation hadn't been her idea. In fact their mother's insistence she join Alessia was the only reason for her presence. Uh huh, weird to be chaperoning her full-grown sister? Maybe. Given the catalyst for the trip, their mom's apprehension was natural. But, seriously, did it have to be her? The question was kind of rhetorical. Alessia had plenty of friends, most of them as crazy and gregarious as her. So someone may wonder, why hadn't she brought them along instead?

The answer to that question was revealing in itself.

Best to start at the beginning. Cliché but necessary. Alessia won the tickets through an online contest. And the vacation wasn't the only prize. No. Thirty days on a private island south of Hawaii was just the beginning.

"Meet Roman Lowe!" Some Hollywood star Alessia was beside herself about meeting was the real prize. Never mind that the only reason she'd even heard of the guy was his negative image in the press. Fights. Drugs. Dramatic episodes. God only knew what the next thirty days would hold.

Okay, so, yeah, this Roman guy was supposed to have cleaned up his act. "Supposed to" wasn't exactly money in the bank. The purpose of this stunt had to be rebuilding the actor's image. Would it go off without a hitch? If anything went wrong, her little sister could have her heart broken and need support. Hence why their mother demanded she be Alessia's plus one.

For a decent spell, this Roman guy's reputation bumped from one mishap to another, blow after blow. Her awareness of that was significant given she spent about as much time reading celebrity news as someone without a yacht would spend at a marina. The details were hazy. Run ins with law enforcement, substance abuse issues, and various high-profile fall outs with his girlfriend, the glittering beauty Sway Sheridan, dominated the entertainment headlines. According to what Alessia told her on the plane anyway.

The real prize lay before her. Until witnessing it, she hadn't known the environment would be so renewing. Curling her fingers around the deck rail, she arched into her breathing. Beyond the vast ocean, someone, somewhere, could be looking right back.

The island felt a million miles from anywhere.

Felt, but it wasn't.

After a flight to LA and a night in a hotel, they'd boarded a plane to Honolulu, then another, small, private luxurious plane filled with other competition winners.

Ten, apparently, each with one companion.

That they were all female wasn't much of a surprise.

Roman Lowe's incredible physique had been a popular topic of conversation, and his charm, his talent, his love of the ladies. Yadda, yadda… The excitement passed her by, but she was happy to see Alessia happy.

Sway Sheridan, Roman's girlfriend, if she was still his girlfriend, came up more than once too. Were they still together? Was he single? Would his rockstar brother make an appearance? Maybe they could share. As long as talk stayed talk, the frenzy could pass her by.

On finally making it to the island, a bunch of glorified golf carts transported them to check-in. To cocktails and flowers, promises they'd have the trip of a lifetime. So far, so good.

The main building was just a couple of floors high, surrounded by a tranquil pool, crisscrossed by wooden walkways. One of the paths led to a separate structure where the rooms lined up together.

With lots of pale wood and fabric, maximizing their natural environment must've been a conscious choice. And what an amazing one.

Tearing herself away from the aroma of flora and the beckoning surf, she went back inside through the sliding door. A double width square arch displayed Alessia's adjoining room, a mirror image of hers.

Busy, Alessia spread clothes from her suitcase on the bed. "What do you think I should wear tomorrow?"

"Tomorrow?" she asked. "Today isn't over."

"They said we were eating in the dining room tonight. Just us. The competition people. We don't meet him until tomorrow."

Going to admire the delicate fabric draped across the bed, her sister's excitement was palpable.

She swayed sideways to bump Alessia's hip with hers. "Like you haven't already picked out exactly which outfit you want to wear."

Alessia's grin glittered. "I went through about fifty different combinations. I really don't know… I keep second-guessing myself."

"The light is different here."

"Mm. Yeah!" Excitement burst from her sister. "Yeah, uh huh, it so is!"

"Why don't you try some on?" The suggestion gave Alessia the excuse she wanted. "They said we had an hour before dinner."

All her life, she'd admired her sister playing dress-up, trying on this outfit and that. Their minds were different, they viewed things in different ways, but when it came to supporting her sister, Thea did everything she could, with the little things and the big, and always would.

TWO

DINNER WAS WONDERFUL. In a curved dining room, a circle of water beneath and glass ceiling above allowed them to witness the light fading from the sky. Delicious food, gracious staff, beautiful environment, tick, tick, tick.

The mood was high and why wouldn't it be? By design, the prize winners shared a passion. One they were eager to gush about. Here and there, spirits were tainted by the occasional glimpse of women circling, assessing, inspecting. Did they see each other as competition? Even the companions brought along for the ride threw an elbow here and there. Some were flat excited, others subdued. This would be an interesting month.

After food, music started. In true Alessia style, she'd already found herself a clique. They'd been huddled at the bar for the last half hour. Though relieved probably wasn't the right word, pressure eased from her shoulders. She went to her sister's side and rested a hand on her back to get her attention.

"Oh! Thea," Alessia said, hooking an arm around her to bring her into the group. "Meet my people, this is Keri, Lark, Alana, and… Francesca!" Her sister sucked in a big breath. "Girls, this is my sister, Thea."

She'd never remember those names. "It's great to meet you all."

"Let's get you a drink!" Alessia exclaimed.

"No," she said, intercepting her sister's arm before it could get the bartender's attention. "Thank you for the offer. I'm tired… I'm going back to the room."

Alessia didn't hide her disappointment. "Oh no, please stay. Stay and party with us."

"Thank you." A smile would settle any offense, that was the idea anyway. "I appreciate the offer. We're here for a month, I'll catch up with everyone in the morning." She kissed Alessia's cheek. "Be good, little sister."

At home, leaving Alessia alone in a bar would be unthinkable. Being on a private island put her mind at ease. The only guys around were staff and none of them had been inappropriate. Their room wasn't a city away either. If something happened, she could be with her sister in minutes.

Strolling out of the dining room, she crossed the ring of water without seeing another soul. Tiredness wasn't the only reason for retiring. The noise and atmosphere were great, for Alessia and the like. In contrast, the beach was the only thing on her mind.

Okay, being there for her sister didn't require embracing the vacation part of the equation. Not that it actually was a vacation; her boss, Anika, enjoyed reminding her of that. Like the show, work must go on. She couldn't complain. What kind of job would allow anyone to duck out for a month straight? Not many. Her work could be done remotely, and that was exactly her plan. Sort of.

Since standing on the deck earlier, one urge tickled her consciousness. Embracing it, she kicked off her shoes at the end of her bed and kept on going to slide back the glass to the deck. Instead of going to the barrier that held her back earlier, she descended the smooth wooden steps to the beach.

Sinking her toes into the sand, she stopped, wiggling them deeper. The gentle crash of the mighty ocean worked the knots from her shoulders. Something about it invigorated her while at the same time grounding her. The ebb and flow suggested the great blue was in a good mood, a welcoming mood. Lethal as it could be, that night, right then, it received her in friendship. The coast was one of her favorite places; the ocean was something different to what she got at home.

Its vastness. Its foreverness. Excited by the senses overload, she scampered toward the waves, like a child released from the constraints of civility. The tickle of water on her toes tempted her deeper. She wasn't nuts enough to swim in the black void rippling beneath the moonlight. It just went on and on. Possibilities were endless. With the sea at her ankles, she walked through the surf, parallel to the beach.

The water's massiveness put her insignificance into perspective. So much about life was unknown; anything could happen any time. Were they in control of their own fates? If this ocean decided to take her, there were only so many ways she could fight back or escape.

Optimism was a battle some days. In the city, surrounded by the rush and stress of everyday problems, concentrating wasn't always easy. One thing kept her going: the unexpected. Every day was an adventure, if she stayed open to possibilities. No one knew what was right around the corner. If the worst happened, she'd face it head on. And something good was always welcome, especially if it was a surprise. A good surprise.

Like the ocean.

Being out there, in a remote corner of the world few people knew existed, excited her. Unexpectedly. Vacations had never featured in her life, as a kid or an adult. For the first time, she got it, how refreshing it could be to split from the day-to-day humdrum. Work wasn't gone, she'd still have to clock in, as it were, but doing it there wouldn't be the same as in the office.

People in the wider world rushed around, worrying about their lives, about deadlines and appointments, about hitting targets. On the island, she could breathe without all that. Concerns about parents or colleagues washed away in the surf. Even her boss's demands seemed a world away.

Night on the beach didn't scare her. Not out there. No one could hurt her. There was no one to try. How long had she been walking? It wouldn't be a great idea to go too far. Was that a light up ahead? In the trees a ways away? Continuing, she kept an eye on it. The brightness cut through the trees, flashing as each leaf and trunk swayed, covering and revealing it depending on the breeze.

Hmm… what could it be? Closer, the water became less interesting as curiosity grew. The hotel was gone. When she glanced back, the lights of it were lost to the curve of the coast. There was a faint glow, but no building.

The light in the trees was too far from the hotel to be part of that main structure. Maybe employees lived somewhere around there. Details were difficult to pick out in the dark. Whatever it was attached to couldn't be large, there was only one light.

With twenty guests arriving, rooms to service and meals to serve, how many staff members would a place like that need? Could five handle it? Ten?

"He's not here."

The male voice stopped her dead. Uh… Scanning the beach, looking for its owner, she came up short. Where the hell did it come from? Moonlight aided her walk but neglected to highlight any signs of a person on the sand. Maybe looking into the light for so long had messed with her eyes.

"You shouldn't walk so far at night."

Again, the voice, and closer. Except it didn't sound like… Whipping around, she zeroed in on him striding from the waves. Whoa, boy, nothing wrong with her eyesight. Damn, that was a body, a cut body more impressive than any she'd seen in real life. The lines of his form were so mesmerizing that he was practically upon her before she even thought to look at his face.

"I… *You're* out here," she said, giving herself a mental slap. "Why shouldn't *I* be out here too?"

He stopped. The previous purpose in his gait and trajectory suggested he'd intended to carry on up the beach. Her words changed that plan. Maybe fifteen feet in front of her, a little deeper in the waves, his attention cut to her. With his back to the moon, she couldn't decipher his expression. He was tall. She liked tall men, always had. Though that was a totally inappropriate thought; one that completely shifted her perspective.

The seductive island just delivered this random guy from the surf like driftwood, as though he was some kind of offering to her agitated hormones.

"I have permission to be here," he said. "Do you?"

"I didn't know I needed it."

"So you thought you'd go wandering and just happen to run into him?" he asked, exhaling a sneer of pity. "Sorry to tell you, he's not here."

"You keep saying 'he' and I have no idea who you're talking about."

"Yeah, right."

"Hey," she said, kicking at the waves. "Don't dismiss me. Do you know how disrespectful that is? You've made an accusation, either back it up or apologize."

"Excuse me?"

"You heard me. I was having a perfect evening until you rudely interrupted with your assumption. I am here because I like listening to the waves and spending time with my own thoughts. I shouldn't have to justify myself to you; I don't have to justify myself to anyone. Am I doing something illegal?"

There was a long pause before he answered. "No."

"Am I being offensive or unruly? Causing mayhem or harm?"

Another long pause and a more incredulous answer. "No, but—"

"The polite thing would be to go about your business and leave me to mine. Or if you couldn't help yourself, say good evening or ask if I need assistance, don't bark at me."

"I—"

"How would you feel if I assumed your business or interrupted you without invitation or respect? You wouldn't like it, I'll bet. No one likes it."

"Damn you're scrappy."

"Why does a woman asserting herself need a label?" she asked. "Can't I just be right?"

"Uh…"

"It doesn't matter," she said on a sigh. "You've ruined it now. My bubble burst."

Spinning around, she went back the way she'd come. The hotel would appear eventually. The spell had broken, for the night at least. The driftwood dude might be right that she was in the wrong place or even that she wasn't allowed to be there. That didn't mean he had any right to be rude.

Whoever he was, employee or supervisor, it didn't matter. Even if she had intruded on him, it had been accidental. He could've gone about his business and ignored her. She would've been out of his way just a few seconds later.

The island had her. Its people still had a way to go.

THREE

EVERYONE WAS ON high alert the next morning at breakfast. It was the day. *The* day the competition winners would meet their prize. For them, the island was secondary to the man, as revealed by Alessia's agitation and that of the others at the breakfast buffet too.

"Sit still," Thea said, reaching over to lay a hand on her sister's wrist.

Alessia's posse from the bar the previous night had joined them. They were as twitchy as her younger sister.

"This is so exciting!" Alana exclaimed so loud that she drew the attention of other tables. "I can't believe it's real."

Thea smiled. Just like Alessia, the other women were in their early twenties. Their over-the-top enthusiasm was sweet. Being so aroused by anticipation was usually reserved for children. In her opinion, every excuse to let loose and embrace happiness should be snatched with both hands.

Lark leaned in and lowered her voice. "You

know what I can't get over?" The women slanted closer, bubbling with anticipation. "He's somewhere close by. He's actually on the island right now, he has to be."

"I can't believe it," Alana said. "I still can't…" She laid both hands on her chest. "God, I think I might die."

Before they could say more about their joy, a woman came in, clutching a leather binder to her chest. "Hello, everyone!"

Screams, followed by hushes, went around the room as the prize-winners reacted to this incremental progress. A few people said hello back, they weren't quite a cohesive group, maybe because they were so overwrought.

"My name is Mieux, I'm Roman's coordinator for this event." A holler of approval rose, and the woman laughed. Yeah, that was her feeling too only she kept hers in for Alessia's sake. It was like being on a rollercoaster ride without experiencing it while everyone else went nuts. "I know!" Mieux raised a hand to silence them, though it took another few seconds for the crowd to calm down. "He's excited to meet all of you too. We have a few pieces of housekeeping to deal with before he joins us. But…" Mieux backed away. "No point being stuck inside when we're in such a beautiful location. If all of you will follow me, we'll take this outside!"

People scrambled to leave their seats. She was the only one who didn't move. Alessia was halfway up before she noticed and rebounded.

"You're not coming?" Alessia asked and tilted her head. "You want to work?"

She winced. "Do you mind? I'll come if you need me to."

Alessia grinned as Keri and Alana caught her arms.

"Come on!" Alana exclaimed. "We don't want to

be last."

"I'm good," Alessia said. "I know you won't enjoy it. I have my peeps." She pulled away from Keri and Alana to throw her arms around her sister to whisper in her ear. "Besides, while they have to share their time, I'll get to meet him alone."

She smacked a kiss on her cheek and grabbed for her new friends. The three of them hurried to catch up with the others pouring out the back. Alessia waved once more before disappearing through the doors that swung shut behind the rabble.

Ah, peace.

Picking up her juice, Thea finished up. She hadn't read the Roman itinerary too closely the previous day. Roman Lowe was probably a very interesting person and was renowned for his charm. However, knowing herself the way she did, she'd be aware of every second of work lost while meeting the stranger, and obsessing about how she might make it up.

Another set of doors opened, and a couple of servers came in. When they saw her, they hesitated.

She put down her glass. "Sorry. I'm finished."

Leaving her seat, she respected the schedules of others too. The staff would want to get the dining room cleaned before whatever they had to set up for next. The grand round room had to be used for other events. Even if it wasn't, lunch would be just around the corner.

Which reminded her of something else. On departing the dining room, she went to reception. No one was there. Hmm. What should she do? Most places had reception manned twenty-four hours, but this island was not a resort open to the world, not at that minute anyway.

She only had to loiter for a few seconds before a guy came hurrying out of a side room.

"Yes, ma'am, can I help you?" From the guy's

expression, she guessed he was torn between his customer relations training and sheer confusion. "You didn't want to join the group?"

"I have work to do," she said, laying her hands on the high desk. "I didn't see the Wi-Fi password anywhere and I can't get cell coverage."

"No, you won't get that here," he said, doing a terrible job of hiding his amusement.

She exhaled. "But you do have corporate facilities. I read it in your brochure last night."

Which she'd picked up when trying to check her emails and come up blank on how to access the internet.

He frowned. "Yes, we do, but…"

Her brows rose when he didn't continue. "But… what?"

"Well, they're not… serviced at the moment. We have a building on the north shore, but—"

"I can walk," she said. "If you give me directions."

"There are carts, but…"

Another but, a smile warmed her lips. "Is there a problem?"

"I… I don't know."

Poor guy hadn't expected this. Given the other activity on offer, her desire to work put her in the minority. She enjoyed what she did, most of the time. It wasn't easy, but she liked being thorough. Who didn't want to do things well?

"Guests aren't allowed… During their stay… Mr. Lowe's team are the only press allowed. It's an exclusive event."

Her mouth opened in understanding. "Let me assure you that I don't work for any media company. I also have never met Roman Lowe and am passing up that chance to get on with my day job." The guy didn't seem convinced. "To be honest, I'm more interested in receiving email than sending anything out. I shouldn't need to make calls." Though her boss would just love her being unreachable. "All I need to do is pick up my emails and pull a few things from my cloud… Can I do that?"

"I… don't know. I have to check with my supervisor."

"Okay." What the hell would she do if they denied her access? Her hard drive contained most of what she needed to get started, but the cloud documents would become necessary along the way. "How about I go grab my things and come back? That will give you the chance to talk to whoever you need to talk to."

And for her to come up with a few arguments if she had to push the issue. It wasn't like she could just leave. The plane that brought them didn't appear to belong to any commercial airline.

The guy relaxed a little and nodded. "Yes, that would be great. Thank you."

"No problem," she said, pushing away from the desk. "I'll just be a few minutes."

She returned to her room to retrieve her laptop and folders. Everything was in the same place in her closet. Killing some time, she sat down to undo the sandals rubbing at the back of her ankle and switched them out for slip-ons. Giving the guy a few extra moments, she reapplied her sunscreen, put some shimmer on her cheeks and swiped on a little gloss.

Earlier that morning, Alessia spent half an hour putting on makeup. Should she make more of an effort? All she'd done was smudge on a little gold eyeshadow. The preened women at breakfast were so glamorous it was difficult not to be aware of her hang-ups. Still, she didn't mind fading into the background when the others were so eager to be noticed.

When there was nothing else to do, she scooped her work things into an oversized beach-bag and grabbed her sunglasses and hat. If there was time at lunch, she might go for a walk on the beach or lounge in the sun a little. Should she put on a bikini beneath her clothes? No, then the temptation of the water would likely win out. If she wanted to swim later, she'd return to the room and change.

Back at the reception desk, she reconsidered that decision. If she was going to be away from her room to work, it would be nice to have the bikini as an option. The guy from earlier came scurrying out before she could progress beyond the contemplation stage.

"You have to sign these," he said, putting a stack of papers on the reception desk in front of her.

"What is it?" she asked, scanning the first sheet. "It's an NDA."

Thea answered her own question before he could. Glancing at his badge to check his name, she read *"Tom."* Her ex's name was Thom, pronounced the same, spelled differently. That was a shame for this Tom, she wasn't likely to forget him.

"Yes," he said. "Everyone else is signing them. It says you can't talk to anyone about anything that happens here. It includes electronic means too." His eyes rose like he was searching his thoughts. "Oh, and I was also told to remind you that the Wi-Fi can only be used at the corporate suite, and you'll be the only one on it other than our staff."

Reading between the lines, she smiled. "So if any secrets get out, you plan to blame me."

He shrugged. "Honestly, ma'am, I'm parroting what someone else said. Feel free to read the NDA and sign it at your leisure. Though anyone who doesn't sign will be transported off the island."

Did that mean their plane was still there? Interesting, but not really relevant. Not like she was a pilot or would be able to afford so much as the fuel costs, if the staff wanted to charge her for using it to leave.

The NDA seemed standard. Anywhere else, she'd send it to lawyer-ex Thom to check it out. This time, given she had no intention of spilling secrets to anyone and hadn't even met the big star, it didn't seem like a big deal to sign it.

The page underneath gave more cause for concern. "This is a release," she said. "Allowing you to use my image or words in marketing materials and/or press related to the event." Tom remained blank. She pushed the NDA back to him. "Keep this one. I need a day with the other one."

"Oh, I…" His color rose as he looked around. For whom? No one else was there. "I'll have to check."

She smiled and tucked the release into her beach bag. "You do that. I'll make my way to the corporate suite… Can you point me in the right direction?"

"There will be a cart waiting for you in the main lot," he said, picking up the NDA. "Without the release, I don't know if you can…"

Shame for this guy. Obviously a worrier, his day wasn't getting off to an easy start.

"I haven't met your big star. No one has taken my picture, and I haven't been asked anything. The release is irrelevant until any of that happens." He thought about it for a few seconds then seemed to calm down. "Okay? Can I go now?" He nodded. "Thank you."

The hotel faced the beach. The lot where they'd arrived in their carts was tucked in at the side of the building. It wouldn't do much for the view to have a big, ugly circle of concrete between the serene pools and lush greenery that separated their flagship building from the beach. She got it.

Tom was right. A cart awaited her outside, driver and all.

"Honi," he said, wearing a broad smile.

"Thea."

"Good to meet you, ma'am."

She sat down, and he got moving. There wasn't really time for small talk. Absorbing the sights and sounds of the tropical place required all her attention. Did people get used to living there? In the city, it was easy to forget the culture and significance of the environment when it was gray and dull, even in the sun, it all seemed dreary. It couldn't be the same there. Somewhere like that, so lush and green, it had to be a treat every minute.

The track to the corporate suite, at the north of the island, split off the same curving road they'd traveled from the airstrip. Maybe that same road ran around the whole island.

They stopped and she hopped out.

She should've been better prepared and fumbled around in her bag for her wallet. "Thank you."

"You're welcome."

With a wave, Honi drove off without waiting for a tip.

Huh.

Trees offered some welcome shade in her approach to the back of the corporate suite. At least, she guessed that's what the building was, Honi hadn't confirmed it.

Inside, stairs led up left and right from a small foyer. Straight ahead, one of two double doors was open. The view of the ocean beyond that room beckoned.

The crash of the waves lightened her soul. The broad room led out to some kind of wide terrace with loungers. A perfect place to work.

View in her sights, she headed through the doors to—the intrusion of another figure in her peripheral vision stopped her dead.

A person. She hadn't even considered someone

else might be there. Surprised, she stood there, saying nothing.

On his feet, behind a desk with shelves at his back, the guy mirrored her in silence and stance. Maybe he was waiting for an explanation; she had just walked in on him. Wearing board shorts and a casual button-down only partially buttoned over a tee-shirt, he wasn't like desk jockeys back home. But then, who would be comfortable in a suit or tie in that environment?

"Tom…" she started, pleased to have at least remembered how to talk. "At the desk…" Raising her fist, she jabbed a straight thumb toward the door. "In the hotel said I could…" Her thumb curled in as her forefinger sprang out. "I can go upstairs."

"You're the scrappy wanderer."

Confused, she blinked her wide eyes. "I'm… I'm what?"

"The beach last night… That was you."

What was he…? Oh wow. Took her a second, but yeah… Words failed her again. The guy in the surf last night. She'd paid more attention to his body because his features were difficult to pick out in the moonlight. Yeah, that was the reason. After he'd made the connection, she got it, his shape, the height, the breadth of his shoulders…

"You're… the driftwood…"

He smiled. Wow, damn, that was… unfair. Any animosity she held for the guy who'd startled her with his rudeness dwindled in the light of that killer smile.

"Carried in from the sea," he said, nodding. "Yeah, I guess it probably did look like that." What should she say? "I see now you were telling the truth."

She was ten steps behind. "About what?"

"Last night," he conceded. "I thought you were looking for Roman."

Oh, her mouth opened, exhaling understanding.

So Roman was the enigmatic "*he*" the driftwood referenced.

"Nope," she said, curling her fingers around the strap of her bag. "Sorry to disappoint."

"No, I'm not disappointed, just surprised."

"Because you're always right?" she asked, finishing the question with a smile, so it didn't come off too confrontational.

He breathed out a laugh. "It has been known… maybe once or twice." When he smiled, her own widened. "Why would you come all the way here if not for him?"

"He's a stranger. Why would I come here for him rather than someone I know?"

"He's a stranger to all of the winners, as far as I know, but they're here for him."

"Then I don't suppose his ego needs me," she said. "I came here because my sister is not worldly and I want to support her."

His eyes narrowed as he considered her for a few seconds. "Your sister?" She nodded. "Doesn't she have any friends?"

That made her laugh. "Alessia has a lot of friends, but each of them would be as interested in Roman Lowe." Tipping her head to the side, she crooked a brow. "I'm not competition."

"Ah," he said, apparently enjoying that revelation. "Why is that? You're married?"

"No," she said, shaking her head.

"Engaged? Involved?"

Again, a head shake. "No. Neither."

"So you're not competition because…"

He drew out the last word to prompt her.

"Because I have no interest in throwing myself at a stranger. Because money, for me, doesn't equal happiness. Because the idea of being plastered across the television and internet is genuinely terrifying… Can you imagine that kind of scrutiny? I don't envy him it."

"Your sister doesn't mind any of that?"

She shrugged. "We're different. Doesn't mean we don't love and care for each other. So she's happy watching makeup tutorials and trying out different hairstyles? It doesn't mean she's not a good person, just that she values looking good and spending time with her friends."

"And you don't value those things?"

"I'm more… work-oriented… and much more interested in what a person says than how they look while they're saying it." His head bobbed like he was taking it in. "Anyway… Like I said, I can go upstairs."

"It's nicer down here," he said, stalling her before she could retreat. "Up there it's just boring boardrooms and uncomfortable furniture." He put down whatever he'd taken from the shelf and turned himself more toward the room. "Here we have couches inside and loungers on the terrace… Could probably even rustle you up a hammock, if you feel like working on the sand."

She laughed. "Thank you, but my sunscreen's supposed to be just in case rather than a challenge…"

"Then you should work here," he said, rounding the desk to come her way. "We got off on the wrong foot… We should start over." He offered her a hand. "Zane."

Sharing a workspace didn't bother her. She worked in an open-plan office most of the time anyway.

Sliding her hand into his, she shivered when his fingers closed around it. "Thea."

"Pleasure to meet you," he said. "Wanna get to work?"

She nodded. Having a colleague wouldn't be so bad. While he did his hotel business stuff, she could get to work on her project. Maybe they'd motivate each other. With the sun glittering off the ocean, it wouldn't be easy to resist temptation. If he was working, she'd be working, the setup would do just fine.

FOUR

ZANE LET HER WORK at the desk. He spread out on the opposite side of the room, where two couches faced a low table.

They worked with little interaction beyond the tip-tap of their keyboards. His preference was to work with his laptop on his legs. Sometimes his feet ended up on the table. He'd even been sitting on the floor for a while.

When she worked at home, she liked to spread out too. Usually on the floor or the bed. Building a new training course meant tying together a bunch of strands. Increasing intensity without scaring participants, making sure everything was covered, was a complicated process. One that required concentration.

"Lunch!" His exclamation startled her. Sitting on the far away couch, he stretched to flex his back. "Damn," he said. "Shouldn't have doubled my run this morning."

She frowned, breathing out as her head dropped to the side. "Was that a humblebrag?"

He laughed. "Could've been."

When he surged to his feet, she bowed back, an inhale catching in her throat. Even from twenty feet away that body was impressive.

"What are you in the mood for?" he asked.

Mmm… Loaded question given her current line of thinking.

Somewhat reluctantly, she dragged her mind from the gutter. "Work. I'm in the mood to work."

"Someone very smart, much smarter than me, taught me that breaks are important. If we don't take breaks, we lose perspective. We forget what's important… So what'll it be? Sushi?"

"Sushi?" she asked, perking up as her mind shifted gears.

Her interest put another smile on his face. He wasn't shy about showing his feelings.

"Absolutely. We've been sitting in here all morning. Why don't you go out and get some air? I'll arrange lunch."

"Maybe we should go back to the hotel. I don't see a kitchen anywhere around here."

And definitely no sushi, she'd have noticed that.

"Go back if you want, but I guarantee the servers have enough going on with Roman's entourage."

Good point and with Zane being staff, his colleagues wouldn't appreciate serving him in the dining room. As she was a guest, it was probably against some health and safety rule to let her eat in the kitchen.

"Okay, here is good," she said, slipping off her shoes and kicking them under the desk. "I'm going to breathe."

The doors to the terrace had been open all morning, teasing her with refreshing sea air and the whisper of waves. Just after one p.m. was a good time to give into temptation. Striding out, she opened her arms wide, and her head fell back. But she didn't slow down. Nope. How often did she have her lunchbreak in such a beautiful setting? The semi-circular terrace was surrounded by a broad waist-high wall. That was the obstacle holding her back from the beach.

The grass bank below was just a few feet wide and a clear path to the sand. On either side of her view, gray rocks extended into the water and trees hung low in the lush tropical forest surrounding them. It felt like the last place on Earth. The last paradise.

"You like the beach."

His voice, low and deep, rumbled like the distant waves out there on the horizon. It washed over her in a cleansing tide.

"I like forever," she said, curling her fingers around the far side of the terrace wall. "I like looking out there and imagining all that will be, all that could be… all that's ever been."

"That's a lot of imagining."

Spinning around, she caught the wall to jump up and sit on top of it. "These are the same waves people have looked out on for millennia. And these rocks we stand on? This land, it's lush and fertile, borne of volcanic commotion rooted deep beneath our feet. It doesn't blow your mind?"

He dropped down onto one of the outdoor sun loungers, extending his legs and tossing his arms over the back behind him.

"You blow my mind," he said. "How do you switch from whatever you were doing in there to these broad existentials in less than two minutes?"

"It's the air," she said, opening her arms and leaning back. "Don't you just feel cleaner here?" Sitting straight, curiosity got the better of her. "How long have you been here? You know there's more to the world than this, right? It's not all clean nature and sea air."

"Unfortunately, I do," he said. "I like seeing it through your eyes though… You're so… open."

"And you're used to guarded people?"

"I'm used to people being less… impressed… Sincerity is a trait I value."

"Doesn't everyone?" she asked.

"It pours from you. In the way you act, the words you say, your tone, your expressions. You're so… bare."

She laughed, making a point of looking down at herself. "And this isn't even my most revealing outfit."

"I can't wait to see the others."

They shared a smile.

"Do you work here every day?"

"Most days, yeah. What are you working on?"

"I'm putting together a training package," she said. "I work for an HR consultancy company. On their training team. Companies hire us to go in and train their people on whatever. Some are standard packs, like if there is new software or hardware people need to learn to use. Those tend to come from whoever produced it. We go through them and customize the set as we have to, then we go in and deliver them."

"Others aren't standard?"

She smiled. "I do a lot of studying. A lot of online courses. We build our own packages, for confidence and development. We do things like sexual harassment seminars and go to various conventions and things as well… If your people need to learn it, we can teach them."

"Putting the packages together is your job?"

"I build them and go out to deliver them too."

"A jack of all trades."

"Something like that. What is it you do?"

"Nothing as exciting as that," he said. "How long have you been with them?"

"A couple of years," she said. "I did in-house

training for a multinational before that."

His arms slithered down to the chaise at his sides. "You didn't enjoy it?"

"Less latitude," she said. "A lot more layers and bureaucracy to deal with. Plus, it was the same thing over and over. I prefer variety."

"So you have your dream job? Great! Not something many people get. And it gives you time off to go places with your sister."

"Our offices are being refurbished. There was a flooding issue. Working away was sort of ideal timing."

"Can't say it didn't work out for me too," he said. "Is it just you and your sister?"

"In the family?" she asked and nodded. "Yeah."

"She's younger than you?"

"Yes," she said, picking up her legs to cross them in front of her. "You interviewing me for something?"

He laughed. "Just getting to know you. What about your parents?"

"They're teachers. Met in college. She was a freshman, he was a junior. I was a surprise in her junior year. They got married just before I was born and had Alessia three years later… My grandparents helped out a lot."

"I bet. What do they teach?"

"High school. My mom is an English teacher. Dad's a history buff."

His head bobbed. "Your grandparents still around?"

"My mom's parents, yes. They live just a street over from my parents. My dad's parents died when I was little… car wreck."

His eyes drifted to the sea. "I'm sorry… I know what that's like."

"How do you know what that's like?" she asked, sliding down from the wall when it was clear his attention was elsewhere. There was nothing out on the waves, she double checked, so it had to be something in his head. "Zane?"

Like he'd forgotten she was there, his focus jumped to hers. "Sorry, I was somewhere else."

"Tell me," she said, sinking down to sit on the edge of his lounger. "Where were you?"

"My mother died in a vehicular accident."

"I'm sorry," she said, sensing it was still raw for him. "Recently?"

He smiled and breathed out a laugh. "No… A long time ago."

Slipping a hand under his, she curled her fingers around his palm to take it to her lap. "You were close?"

He shrugged, fixated on their joined hands. "I was a kid. It blindsided me. Blindsided all of us… Didn't appreciate what I had until it was gone."

"We're all guilty of that. Do you have siblings?"

"A brother," he said. "Stepbrother."

"Your father remarried. Do you get along?"

Bright amusement lit his face. "Rourke's a law unto himself."

"What about his mom?"

"Was she a good replacement for mine? Truth is we were sent off to boarding school. Most of our raising was done there."

"By teachers?"

"Let's go with that."

"Now I'm intrigued," she said. "My parents are still together. They can be pretty zany sometimes, but we had stability."

Clearing his throat, he adjusted his angle. "Do you have a big family?"

"Not that we're close to. You?"

"Rourke, cousins on my mom's side."

"That's good. That you kept in contact with

them."

One side of his mouth tilted. Was there something more to those relationships? Watching him intently, drawn in, his eyes ascended to hers, his smile creeping higher. Yes, she was definitely missing… something.

"That mind of yours is working again," he murmured, his voice a deeper purr than before.

She conceded a smile of her own. "You're staring… at me."

"I am," he said without any hint of contrition.

In fact, he might actually be proud. Taking control of their joined hands, he guided hers up, laying it flat in the center of his torso. No colleague would do something so… intimate. Yet, as she watched his hand flatten over hers and felt its warmth, she admitted, only to herself, that she liked it.

Swallowing hard in hopes of calming the quickening of her heart, she took a slow, measured breath. "When will our sushi arrive?"

"Might be a while," he said, sinking lower. "But don't worry, we've got a lot of ground still to cover."

Getting to know each other? It might be the longest lunch break she'd ever taken in her life, but they were in a tropical paradise—nothing was business as usual.

FIVE

WORK DIDN'T GET their full attention for the rest of the day. Any attention to be honest, neither of them returned to their computers. They stayed right there on the loungers until the sushi arrived an hour later. And it wasn't just any sushi, oh no, it was the most incredible sushi on the face of the earth. These finer things were something else. Maybe she'd suggest sushi day back at the office and make this a regular thing. Though the amazing experience may have had something to do with the company too.

While she tried to make the point that sake wasn't a great idea during a workday, Zane rearranged the furniture, facing their loungers opposite ways, and putting the table between them. They sat, they ate, they talked.

And, yes, he won the sake argument. Though it wasn't the only treat. They enjoyed green tea and fresh made lemonade too. After sushi, crepes filled with ice-cream and fruit were brought out to the terrace. The resort was beyond full-service. If this was how they treated staff, imagine what guests experienced.

It took the sun sinking in the sky to clue them in the day was over. Or her anyway. Zane's conversation turned to the perfect place on the island to watch the sunset. Shit, sunset! She'd made quick apologies and darted inside to gather up her things. In some sort of weird serendipity, Honi waited in his cart outside, ready to return her to the main building in time to catch dinner with her sister.

Though after such a sumptuous lunch, she hadn't been hungry and only picked at her plate. Not that anyone noticed. The contest women chattered and swooned over their big day. She only caught bits and pieces; her mind was on Zane.

Later, after considerable effort, work became her priority. While Alessia got ready to spend the evening drinking with new friends, she settled down to finish what should've been done during the day.

The following day, Alessia was ecstatic, practically bouncing off walls. Breakfast seemed to be infused with hormones or amphetamines, the room was a potent soup of enthusiasm and heat. Meeting Roman hadn't quenched anyone's thirst for him. Eager, all rushed out as soon as Mieux arrived.

She, on the other hand, got her things from the room and set out to return to the corporate suite.

Honi wasn't chatty, which could be a good thing. When Zane turned out to be chatty, it took her until midnight to make up the time she'd lost reciprocating. Though she wouldn't admit it out loud, she'd done some of that day's work too. Just to take the pressure off if Zane commandeered her at lunch again.

She sprang out of the cart. "Thanks, Honi."

In the entryway of the corporate suite, she stalled. Work. They were there to work. The previous day was an anomaly, she couldn't dwell on it. A man like Zane, hot, smart, funny, he was probably looking for excuses to bunk off work. Having a colleague may be a novelty for him.

He lived in the middle of the Pacific and she lived in the Midwest. There was no future to their friendship. Nothing but the moment. Both of them had work to do; work that would carry on after her month on the island. Something their relationship couldn't do.

Damn. They'd held hands, that was it. He'd made no move or suggestion he was interested in her beyond friendship.

She hadn't been with a man since Thom.

Shit, pull it together. She wasn't a swooner. Zane was a friend. A fun friend… who liked sushi. It couldn't hurt to have a friend who lived on a tropical island… though the long-distance charges may kill her.

Continuing into the large office, she spied him exactly where he'd been the previous day. Sitting on the couch, legs propped on the table, typing on the laptop, glancing occasionally at paperwork on the couch at his side.

With a pen in his teeth and a furrowed brow, he didn't acknowledge her.

Okay. See? Work.

So much for the pep talk. Her disappointment was disappointing. He was working, showing work was the most important thing. She couldn't fault that.

Work. The desk. She set her focus without distracting his. Sliding the bag from her shoulder, she dumped it on the desk and… What was that? A brown drink in a tall glass mug, brimming over ice. Had she mentioned… She swooped around the corner of the desk to sink down into the sumptuous chair and sipped the drink. Iced coconut latte. In their conversation… he'd remembered.

Her favorite right there. He'd delivered it… somehow.

The taste was still on her lips when she glanced up and caught him peeking from the top of his eyes. Letting her head drop to the side, she assessed him for a second before showing him a smile. He wasn't so shy with his, though it was pure mischief. The guy was full of surprises and flashed a quick wink.

A wink. Huh. She hadn't thought of him as a winker. Her smile grew, but by the time she focused on Zane again, his attention was back on work. Work. Yes. It was work time.

SIX

"LUNCH!"

Second time around was just as startling.

Zane closed his laptop and dumped it on the couch to pounce onto his feet. "We're going Mediterranean today… I saw the ciabatta proving last night."

She sank back in her seat. "If I eat with you, will I get back to this desk today?"

On his way over, he pushed his linked fingers away from his body, cracking his knuckles. "Probably not, I have a whole bunch of questions lined up for you."

As he came around the desk, she turned her chair his way and didn't argue when he bowed to pick up her hands to ease her onto her feet.

"I have work to do."

"Me too," he said, linking his fingers between hers. "Something we have in common."

Funny.

On the terrace, the chaises remained in the same position as the day before.

"We should've fixed this before we left." Though she had been the one to rush out in a hurry. "It's not our place to rearrange the furniture."

"No one cares about that," he said. "Do you want wine? I can have them bring a selection."

Laughing as he directed her down to her chaise, she kicked off her shoes and raised her legs to the soft, warm cushioning beneath.

"You're determined to get me drunk in the middle of the day," she said. "My boss would kick your ass."

"Nah," he said, settling on his own chaise. "I can be charming."

"Anika is not the type of woman to be charmed… no matter how good-looking the guy doing the charming is."

He stopped straightening the table to make eye contact. "You think I'm good-looking?"

Pushing her shoulders back, she wriggled deeper in her seat. "I think you're a goofball."

The large parasol next to his chaise offered shade that protected hers too. The one on her side, which had been there the previous day, was gone.

He laughed. "Can't say I've been called that in a while."

"Where's my parasol?" she asked, looking around.

Zane pointed up. "What's wrong with this one?"

It wasn't like there was anyone around to steal it. "If it blew away, it would be our fault."

"I think we're safe, no storms last night. Can we get back to you thinking I'm good-looking?"

Yep, a goof.

"You don't need me stroking your ego, Mr. Humblebrag." Forgetting the parasol, she shifted to rise. "You know exactly what you look like."

He braced, tossing a leg off his chaise like he intended to leap up. "Where are you going?"

"I'm going to get my bag," she said, heading inside. "Is that okay?"

Without waiting for his response, she went in to retrieve it. Outside, she donned her sunglasses and left her bag between the chaises to go to the wall again.

"And now you're ditching me," he said. She flashed him a smile over her shoulder then climbed up onto the wall. "Whoa, where are you…"

Jumping off the other side, she made short work of running down the grass bank and into the sand. Scrunching her toes in it, the heat of the grains seeped up through her. When she heard what sounded like someone landing on the grass behind her, she started to move again. Running the width of the beach, she didn't stop at the water's edge. Gathering up her maxi skirt, she waded in until the water lapped her thighs.

Spinning around, her co-worker remained at the edge of the tide.

"Makes me feel better!" she called back to him.

Since arriving, all she'd wanted to do was dive into the water. With work and Alessia and Zane and everything, there hadn't been time. The horizon appealed. She was so small in something so vast, yet, somehow, it made every breath seem vital.

The sound of movement in water preceded a hand sliding onto her shoulder. It kept on going along her clavicle until it hooked around her other shoulder. His forearm felt good, solid and secure, resting on her body.

He pulled her back and must have crouched because he murmured above her ear. "Your boss would let you do this at work?"

Her skirt was still in her fist, but with the other hand, she touched his wrist. "My boss isn't here."

"No one is here."

That bassy truth vibrated through her. Why did his voice get deeper like that?

Relaxing the weight of her head, her cheek made contact with his hand just above hers when she pushed up her shoulder.

"Don't you feel better?" she asked. "Out here, in the air, surrounded by life."

"I sure feel something."

Were those words for her? Closing her eyes, she inhaled through her nose. Her head went back, bumping against him, but he didn't retreat. If it was up to her, they would stay out there all day. But, sigh, that wasn't possible. She couldn't ask him about getting back to work and then not even let the guy eat lunch.

"I'll need a vacation after this," she said, patting his wrist, then easing his arm away to head back to shore.

"Where are you going now?"

"The Mediterranean," she said without looking back.

As she walked up the beach, sand stuck to her feet. That was okay, the grains would fall off as her legs dried. Still holding her skirt at her hip, she got as far as the wall, and then… huh. It was higher than she'd thought, would she be able to reach it? With greenery all around the rest of the building, getting back without footwear might be difficult.

"Didn't think about that, did you?" Zane said, coming to her side.

She grabbed his shoulder. "You can give me a boost."

Laughing again, he bent down to offer her a foothold. "Here to help."

Slipping her foot into his linked fingers, she whooped when he did as she asked and boosted her up. He was strong. Damn, the guy was maybe too capable.

Her skirt dropped, probably over his head, as she grabbed the wall and hauled herself up onto it.

"Got it?" he called out.

"Yeah, I'm good."

On her knees, she brushed her hands together, catching her breath. It took him seconds to not only get onto the wall, but over it. She was still kneeling there when he returned to his seat and raised a large plate of food.

"Lunch is here." He picked up a bottle of wine next. "Sure you don't want some?"

"We had sake yesterday and never got back to our work," she said, climbing off the wall to go to her chaise. Sitting on the side, she curled her legs beside her. "You think people will get mad if I get the chaise sandy?"

With two glasses in one hand, he used the other to pour the wine. "No. No one will get mad at you, Wanderer." Holding the glasses toward her, he let her take one and put the wine back on the table. "You want to drink to something? Your imaginings?"

Smiling, she held her glass to his. "I say we drink to the possibilities. To everything that came before us and to everything that will come after."

"That's a lot of possibilities," he said, touching his glass to hers. They drank and he pushed the plate toward her. "You see it all. See the good in everything."

"I try to be optimistic," she said, picking up a bruschetta. "It's better than the alternative."

"So I have a question for you," he said. He hadn't even looked at the food. Her mouth was full, so all she could do was raise her brows and nod. "Why aren't you married?"

Swallowing the mouthful, she put the rest of the bruschetta on the edge of the plate. "I'm twenty-seven, think I'd count as a spinster?"

He laughed. "That's not what I was… You seem

like the kind of woman who'd attract men like flies."

"To dung?"

Another laugh. "Or to light. That's what you are, Thea. You're light. You light up everything around you."

Unsure if he was teasing or hitting on her, she just topped her shrug with a smile. "Life happens, I guess. How come you're not married?"

"How do you know I'm not married?"

She nodded at his hand. "No ring."

"Maybe I lost it in the sea."

"Maybe you did," she said. "Is that why you were out there in the dark? Looking for it?"

"It gets dark early around here."

She sipped her wine, trying to subdue her ridiculous disappointment. "What's she like? Does she live here on the island with you?"

The slant of his lips climbed again. "I'm not married. I'm not involved at all… yet."

"Relationships aren't easy to navigate… I think to make one work, we have to find our equal. Too many people think that means equal in society or in salary or having things in common. Sure that helps, but you don't have to be the same as someone to be their equal."

Interest narrowed his eyes. "What makes two people equal?"

"Values. Respect," she said. "You have to find someone who respects your outlook the same way you respect theirs. Someone who wants the relationship to work as much as you do. Doesn't mean running out and getting married or rushing anything, just that you both understand what the relationship is. That you both place the same value on it." Conscious of her rambling, she laughed. "Though, if I had a foolproof way to make relationships work, I wouldn't be single, would I?"

"Guess we're all learning as we go."

"Exactly," she said, presenting a hand to him.

"That's what I mean. Two people have to want to learn together. They have to appreciate mistakes will be made and want to fix them together. The commitment should be real."

"And you haven't found a guy who wants to learn with you?"

"I'm not always the easiest woman to be in a relationship with," she said. "I'm headstrong. I have a habit of sharing my point of view… I can be quite demanding."

"Now I am intrigued," he said. "What do you demand?"

"Respect. Communication." She pointed at him. "I'm big on communication." She shrugged and drank some wine. "I'm in no hurry to get to the end. When it happens, if it happens, I'd rather wait to be in a relationship that made me happy than be in one that made me unhappy just for the sake of it."

"And you don't have any qualms about telling a guy that."

"Right," she said on a single nod. "Somewhere…" She swept her wine around in the direction of the ocean surrounding them. "Out there in the world, there's a guy who will put up with me calling at three a.m. to tell him something trivial… who won't care that I love karaoke, even if it is embarrassing when I insist on standing up. A guy who won't mind that I run into the ocean without notice. A guy who'll kiss me, even if there are people watching… A guy who will laugh with me, even when no one else gets the joke… A guy who'll let me breathe, even though I need him with every breath…" She sighed and looked at him again. "Sorry, I'm rambling."

"I like rambling," he said. "All of that is coming from someone… someone who hurt you."

She shook her head. "I'm not hurt. Not anymore.

But there's a bit of everything from the men in my past, I guess. Like I said, I'm not easy to be in a relationship with."

"I didn't hear anything unreasonable on your list…" He peered closer. "Though, I guess it depends… what kind of karaoke?"

Zane always eased the tension, always relaxed her, made her laugh. She was a bold woman, not too easy to handle. She knew her own mind, and definitely knew her heart. Some men were intimidated by her confidence. Some sneered at it. She wouldn't apologize for being who she was, and it didn't seem Zane wanted her to either.

SEVEN

"SO WE ENDED IT."

With her arm curled under her head, she'd been lying on her side, listening to the story of Zane's last relationship for a while.

She sighed. "It's so sad." He frowned. "I feel sorry for her."

"For Arden? Why?"

"Because she loved you," she said. "She had this picture in her mind of what her life would be and you were in it."

"You think I should've stayed with her to complete the picture?"

"No!" she said, pushing her upper body away from the lounger.

"I trust my instincts. I believe a relationship should progress, decisions should be made because they feel right and both parties are ready, not because of some arbitrary timeline."

"I agree completely," she said, her lips curling. "She loved you. I can feel sorry for her without judging you for your choice." She laughed. "I have a lot of respect for her, for what it took to be with a man like you. You probably did her a favor."

"Oh, did I?"

"Sure," she said, appreciating the warmth he exuded. "A man like you in a place like this. Out in the middle of nowhere, sparse phone signal. I don't know what the island is most of the year, but there's a hotel, an exclusive, like seven-star hotel… I bet it's filled with gorgeous, rich women all the time. It would take a very secure woman to be with a man living in the ocean surrounded by sirens."

He laughed again. She adored the sound. Every single time she heard it, more of herself surrendered itself to him.

"Something you haven't figured out about this guy yet," he said, sitting up, pushing the table aside to set his feet on the terrace beneath them.

She sank onto her back. "What's that?" she asked, arching her body, working her muscles.

Relaxing, she tilted her chin his way when he swooped over to sit on the edge of her lounger.

"When he commits, he goes all the way."

Seductive claim. Either completely true or absolute bullshit, but he sold it well. He pinched her chin between a curled forefinger and the pad of his thumb. Before she could process, he bowed, and then…

His lips met hers. Gentle, a delicate meeting, he gave her time to get used to him being there. And what did she do? Froze. How did—what did—oh, damn, she hadn't expected this. Imagined it? Maybe. In her head. Not in reality.

Angling his head, he pushed harder, asking for more in the way his lips moved, beckoning hers to reply to his want.

He wanted her. That's what he revealed. Exactly

what she'd thought that morning he hadn't shown her. His mouth. That mouth.

Dismissing her overthinking, impulse took control. No permission needed. Not from her consciousness. The texture of his shirt under her fingertips registered first. They slid up his chest, toward his throat. As she grazed a button and found his tee-shirt, she slipped her hand flat under his outer layer, testing the resistance of his chest beneath.

His muscles might be hard, yet there was a heat within him, passing her a soul-deep glow.

Oh, his mouth. It was hers. Right there, in that moment, it belonged to her. For those seconds, they were each other's. She was kissing him back. More. She wanted more and didn't want to sacrifice him to the world again. As soon as they stopped kissing, as soon as he took his mouth back and her hand slipped away, he'd be his own man again. Thea didn't want that. She wanted—

When the truth hit her, she pushed him back. Goddamnit. She couldn't even look him in the eye. Searching her own insanity, she pushed him further and jumped off the chaise.

"Thea," he called. Grabbing her bag, she didn't care about her shoes or the things she'd left behind. "Thea!"

She kept on going.

She snagged her laptop and left, Honi was waiting and didn't ask any questions when she requested a ride to the hotel. Dinner was only a half hour away, time to get it together. Alessia would want to talk about her day with Roman.

Worrying her sister was the last thing she wanted. If she couldn't get the incredulity from her head, Thea would be a walking billboard. She wanted him. Damn. Her attraction was obvious, and allowed, but to act on it…

A vacation fling would be one thing, but it hadn't been that. The stirring in her gut evoked an awareness beyond basic sexual attraction. He was hot, a lot of women would be attracted to him. Why couldn't she be one of those women who could use a guy for sex, then walk away without a second thought?

Casual sex. She had never been good at it. In college, she'd tried it. Even had a couple of one-night stands. After the initial thrill, it was horrible. Everything about it. From the awkward lying there pretending to sleep, wondering if she should leave, to the uncomfortable morning after and creeping home, she hated it.

People who could do it, great, well done, she didn't judge. Many folks could go through partners and live it up, be spontaneous. She just wasn't one of those people. She'd rather go without sex than do it just to pass the time.

A tropical island in the middle of the ocean was not the place to consider rethinking a life choice she'd stuck by for years. Dating was fun. Conversation great. Who didn't like flirting and playing? And sex, yeah, she even liked sex. Often, when she was with someone.

She couldn't do it. Already captivated, not only did she want to get physical with him, feelings were creeping in too.

Damnit. She should've known better than to spend two days talking and playing with such an alluring guy. What did she think would happen? They were supposed to work. Supposed to be focused on their occupations, not each other. What was with the food and the drinking? The laughing and sharing. It was nuts.

It took her a second to get out of the cart at the hotel.

Before she got up, she decided. That was it. She'd

go back the following day to pick up her things and from then on, she'd work in her room. Alone. Without distractions… Without Zane.

EIGHT

AFTER MAKING HER decision, it was easier to fake it in front of the exuberant Alessia. She even went for a drink with her and her friends after dinner. They talked constantly about how incredible Roman was during their hike that day. He was so strong and fit and amazing. Even Thea started to believe it.

No one asked about her day. Why would they? As far as everyone else was concerned, all she did was work. Their focus on the star and excitement about what was to come gave her a break. No one was looking at her, so she could almost forget what happened.

It all came crashing back to her upon opening her eyes the next morning. There was no avoiding it. Her notes were in the corporate suite. She could start over without them, but she'd mapped out some good pathways. A second swing wouldn't do them their original justice.

Plus, you know, Zane might get the crazy idea about bringing them to her room. Shaking that notion wasn't quick or easy.

All she had to do was go there, collect her things, and apologize for sending him any signals. There could be no more signals.

Except when she got there, Zane was on the terrace, talking on what appeared to be a cellphone. She didn't look too closely; he was moving around and could turn her way any second.

It was best. Perfect, actually. While he was out there talking, she could gather her things.

Hurrying over to the desk, intentions clear, she paused at the sight of the latte in the same place it had been the previous day. Damn. That had been good latte. She'd miss the latte. Yeah, that was the root of her sorrow.

Shaking off her disappointment, that wasn't really about the drink, she pulled her bag across the desk to collect her things into it.

"Wandering away, Wanderer?"

She hadn't heard him approach, probably because he was only just inside the tall terrace doors.

"It'll only take me a minute to get out of your hair."

So much for the speech she'd been mentally writing all morning.

"You don't have to go," he said, coming closer.

Still, she couldn't make eye contact. Nothing had changed since she'd abandoned him on the chaise the previous day.

"It's okay. I can work anywhere."

"Thea," he said from the other side of the desk. Unable to look up, she kept stacking her things, stuffing them into her bag. He came around to her side. "Thea."

That time he accompanied the murmur of his name on her lips with his fingers combing into her hair to scoop a hand around the base of her skull.

"Don't," she said, wincing as she raised her

shoulders in a recoil. "Please."

"I should've realized you were a runner," he said, taking his hand from her hair like she'd asked.

Except the minute it was gone, she wanted it back. Right then, it hit her how much trouble she was in.

"I have a lot of work to do."

"I know and this is the best place to do it."

He put the phone on the desk as she stuffed the last of her things in her bag.

"I thought there was no cellphone coverage around here."

"There will be by next summer. But that's a sat phone."

Much smaller than she thought they were, but what did she know.

"I've taken over your space for too long," she said, intending to leave.

Zane caught her shoulders to halt her. "Can we not pretend you're running out of here for any reason other than what happened yesterday?" She didn't say a word, but he smiled. "I kissed you."

"Zane…" she said and tried to pull away.

He tightened his grip. "Something scared you; I want to understand what it was."

"Nothing, no, I—"

"Come on, babe. We got past the barriers and gave each other a second chance… What did I do wrong?"

"Nothing!" she exclaimed, horrified he'd think that.

"It was a good kiss," he said, somehow moving closer. "We felt good together."

Her gaze floated up to his. "Yes," she conceded in a whisper. "Too good."

"Help me understand, baby," he murmured, his palm skimming upward until the edge of his thumb grazed her jaw. "What's going on in your head? You don't want this…? Don't want to see what this is?"

"I don't do casual sex," she blurted out. "I'm sorry, I… It's not a big deal, I've done it, didn't enjoy it, so decided not to do it again… Years ago, I mean, not because of you, just…" She shrugged. "You're very attractive and I know we have chemistry, but I can't. I just can't do—"

"Hey," he said, cupping her face. "Who said anything about casual?" She blinked at him. "Baby, I think you're amazing. You're hot and so… alive. I wasn't looking for you, for anything… You know how they say as soon as you stop looking for a relationship, that's when one finds you? Babe, I flew thousands of miles to a basically deserted island and… here you are."

"We've known each other three days."

"I know," he said on a short laugh. "I'm not suggesting we fly to Vegas and make it official, just…" His focus shifted as his fingers rose to a tendril of hair hanging by her face. "This isn't nothing."

It wasn't. Thea was drawn to him. Something in her had connected itself to something in him.

The incredulity just wouldn't go away.

"It's been three days," she said again.

His broad smile heralded an exhaled laugh. "I know it would sound nuts to anyone else, but…" He peered deeper into her. "It isn't just me, is it? All you wanted from me was sex?"

Locked onto his gaze, her hands somehow found their way to his chest. "I don't know what I want from you… But if we hook up for a one-night thing… We have the next twenty-something days here and—"

"We don't need an expiration date or to put any pressure on each other," he said, wrapping his arms around her shoulders to pull her closer. "Until we decide otherwise, you're mine. I'm yours. We're together.

Nothing casual. Doesn't make forever inevitable, we just be… together."

The idea was tempting. "It can't be that simple."

"You don't want to be mine?"

He squeezed her so tight she felt it in her lungs. The depth of his possession finally relaxed her enough to smile.

"Is this your idea of a shortcut into my panties?"

He bobbed his chin toward the desk next to them. "The desk could probably hold us."

Wrinkling her nose, she pushed her shoulders back against his embrace to get a better look at him. "You said there were tables upstairs. The chaises are still outside… And the beach is just over the wall. You lack imagination, Drift."

"Do I?" he asked. "Maybe imagination can be your department."

"So what's your department?"

"I come up with the ideas, you figure out how we execute them."

"Oh yeah? So your idea is…"

"Getting into your panties."

Bending his knees, he sank lower to grip her ass. His audacity wrought a shriek of a laugh from deep inside her.

"Zane!"

His mouth stole hers and everything else faded away. When he boosted her onto the desk, she heard her bag fall, and shoved it to the side, getting it out of their way. He urged her further onto the desk, pushing himself hard against her, the imprint of him betrayed how much he wanted her, how hard he wanted it.

Driving her fingers into his hair, she held his head, pulling him to her, begging for the intensity of their kiss to keep on going all the way to the end of—

She tore her mouth from his. "Wait."

"Wait. Wait?" he panted. "Baby—

"I know," she said, bringing her hands to his cheeks. "I know, me too, but we…" She had to stop and take a breath. "If you're serious about this being more than a one-time thing… Don't you want to date me?"

His mouth opened, but his expression exposed a conflict between the honorable answer and what his body wanted.

"I… yeaahh," he said, dragging out the begrudged word even though it sounded painful.

After another few seconds, he groaned and conceded the transaction wouldn't be completed.

As he backed off, and turned away, she shimmied to the edge of the desk, pulling down her skirt. Sitting there, she gave him a second to calm whatever he needed to calm. If they were together, she might tease him… and one day, if together became a more tangible thing, she might help him out with the calming.

Glancing around to check how far her bag had gone, everything was scattered. Her laptop hung precariously on the corner of the desk, just beside a pool of brown liquid and ice.

"Damnit," she said, hopping off the desk to rush to the restroom.

Grabbing up as much tissue as she could, she hurried back to the mess to mop it up.

"Babe, you don't have to clean."

"What a waste," she said, tossing the sopping tissues into the trash. "No sex and no latte. What did I do to piss off fate today?"

"There's a spot on the west shore, a cabana with a grass roof. It's not much more than a room with a deck, but it's quiet… it's private."

"You want to have sex there?"

"I want to date you there," he said, coming over to stop beside her. "Go outside and wet your toes… I'll clean up in here."

"You don't have to—"

"Babe," he said, extending a hand to her. "You want to date. You love the beach and your work is important to you."

She looked up at him. "Why are you telling me about me?"

"Showing I pay attention," he said, smiling.

When her hand slid into his, he pulled her to her feet. "I can clean up a mess."

"We work in the day," he said, tucking her hair behind her ear. "It's important to you, I won't get in the way of that. We date at night or in the afternoon, whichever you prefer." He guided her hand onto his chest. "I respect what you value."

Picking up on his meaning, she touched his face. "You're my equal."

"Yes, I am," he said, descending slowly to kiss her quick. "Now get outside and feel better while I take care of things in here. You have work to do."

He was right. About everything. More than once or twice, it was becoming a habit. She went outside to be confronted by a large block of stone in front of the wall. A block…? No, a step. Her lips curled as she ascended the block to stand atop the wall, then she laughed. There on the other side were more blocks. A stack of them: descending stairs.

Taking advantage of her new route, Thea needed the chance to center herself. Having a date didn't give her permission to be distracted. She had to get her work done and then… she could let loose.

NINE

"YOU HAVE TO COME," Alessia begged after dinner that evening. "You came last night."

Because she didn't have work… or a date.

"I can't," Thea said, looking through her cosmetics case.

"You work all the time, like all the time. You came here to hang with me."

"You have your friends." Thea tossed an eyeshadow aside, then caught her sister's reflection in the mirror above the dresser in front of her. "Have you fallen out with them?"

"No! The girls are great," Alessia said, hurrying to hug her. "I just feel bad for you. You're always working. We're always having fun, *and* we get to hang with the coolest guy on the planet." She pulled back to wiggle her brows. "The hottest guy on the planet." Thea's automatic smile betrayed her; Alessia came over all curious. "I haven't seen you smile like that since… maybe ever." She gave her a shake. "Spill. Come on. Why are you smiling like that?"

Okay, deep breath.

Taking her arms, Thea guided her sister back. "I may have… met someone."

Keeping it secret might be fun, but there was no real reason for it.

Alessia frowned. "Met someone?" She gasped. "A guy! You met a guy? Here? How did you—" She shrieked. "You haven't been working at all! You've been…" Alessia lowered her voice to a whisper. "You've been having secret sex."

Thea laughed. "No, I really have been working. He works here too. Over at the corporate suite."

Alessia already knew she worked in a different building during the day, which was why she wasn't in the room anytime her sister popped in for whatever.

"Ooooh, office romance."

Just like Alessia to swoon. God, she loved her sister.

"Maybe," she played it a little coy. "We're going to spend some time together tonight… see if maybe…"

"You could be something," Alessia said, bouncing up and down, grabbing her wrist in both hands. "Oh my God, imagine you fell in love! That would be amazing! You could live on a tropical island." She frowned. "Mom would hate that. Oh my God, she would go crazy!" Perking up, she tugged her arm. "Maybe she would move all of us out here."

Thea laughed. "You'd go nuts here permanently. There are no stores for clothes or those little boutique wine bars you and your friends love. And your friends… Alessia, you love your friends."

Despite her sister's enthusiasm, Thea chilled. Zane and she had said together like it could mean something. Except… how could it ever mean something? She would never leave her family; she needed them like they needed her. Her breath stalled for a minute. No. She was going to be positive, optimistic, they had to find out if their zing could be a real thing before long-term planning.

"It'll all work out," Alessia said, pulling her into another hug. "I'm so excited for you."

A knock on the door took Alessia from her side. Her friends were there to get her, so after some quick goodbyes, they disappeared in a cloud of fading laughter.

Alone in their room, she turned to the mirror. Zane would pick her up in less than an hour. If she went out with him, falling for him was a real possibility.

It was an experience. That was a better perspective. Whatever happened, even if she got her heart broken, it would be amazing just to get to know him. That was enough… wasn't it?

Optimism. Optimism. It was the key. What she needed to keep her going. Life choices had to be approached with a positive point of view.

After showering, she did her hair and even her makeup, going through the regular date ritual. But as she stood there in her underwear, looking at her dress, she couldn't make herself feel it. Was she setting herself up for heartbreak?

Her attention leaped around when someone knocked on the door. Someone? Zane.

Damnit, this wouldn't work without positivity. If she couldn't find her optimism… Why had she thought dating Zane was smart? Where had her optimism come from earlier?

The next knock reminded her.

Ah ha! Leaping from the spot, she ran to the door and didn't think twice about opening it.

Zane's mouth was open, but the happiness meant to accompany his quirky opening line died on his lips as his eyes dropped.

"Best date ever."

"I need you to kiss me," she said, grabbing the back of his neck in one hand to pull him down to her level. "Please."

It took him a second to catch up after she laid one on him. In true Zane fashion, he got with it quick smart. Stooping, he hooked an arm around her waist, pulling her body to his, taking control, giving her his confidence.

That was it there. The pressure of his mouth, the joining of their tongues, right there in his kiss was all the optimism she'd ever need.

Planting her hands, she pushed him away. "Thank you."

Leaping backward, she slammed the bedroom door in his face and ran over to grab her mini wrap dress from the hanger. It had spaghetti straps, and the chiffon was just transparent enough to tease what was beneath. Not that she had much left to tease, he'd just seen her underwear.

Dating on a practically deserted island had its perks. No need to worry about cash or a purse. There was nowhere to spend money and no cellphone signal. She could take one for lip gloss, but that seemed ridiculous. A whole purse for one tube? Hmm, if there was a chance her bra would come off, she couldn't just slip it into her cleavage.

Almost at the door, she paused and whirled around to rush back to her cosmetics. Grabbing for her lip gloss, she stuffed the tube into her cleavage. Bra was staying on. Decision made.

In the hallway, she caught the bewildered Zane's hand.

"Ready?" he asked, a glimmer of amusement behind his confusion.

"Yes," she said, smiling up at him like she hadn't done anything peculiar at all. "Let's go."

One step forward, he pulled her back.

"Not that way," he said, drawing her away from the typical route to the main hotel. "Down here."

"I have never been this way."

"Dating me, you'll get to know all the secrets," he said, guiding her to a door at the end of the hallway she'd never noticed.

Unlocking it with his thumbprint, he led them through foliage encroaching on an external path to a small concrete square. Ah, hmm, a bunch of carts were parked in rows like this was their depot area.

Zane led her to one and helped her into the passenger side. It was thumbprint enabled too and started without a hitch. When he drove them out of the lot onto the road, she had to grab for the frame. This guy liked speed, apparently.

"You know, I could just loop around and take you home. Unless you want me to take you out some time."

"What?"

He flashed her a grin. "I'm asking you out. Everything's backwards, so I figured that's where we're at."

"Backwards?"

"I saw you naked, then kissed you, then I got to pick you up... so it must be time to ask you out." Yeah, well, when he put it that way. "Are you okay?"

"Am I...? Yes. I'm okay... Why do you think I'm not okay?"

"You came out in your underwear and asked me to kiss you."

At the time, he didn't seem to have a problem.

His query put a smile on her face. "And you're complaining about that? What kind of date are you?"

"Is that what you were doing? Getting the awkward doorstep moment over with?"

"Awkward?" she asked, playing to his teasing. "I'm never awkward on the doorstep."

"Never?"

"No."

"What if you want a guy to kiss you and—no, wait, scratch that. I've experienced what you do if you want it and a guy isn't delivering."

"I'm not shy in asking for what I want. Any man is at liberty to say no."

"Any man? No. This man," he said, reaching over to squeeze her thigh to encourage her closer. "We're us, remember? Just us."

Coiling her arm around his, Thea enjoyed the weight of his hand on her leg. The reassuring heat of his body against her side was a comfort too. Sitting beside him, it felt like anything was possible.

Resting her head on his upper arm, she enjoyed the air on her face and closed her eyes, appreciating why he liked the speed of the cart whizzing along the road.

"Are we going to work?"

Although it was dark, the moon and occasional muted overhead light kept them company.

"You want to do it at work?"

She laughed and nudged him. "We are not going to have sex tonight, Drift."

"Even if my wood happens to drift toward—"

"Zane," she said, lifting her head. "Be a gentleman."

"Okay, gentleman… Did I tell you how beautiful you look tonight?"

"No, you didn't."

"Well, you're gorgeous… You're always gorgeous, but I don't like to get too focused on the physical."

"Why not?"

"'Cause there's more to you than what you do to

my pants."

"Oh yeah?" she asked, propping her chin on his arm. "What do I do to your pants?"

"You'll find out when we take off the training wheels."

The curve of his lips delighted her. Every time. Every minute they were together, happiness filled her. That was it. He was her optimism. Her hope. Her happiness. On the island anyway.

"If we do," she said. "I'm making no promises."

"I have confidence."

"In your abilities of seduction?"

"In how much you want me."

They'd passed the corporate suite and the airfield. Inland, there was another building in the trees up ahead.

"What's that?"

"Employee steadings. We've got another couple of miles to go."

The road was a good landmark, easy to find. From near it anyway. If she was in the center of the island, she wasn't sure how fast she'd find her way out.

"How long have you lived here?"

"I don't live here," he said, a snicker in his voice.

Maybe the job was seasonal. Or they only had employees there whenever visitors resided in the hotel.

"Coming here then, how long have you been coming here?"

"Three years," he said. "Thereabouts."

"Three years. It's a beautiful place. You're lucky to have a position here… I guess this is a dream job for you too. How do you keep in touch with your family? That sat phone?"

"If there's an emergency, yeah," he said. "I email and there's a plane in and out a couple of times a week."

"There is?"

"Where do you think we get supplies?"

"I hadn't thought about logistics… That's good to know… a plane, hmm."

"Why is that interesting? Thinking about leaving?"

"I might stow away… depends how the next couple of weeks go."

"I'll tell the guys to check out the cargo holds before departure," he said, slowing down to pull off the road.

"Is this it?"

"This is it."

He brought the cart to a stop and both of them got out at the same time. Though she tried to peek into the shadows of flora up ahead, there was no hint of what awaited them.

"Where is it?"

"This way," Zane said, linking their hands to lead her onto a dark path.

It wasn't too long. After a few steps, the path swept around in a curve. That was when she noticed the light. Moonlight. No, not the moon, there was a golden glow. The moon wasn't gold. What could that be?

They kept going toward the light until a wooden structure came into view. Round with a dried grass roof, it was circled by a deck. The path blended into that deck. Tiki torches! That was the light. And, oh, the beach! A small, secret cove protected by rocks and plants with the structure at the back. Wow, it was perfect!

"Oh my God," she whispered as they got around to the large patio daybed in the cabana.

That he'd brought her to a bed with little else provided plenty of teasing material, but it would wait. The waves were too captivating.

Stopping by the stairs at the edge of the deck, she squeezed the wooden railing, transfixed by the view.

Zane came up behind her to bow and hold the barrier, his hands next to hers, trapping her in his embrace. "Am I winning points?"

She smiled. "Too many to count."

"Come sit down."

Thea didn't object when he took her hand to lead her over to the daybed.

"Your seduction technique isn't subtle," she said. "Did you forget you're not getting laid?"

"I didn't forget," he said, smirking. "Get on up there."

The round bed was in the middle of the space with a table around it. At one side was an ice-bucket and various bottles.

As she kicked off her shoes to crawl up onto the bed, Zane fixed their drinks.

"That ice will run out quickly."

He stepped aside to pull the handle just beneath the tabletop. The bottom was hinged so only the top section opened to reveal a unit full of ice.

"You want it? I got it."

"Is that right?" she asked, smiling as he came onto the bed with two glasses.

Propping himself on the mound of pillows facing her, he handed over a glass. "For you?"

"What is it?"

"Taste it," he said.

She sipped the liquid only to be delighted by its taste. "It's rum."

"Tropical punch," he said. "Guava and mango."

Holding her glass aside, she leaned in. Anticipating it he moved to accept her brief kiss.

"I love it."

"I have other recipes. Gifted to me by a friend," he said, combing his fingers into her hair to tuck it behind her ear. "You said rum was your go-to."

"It is," she said, drinking some more. "I love it."

Scooching closer, she nestled against him, gazing out over the ocean.

Zane's arm came around, holding her back against his chest. "You feel good," he said, kissing her hair. "Want to tell me before's problem?"

"There are no problems here," she said, stroking the back of his forearm draped across her. "Just tiki torches and the tide. It's beautiful. Why would you ever want to leave here?"

"Maybe now you're here, I won't."

Despite denying an issue prompted her frantic request for a kiss, now that it had come up, she couldn't ignore the opening.

"My family are important to me… and I'm important to them. I have friends at home. People who rely on me."

"My family are important to me too," he said, then there was silence for at least ten seconds. "You thought about backing out… because you can't see a future." Nail. Head. Yep. "Can I tell you something?"

"Mm," she said, enjoying her drink, before settling her head against his arm.

His lips moved deeper into her hair. "I'm a problem solver." She exhaled a laugh. "I'm serious. It's my superpower. If there's a need, I'll find a way to satisfy it. Necessity is our friend. You don't have to worry about anything so long as you're with me. Just live in the moment. Don't focus on what might come next, focus on what you want to do now."

"Well, that's dangerous." Peeking over her shoulder, she didn't have to say anything to convey her thoughts. "Tell me about the island," she said, settling against him, drinking more. "Do we have more of your yummy cocktail?"

"As much as you want, Wanderer." His embrace

tightened. "You can have anything you want."

"Then talk to me," she said. "I want to know about the island… about the hotel. When is it open? Are there guests year-round?" She tilted her chin toward her shoulder. "Do you have like a budget week? A charity weekend? Maybe I could save up for five or ten years then come visit you again… if you're not married by then. Do you live in those employee quarters we passed?"

"You can come visit the island any time you like."

"If that was true, I'd never leave," she said, resting her face on his arm. "Say things, Drift. Your voice is like the waves."

"Anything you want," he said, losing his mouth in her hair. "Anything at all."

TEN

FOR THE NEXT THREE hours, he regaled her with island facts. Facts about its geography, the building process, the facilities at the hotel. It was open, at the island owner's discretion. If anyone wanted to stay, or have an event there, he'd open the hotel. Other than that, availability was severely limited.

Apparently, there were a bunch of instructors on call from Hawaii who'd fly in to take groups out on the water, and trekking in the interior of the island.

Anything was possible there. Anything.

Including drinking too much.

Zane took her glass for what could've been the tenth time that night. As his focus went to their bar, she rolled onto her knees.

"Oh, Drift," she groaned. "No more. I've drunk too much."

He looked over his shoulder. "You feel ill?"

"No," she said, her chin descending as her gaze heated. "I feel invincible. Come over here."

On a smile, he exhaled a laugh. "I don't think

so.”

“Come on,” she said, stroking the bed between them with both hands. Leaning forward, she opened and brought them back together in large arcs. “You brought me to bed for a reason.”

“No,” he said, putting down the glasses and leaning back to prop himself on a hand. “No. No. No. Definitely not that reason.” Rising high on her knees, she untied her dress. “Babe, you’re drunk.”

“What have you lost?” she asked, catching the edge of her dress to peel it aside. “Come over here.”

“If I come over there, you won’t like me in the morning.”

“Baby…” She opened her dress, dropping the straps to the inside of her elbows. “You haven’t thought about this? About being alone with me…” Sliding one knee closer, then the other, she crawled toward him. “About touching me…” When she got to his side, she curved a hand over his shoulder and kept going, skimming a leg across his lap to straddle him. “About being inside me?”

Capturing his mouth, she gave him a full-on demonstration of what was on her mind. The man was too much. So attentive. So thoughtful. So gentle and yet so desperate… for her. That was what she felt when he gripped her waist and opened his hands to glide them up her back.

His kiss was as sure as hers, as determined. They were there, alone, in the private cabana, surrounded by moonlight, serenaded by the sea.

Coiling her arms around his neck, she basked in the draw, in the magnetism that ached for them to be together, intimate, right there, no delay.

He was ready, growing more ready by the second. The thick, hard length of him was impossible to disguise or ignore. As his hands slid onto her ass to guide her closer, deepening the connection of their bodies, Zane wasn't ashamed or reluctant.

Good. Yes. Oh, her want… she sank her fingers into his hair, determined to have him. She wanted him on his back or over her. Any way he wanted her, she'd submit.

From nowhere, Zane pulled away. "Babe…" that tone sent a chill through her. Pity. That was what she heard as his palms pushed her hair from her cheeks. "I'm going to take you back to your room."

And that was the harsh thud of truth. She'd made a fool of herself. Oh, the cool shame of embarrassment. At the start of the night, she'd asserted they wouldn't get intimate, then thrown herself at him. In the light of day, she would appreciate the rejection. Maybe. It wasn't so easy to be objective while climbing from his lap and wrapping her dress back up. She held it tight, embracing herself.

"Babe, let me—"

"It's back this way," she said, going around the bed, swiping up her shoes to hold them against her, still clasping her dress closed.

Her buzz was gone, replaced by nothing positive. Most of her first dates went well, but no one had a perfect score. Dating Zane with weeks on the island still lying ahead was such a stupid move. Stupid! Ha, and she'd preoccupied herself with their lack of a chance for a long-term future, turned out that was moot. They'd lasted the length of one date.

Their journey back to the hotel was all but silent. Zane tried to talk to her, but her mood was flat. All she wanted to do was get back to her room and crawl into bed. What an idiot. A lush. A ridiculous—she'd never be able to look him in the eye again.

ELEVEN

AT BREAKFAST, she ate next to nothing. Still, she wouldn't be awkward about it. Her shame couldn't get in the way of her work. So when Honi appeared in the doorway of the dining room after Alessia scampered off for her day, she went to the corporate suite as usual. Without hesitation, she planned to stride inside, beach bag on her shoulder, head held high… and with a lot of humility.

Zane paced in the terrace doorway, hands locked at the small of his back.

When he noticed her, he stopped. For a few seconds, they just looked at each other.

Zane was the first to break the silence. "Thea—"

"It's okay," she said, showing his contrition a smile. "You don't have to worry."

His hands swung loose from each other to settle at his sides. "I don't?"

"That's the whole point of dating," she said, going to the desk. Oh, man, there was her lip gloss. He must've found it after… in her defense, her bra did stay on. "We went out to see if we might be compatible." Pulling out her chair to sit, she put her bag on the floor and bent to retrieve her laptop. "Just because the romance didn't work out doesn't mean we can't still work in the same space." After putting the laptop on the desk, she hesitated to look at him. "Does it? Am I being presumptuous?"

"Yes, you are," he said, marching over. "The romance did work out. It definitely worked out."

"Zane," she said on a semi sigh. "Would you like me to leave? I can work in my room or on the beach. I have most of the files I need saved to—"

"Babe," he said, bowing to set both hands on the table. "I stopped because I didn't trust myself."

"You don't have to—"

"Having you in my arms, kissing you… Thea, I had to be a gentleman. I took you to a bed and plied you with alcohol. If we'd woken up there, together, after… You'd never have looked at me again. You'd have been angry and for a damn good reason. You'd have been right to report me."

"Whether you stopped out of respect or just because you weren't as attracted to me as we thought, it's okay." She smiled again. "I had a nice time and you're a good guy."

"Yet it sounds like you're saying goodbye."

Time for humility. "I wasn't sure I'd be able to look you in the eye ever again. I knew I had to try. To come here and apologize for making a fool of myself."

"You didn't—"

"I started the night telling you over and over again that it wouldn't happen. Then I took off my dress and assaulted you." The embarrassment heated her through and not in a good way. "Thank you for not following through and I promise I'll never put you in that position again."

"Tonight we'll have dinner. Meet earlier and then I have a treat for you."

"No." Shaking her head, she opened her laptop to turn it on. "Thank you. You don't owe me anything."

"Somehow, you've got it in your head we stopped because I don't want you. Last night only cemented we made the right choice."

"To stop?"

"To give us a shot. If stopping messes with your head or made you doubt us, come around here…" He boosted his hands off the desk to stand up straight. "Come here while we're both sober and kiss me like you did last night… I promise you it'll end different." What a conundrum. "I want you, Thea. Bad. But I want you more than once. If I'd followed through with you last night, we'd be over already."

"Aren't we?"

"You tell me," he said. "What did last night do for you? Put you off? Are you attracted to me today?"

More than she wanted to admit out loud. "Zane—"

"We're going to be together, Thea. That means sometimes we'll have to step in for each other. Being together for the first time last night, the way we ended up, wasn't right. So I stepped up to keep us right. You did it yesterday when I had you on your back on that desk… We're a team. Equals. We each step up for the other."

His certainty was so seductive. "You've got this all figured out."

Zane shrugged. "I had a lot of time to think about it. I didn't sleep much."

That was troubling. "Why not?"

"Take your pick," he said, running a hand through his hair. "Obsessing about how amazing your body felt on mine or stressing about how quiet you were on the drive back to the hotel." He took a breath. "Tell me I haven't messed this up already, Wanderer. Please, babe. Give us another chance."

She was the screw-up, yet somehow, he was the one contrite.

She sighed, giving in. "Dinner?"

"Yes. Dinner. Yes."

The offer of a do-over. Already they were running out of chances. Too many false starts and they'd be over before they began.

TWELVE

HIS GENIUS PLAN was sort of genius. On their return to their first date cabana, she was dubious. But the bed was gone, completely. In its place was a table and two chairs. They ate the food waiting under silver and then he led her to the beach… to two hammocks set up side by side. They each had a little table attached to the wooden frames, space for their drinks. Virgin. Always.

Zane said the next time she offered herself to him, he wouldn't be a gentleman, so he wanted to be sure she was sure.

For the next seven nights, they did the same thing, and Thea managed to contain herself enough to stick to kissing… and maybe a little stray petting in their cart.

Days were spent in the office. Evenings on the beach. Life was almost perfect.

"A long list," Thea said, gazing up into the stars, her fingers lost in her hair. "There are a million places I want to go."

"Give me an example."

Their hammocks were staggered so they lay face to face, just a foot between them.

"Italy, I always wanted to go there."

"So why don't you?" he asked.

She laughed. "You think I have the time or money to fly halfway around the globe?" With a lazy nod, she highlighted the exception. "Present situation excluded."

"I think—" a buzz cut him off.

When she twisted to see what it was, he was checking his watch.

"What's wrong?" she asked. Alarm crossed his expression. "Zane?"

He rolled out of his hammock and sprang to his feet. "I'm sorry, babe."

"Sorry?"

He came around to her side. "I have to take you home."

"What?" she asked, surprised by the sudden shift. "What happened?"

Bending over to put his arms around her, Zane helped her to stand in the sand. "I'm sorry."

Apologies weren't necessary. His urgency to get her away from the beach and back to the cart scared her a little. Not scared for her life, but scared he was going through something bad.

On the road to the hotel his focus was intense. She didn't get it or like it. Something had happened and she wanted to support him. Were they there yet? Involved enough to share burdens and confide in each other.

They pulled into the side parking lot where the carts lined up.

"I'm sorry," Zane said once again, grabbing her hand to pull her across the front seat of the cart and onto the asphalt.

"Zane," she said, hurrying to catch up when he dragged her to the door and unlocked it with his thumbprint.

The door popped and he held it open. "Babe," he said, bowing to kiss her. "I'm sorry, but I'll see you in the morning, okay? Go to your room, stay inside. Don't come out again."

With a hand on her back, he pushed her into the corridor. Before she could say a word, the door closed.

For a few seconds, she stood there dumbfounded. What a way to end a date? What the hell was going on? She wasn't pissed, or angry, or upset, she was worried. Had something dangerous happened? Something that might threaten life and limb? A natural disaster? A terrorist parachuted in? All kinds of horror scenarios lit her mind. Good thing she trusted Zane. Whatever it was, he'd fix it. He'd never leave her, or anyone, in danger.

Figuring out what his watch alerted him to was impossible, and following him would be ridiculous. If he wanted her to know, he'd have told her. If it was some internal thing, he'd tell her tomorrow, or Alessia would come back with gossip after her excursion the next day.

She went to her room, using her thumbprint to get inside.

"Alessia," Thea called out, expecting all kinds of tales from her electrified sister. The excitement about their host hadn't calmed down a jot since they got there. "I'm back."

Taking out her earrings, Thea slipped her shoes off under the vanity and tossed her jewelry on the surface.

No response. Maybe the excitement had been too much for her sister and she'd passed out already.

She finished removing the pins from her hair and checked how her makeup held up.

Not bad.

"Alessia," she called again.

Still, no response. Usually, after an evening with her friends and their gracious host, her sister wouldn't shut up. Sleep had to be the answer. She went around to check, but Alessia's bed was made, flat, no sign of anyone. Crossing her sister's room to check for light under the bathroom door, she found none but knocked anyway.

Did they have candles on the island? Most likely. Her sister lit them at home sometimes when soaking in the tub. Except, wouldn't there still be some flicker of light?

"Alessia, are you in there?"

No, opening the door revealed…nothing, no one inside. The closet was empty too. Okay, now all bets were off; distress blasted in Technicolor. If there was some drama and her sister was safe, fair enough, she'd let it be. But her sister was out there, and with Zane running off the way he had, trouble, of some kind, lurked. She went back to grab her shoes and put them on while leaving the bedroom.

Drinks in the main dining room, that's what Alessia said, right? Yes, because she'd been ecstatic Roman was hosting a Q&A session. Drinks, conversation, like they were just hanging out, that's what Alessia said. It was only supposed to last a couple of hours. Roman wouldn't want to answer questions all night. Maybe it had run over. That was possible. These things weren't set in stone. Even if Roman had gone, her sister sometimes stayed out with friends. Except usually there would be some sign in the room she'd been back to change her shoes or grab something.

Going up the hallway, confirming Alessia's well-being was all that mattered. Okay, so, yeah, she was old enough to stay out late, but keeping her safe was the whole purpose of them traveling together. Checking was basically her job. And there was no need to panic. Not yet. Zane's drama could be something in the kitchen or one of the rooms. Something with staff or another guest. Maybe there was a wild animal trapped…

Noise from the reception got louder the closer she got. A chill swept through her. Anxiety was warranted, she could feel it.

Striding on, she opened the door intending to find out what was happening. Except as soon as she stepped forward, someone got in her way. A man.

"Go back to your room." The statement was such a surprise, all she could do was blink at the tall blond. "You'll be safe there."

Whoa, hey, concern became alarm in an instant.

"Safe?" she asked, stopping just short of shoving him. "I'll be safe when I find my sister."

Rather than get physical, she swerved around him, continuing on her way to the dining room.

"Wait," he said, darting after her. "Don't go in there now."

"Why?"

"Thea," he said, putting a hand over hers on the door handle. "You don't want to go in there."

She did and couldn't believe the stranger would presume anything else. And how did he know her name? Did he memorize every guest?

"Excuse me," she said, drawing her eyes off him and extracting her hand to grab the other door.

No one would stop her. She gave the door a confident push and marched inside.

The different air brought her to an abrupt halt.

Chairs were arranged around a central platform. The stool up there was empty, but the room wasn't.

Guests crowded in the corner, Alessia included. All close together, no space between. A server on her knees a few feet in front of them sobbed. Something had happened, something shattered their excitement and replaced it with terror.

Zeroing in on what had the women scared, what they stared at wide-eyed, she didn't linger on Zane. He was there, yes, with a couple of other guys, angled toward the man near the head of the room.

Roman.

Thea hadn't met him in person, but she didn't live under a rock. He was a famous actor, she recognized his face.

Though aware of the employee behind her, she didn't pay him any attention either. Roman, the instigator, the man in the spotlight, noticed her. She interested him, or something interested him.

"Get her out of here, Tripp," Zane said, slow and steady, without turning around.

One of the guys next to him glanced at her. "She won't—"

"The elusive Thea," Roman declared. "The woman too good for the masses. Damn, you must be special. Does your pussy sing?"

Who the fuck did he think…?

Anger and arrogance seeped out of him. Entitled didn't do his aura justice.

"Watch yourself," Zane warned in a startling tone.

An employee shouldn't speak to his boss that way. The last thing she wanted was for him to lose his job sticking up for her.

Before she could say that, Roman laughed. "Oh, yeah, you're perfect for each other, cuz. You jump in there and defend her, I'm sure she'll drop to her knees in gratitude later. Gotta have some talent to captivate the Great and Powerful Oz."

"Disrespect her again and you'll be on a flight out

before the sun rises."

"You and your fucking island. He is God here," Roman said, swaying back to grab for the bourbon bottle on the bar. "King and Emperor. That's how you like it, isn't it? You and your fucking brother, your fucking asshole friends." He took a long drink from the bottle then swung it toward the guests in the corner. "You ladies haven't had the pleasure of my cousin's company yet. He's not always the most social guy… does like to tell you everything you're doing wrong at every opportunity though. He's a fucking oracle. Invented that yet? Bet you fucking have."

He started drinking again and wasn't so quick to stop this time.

Cousin. Zane was Roman's cousin? He'd never told her that. And the way Roman was talking… Emperor? King? The island was… She didn't understand. No way it could belong to Zane. Not her Zane. Maybe he was the caretaker, the guy who'd promised his cousin's fans wouldn't cause a riot.

"Time to call it a night," Zane said. "You've had enough… Mieux, take the women out of here."

Thea heard the door behind her open and wanted Alessia and the others to rush out.

Roman lowered the bottle and staggered a few steps. "They stay! They're my women… They're all my women!"

"I can't believe this shit," Zane muttered.

The guy behind her strode past to go over to him. "What do you need, boss?"

"He's the boss," Roman exclaimed. "Boss. Boss. Boss! Always the boss. With his billions and billions. Company rules the globe. He just can't do no wrong. Him and his best, best buds."

"You're supposed to be through with this crap," the guy they'd called Tripp said. "You got access to the island because you swore you were through with bullshit like this."

"Yeah, yeah," Roman drawled.

"Struan left this afternoon," Tripp muttered to Zane.

"Who the fuck authorized that?"

"Man's allowed to live his life."

"Sure about that?" Zane asked. "You seeing this shit? This is what happens."

"Stop fucking whispering! Stop fucking talking. Goddamn!" Anger seized Roman. "She's gonna fucking marry him! Who the fuck is he?"

"Enough!" Zane exclaimed. "You're done. Thea, take the women out of here."

"No!" Roman shouted. "No! They fucking stay!"

Uh huh, like she cared for his opinion.

Turning to the huddle of women, Thea made eye contact with Alessia and gestured her over. Hesitant, her sister paused to reassure her friends before they'd let her go.

Alessia rushed over and hugged her fast. "Hold the door and get everyone back to their rooms," she said to her sister. "Safe."

Her sister nodded and got to work.

"No," Roman said, starting her way. "Who do you think you are?"

Zane and Tripp crossed the room fast to block his route.

While Alessia ushered everyone to the exit, encouraging them on the way. Thea wouldn't back down. Until the others were safe, she'd happily be the focus of this asshole's whatever.

"Who do you think you are?" she retorted. "Because you've made a couple of movies, you think you can imprison and terrorize women?"

"You don't know shit," Roman spat, swaying

forward.

Zane slapped a hand to his shoulder to push him back. "You're too close to the line."

"Fuck the line," Roman said, throwing up his arms to push Zane off as he backed away. "Fuck you, your island, your woman—"

"That's right," Zane snapped. "My island, my woman, remember that when your sorry ass is dragging next time the media tears you apart. I won't be standing there, I won't be propping you up. Me or my best, best buds. I'm done."

Thea glanced back just as the last of the women went past Alessia and out. At least, who she thought was the last until her sister nodded at the other side of the room. The server remained crumpled there, sobbing.

"Get back to the room," Thea said. "I'll look after her. Don't open the door to anyone except me. Lock the slider too. Tell everyone to lock their doors."

Alessia left and the door swung shut. As she headed for the server, Roman noticed he'd lost his flock.

"What the hell!"

Sensing how thin his patience was, Thea hurried to the server and crouched with her. "Honey," she said, stroking her hair from her face. "Honey, we have to get out of here."

Through her swollen, wet eyes, the server tried to focus. "Wh… what?"

"We have to go."

There wasn't time to process her own feelings about the evening's revelations or to tune in to Roman's ramblings. The poor woman had to get out of there before she was subject to more of this insane man's diatribe.

Putting an arm around the server, Thea helped her to her feet.

"She stays!" Roman demanded. "Both of them

stay!"

Not a chance. A couple more guys came through the rear door behind Roman. Their entrance distracted him enough for Thea to get the employee out.

Once in reception, a gaggle of other staff members came rushing over to check their friend.

"Oh my God," one of the other women said, embracing her blubbing colleague. "What happened?"

"He… he yelled at me… He… blamed me for everything. Screamed at me for ruining his life, his career… said I couldn't get anything right… said I was worthless."

The girl was a mess and Roman was an asshole, what a surprise. She didn't need to bear witness to know that. Alessia was by the door to the corridor that led to their room. She went over and slid an arm around her waist.

"You should be in the room."

"I waited for you.

And she could chastise her sister for that, except she understood the need. "Let's get some sleep."

Alessia didn't say anything else until they got into the bedroom. They gave each other space to process. She had questions of her own and didn't fire them at Alessia. Everything had happened so fast. How could so much change in such a short amount of time? She needed to breathe for a few minutes.

Her sister wasn't of the same mind. As Thea went into her half of the room, Alessia stayed just inside the doorway.

"You're sleeping with a billionaire?"

Her eyes closed slowly. Didn't seem fair that Alessia knew the truth only minutes after first sharing a room with Zane. She wanted to scream at him. At least, she should. In truth, she was too stunned to make sense of… any of it. Sleep. Yes, that would help. Maybe she'd wake up and discover it had all been a bad dream.

Sensing Alessia's approach, Thea opened her eyes. The sea was just visible through the doors to the deck, only just decipherable in the moonlight. She needed it to keep her centered and wished it was easier to hear.

Alessia came right around in front of her. "Thea!"

She admitted her shame. "I didn't know, okay?"

"You said an employee. Zane Dyce is not an employee!"

"Did you hear me?" Thea asked. "I didn't know."

"Didn't know?" Alessia said, folding her arms and leaning back. "Yeah, right. Who doesn't know Zane Dyce?"

Calming herself, Thea licked her lips. "And you would've known it was him? I've heard the name in the past, I don't go around assuming every Bill I meet is Bill Gates. Why should I assume every Zane is Zane Dyce?" Her sister faltered, a tiny bit. "I didn't know what he looked like… And the guy I was seeing," or the guy she'd thought she was seeing, "didn't tell me he owned an island… or that he was Roman's cousin."

Her sister dialed her outrage down. "Roman told us."

"You didn't know they were family until after you were here either…" Alessia shook her head. "Did you know Zane was here?"

Alessia's arms dropped to her sides. "No, he didn't say that."

Leaving her sheepish sister, Thea went to sit on the bed. "What happened tonight?"

Alessia sighed and came wandering over. "I don't know. We thought maybe he'd had a drink when we started, but it was fine, you know?"

She wasn't sure she did and raised her brows. "I

thought he was an alcoholic?"

Alessia glared as she dropped down to sit beside her. "It was pain pills and he's over all that."

"Didn't look that way tonight."

"He didn't take any pills," Alessia said. Though she wasn't entirely sure how her sister could know that for sure. "He had a drink… that's no big deal. He's allowed a drink."

Thea didn't like to judge. But if having a drink turned him into a guy who'd berate an innocent woman in public, and hold a bunch more hostage, she wasn't sure he should be drinking either.

"He's the host. He shouldn't get into a state like that. And what did the poor server do to deserve what he did to her?"

"He's stressed," Alessia said, rubbing her thigh. "Sway got engaged."

She frowned. "I thought they'd split up."

Though, honestly? She hadn't given Roman's relationship a lot of thought.

"Doesn't mean he stopped caring about her," Alessia said. "How would you feel if Thom got engaged." She gasped. "Oh my God, Thom! Does he know about you and Zane?"

"How would he know?" she asked. "I haven't talked to anyone from home… except work emails from Anika."

And, also, why would she start calling around telling people she was seeing someone? Anyone? Even if she'd known the truth of Zane's means, she wouldn't have done that. Seriously, who did that?

Solemn and wide-eyed, Alessia nodded slowly. "You should tell him. You should tell Thom before he reads it in the press."

What the—press? Man, that was not what she'd signed on for. It wouldn't be that big a deal… would it?

Thea tsked and got up to get her nightdress. "In the press?"

"Yeah, in the press," Alessia asserted, unbuckling her heels to toss them away. "You date Zane Dyce, people will write about you… they'll take your picture."

The celebrity pages didn't interest her. The business pages tended to be less about pictures. She didn't spend any time perusing the society pages.

"Did you see Zane's picture before we were here?"

"Oh, God, yeah. Not a whole lot, but some. He was with Arden Delgado forever."

And her stomach flipped. Thea hadn't known it. Really hadn't. He'd talked to her about his ex and she'd just nodded along oblivious.

"But, I mean, obviously they weren't suited to each other," Alessia said, maybe reading her doubt. "They broke up, didn't they?"

Yes, and she had some idea about that. Even being mad at Zane didn't prompt her to spill his secrets.

"There's nothing to tell Thom," Thea said. "Whatever it was, it's over."

"Aww, why? I love you two together."

Her sister's exuberance was either endearing or incredibly naïve. "You've never seen us together."

Lunging down the bed, Alessia gripped the covers. "He owns everything. Like everything," she said. "He owns these beds, the linens, the building…" She raised her arms up. "He owns the whole island."

"Thanks, yeah, I got that," Thea said and went over to capture her sister's hands. Pulling her off the bed, she gave Alessia a hug. "Can we please go to bed? I need sleep."

She needed space. With Alessia going on and on, forgetting about Zane's deception wouldn't be easy. Face it, forgetting wouldn't be easy no matter what and sleep probably wouldn't be easy to come by. Still, Thea tucked Alessia into bed, then went to hers to stare at the ceiling.

Zane. He was a stranger. Not who she'd believed him to be. What did the truth mean? What did it change?

THIRTEEN

AT BREAKFAST, they were given a speech about the previous night and sent Roman's apologies. He wouldn't be joining them that day. Oh, what a terrible shame.

Eye roll.

Spending time with her sister was preferable over even thinking about work… and all that entailed. Sand, the ocean, the glorious sky. There was a lot to be grateful for. Roman's groupies may not agree, but from her point of view, the reset was appreciated.

The day was spent on the beach. Servers brought out a picnic lunch and she finally got her chance to swim. All very civilized, benign… though the name Roman Lowe came up more than she'd like.

Where was he? Was he sick? Had he left? Would he ever forgive Sway? For what, she didn't know, but that last one was a popular topic.

The day might've passed for good if it hadn't been for the pervading thoughts about the previous night. Contrary to every other female brain on the island, Roman wasn't the man taking up space in hers.

She'd sort of managed to shrug off her overthinking until she was in the shower before dinner. Washing and blow drying her hair in the bathroom gave her nothing but time to obsess. She came out of her bathroom in a towel only to discover Alessia laying out dresses on her bed.

Thea's dresses on Thea's bed.

"Uh, what are you doing? Picking out my clothes?"

"I've worn all my favorite dresses," Alessia said.

"So you thought you'd pick some of mine?"

The knock on the door turned her around.

Alessia was already scampering across the room. "Lark said she'd bring me some dresses!" she called out, rushing over to answer it.

Turning back around, Thea glanced over the apparel her sister laid out. Why didn't she put as much thought into her outfit? Literally any of them would do.

"Oh my God," Alessia exclaimed.

"Alessia, right?"

Thea recognized that voice. Shit.

"Uh huh, oh my God, you know my name?"

"It's nice to finally meet you," Zane said. "Is your sister around?"

"Oh, God, yeah," Alessia said. "Yeah, come in."

Adjusting her towel to ensure it was tucked in tight, Thea couldn't expect her sister to stand in Zane's way.

Fuck, she'd had a whole day. Why did she feel so unprepared?

Alessia was laughing as she and Zane approached. "Is it funny to knock on a door you own?"

"Money doesn't replace manners," he said, stopping when their eyes met. "Hey, Wanderer."

"It's kind of shocking that you're here," Alessia said. "Isn't it shocking that he's here, Thea? How's

Roman?"

That question broke their stare.

"Oh…" Zane started. "He's doing fine. I apologize for last night… to both of you. None of you needed to witness that."

"Is that all you came to say?" Thea asked. "Are you knocking on everyone's door?"

"No," he said. "I came to talk to you."

Alessia side-shuffled toward the deck. "I'll… go see where Lark is with those dresses."

Her sister went out into the cooling air and silence settled around them.

"I'm sorry, Thea."

Closing her eyes, she shook her head. "An apology changes nothing."

"We were starting something—"

"A relationship should never start on an apology. Not a lasting one anyway," she said and breathed out. "We started in lies, it never had a chance."

"I disagree," he said, coming her way. Thea held up a hand to stall him. "I didn't intend to lie to you about the money."

"You think this is about money?" She went to pull the deck door closed. "You endangered my sister's safety."

After a silence, she looked at him over her shoulder. That was it? He had nothing?

His frown sure suggested that. "Thea, I would never—"

"Why on Earth would you facilitate your cousin's addictions? Strand him on an island with dozens of innocent women? Young, impressionable women?"

"Thea—"

"I know he was addicted to pain pills, and it wasn't alcohol, Alessia told me. But the state of that server… he must have done a number on her. What did she do to deserve that? What if it had been my sister? Maybe next time it will be… I thought… whatever I thought about you…" Whatever she'd felt… "About the man I thought you were… It was a complete lie, a fabrication."

Zane stalked over. "I would never let Roman hurt anyone… He only got access to the island because he swore the addiction, the bullshit, was history. He was in a residential program for months. We got doctor reports, psychologist opinion. Roman swore all of that was in his past." He exhaled, taking his time examining her. "Thea…" His hand drifted to her face. "I would never knowingly let anyone hurt you or your family."

She pushed his hand away. "If that's true, you should get a plane here now and give everyone a chance to leave."

He frowned. "Alessia wants to leave? Of course she or any of her companions will be given whatever they need. They're not prisoners here. My jet is in Hawaii, it can leave within the hour."

"Your jet," she muttered. "I'm not sure I'd be comfortable on that."

"Good," he said, a smile warming his lips. "Because I didn't offer to fly you anywhere."

She crooked a brow. "They're not prisoners, but I am?"

"Only for as long as it takes to persuade you to forgive me."

"Zane, it doesn't matter. We're done. What matters now is my sister."

"Your sister will be taken care of. She'll be given anything she needs. But we have something to work on here."

"Why does it matter?" she asked. "Go find yourself a woman you haven't lied to, or one who doesn't care that your cousin is an abuser."

"I screwed up," he said. "I didn't mean to lie, but it was… When I realized you didn't know who I was… I liked it. I liked the idea that maybe a woman could fall for the guy I am instead of the dollar signs… I would never deliberately hurt you. I've proved that. Proved that I'm not only out for myself or for sex."

She'd screwed up too, the night she threw herself at him. Zane hadn't made her grovel after that.

"Okay," she said and took a big breath. "I'm sorry."

Startled, he blinked. "What?"

"I was scared and when I get scared, I get mad." One confession over. "You don't owe me anything."

"I don't—"

"My mom wanted me here, I came because Alessia isn't what you'd call the most streetwise woman."

"I know this. You told me this."

Except he obviously hadn't been listening. Either that or she just saw this man as a stranger, one who didn't care for her as she'd thought her Zane did.

"I'm not exactly Miss Streetsmart myself…" Her head rolled. "Which I guess you've figured out for yourself. Our parents never beat us, no addiction issues in the family—"

"Thea," he said, stepping in close. "Why are you talking to me like we're strangers?"

"Zane," she exhaled his name. "We were on the beach, drinking, enjoying the stars…"

"Everything was perfect. I enjoy your company, we enjoy each other. Isn't that obvious by now?"

"My job is to protect my sister. Not to drink and talk with hot billionaires."

"You have no reason to feel guilty. We didn't do anything—"

"I'm not interested in your validation. Thank you for coming to apologize, I appreciate your time. I don't want to be late to dinner with my sister so…" His brow came lower. Wow, couldn't this guy take a hint? She gestured toward the door. "I'm late, Zane, go."

"If I tell them not to serve dinner, they won't serve dinner."

Geez, where did this arrogant SOB get off?

"So you'd have your guests starve?"

"If it'll make you talk to me."

She raised her arms, then dropped them. "There's nothing to say. My sister and I have enjoyed the island. Is your cousin still here?"

"Roman? Yes."

And if that just wasn't the answer to the unasked question.

"Family should be important. That's why I'll be taking mine home, as soon as it's physically possible."

"Thea—"

"Can you arrange a flight, or do I have to make my own arrangements?"

Though what the hell did that look like? Maybe she could lash some trees together and make a raft.

"Thea, it's in my power to give you anything you want…" That vehemence didn't suggest the end of a statement. "But I can't let you walk away."

"I'm not your prisoner."

"Your family is important to me."

"No," she said and shook her head. "If that was true, my sister's life wouldn't have been endangered last night. One slip, one fall, one stray fist, or a thrown bottle, anything could've happened with him so out of control. And you know what…?" Her hand came up to gesture. "You know what's really scary about what happened last night? The number of endangered women. Women who don't have their sisters and families looking out for them. Maybe it's okay because you have all this money and think you can pay off anyone your cousin traumatizes—

"

"Thea—"

"Money doesn't excuse bad behavior. Fame doesn't negate responsibility. At least not in my opinion."

"Thea—"

"Some of them will never have been exposed to that kind of behavior. They're young and adore that man. You gave your cousin a platform to abuse—"

"Thea!" This time he grabbed her arm to haul her against him. "I will never disappoint you again."

"No, because I'll never give you a chance." Her fingers splayed on his chest, pushing yet without strength. "You're not the man I thought you were."

"I want to be that man. For you."

"Zane…" his name was an exhale.

"What?" he asked, his voice low. "Read me the riot act, baby." The warmth of his caress fizzed from her temple, down through the rest of her all the way to her soul. "Long as you're talking, you're with me. Keep talking, baby."

"I need to be with a man who…" The weakness in her words came with the loosening of her muscles. "Zane…"

"Yeah, baby?" Shit, she had nothing. He stooped lower. "I'm going to fix this." Her head dropped into the cradle of his hand as it sank into her hair. "I'll make you so happy, I swear it, baby."

Until that moment, the moment his lips made contact with hers in that room, her brain believed they'd been getting closer. That their dates meant something, that spending time together could lead to something else.

In that second, everything changed.

This kiss was different. In the past, he'd held back, restrained himself. This man kissing her was strong, confident, determined. And the funny part? She'd believed he was all of those things before the floodgates opened and the truth spilled out.

Finding her sense, she pushed and leaned back. "No."

"No?"

"I can't—we can't—" The glimpse of movement outside betrayed her sister's approach. "I'm late for dinner with my sister."

As she tried to move, he tightened his hold, and she sprang back against him. "If you're leaving the island, I'm coming with you."

"Don't say things like that."

This time she did get free and hurried to open the sliding door for Alessia and Lark, who'd joined her for some reason.

"Oh my God, Mr. Dyce," Lark said, rushing to him. "It's an honor to—oh my God." Without invitation, the young woman threw her arms around him in a hug. Instantly, he held his hands up at each side, like in surrender. "I can't believe it's really you."

"Yes, it's really me," he said.

His eyes met hers and she sensed the request. Giving the guy a break, she went over to pick Lark's arms away to break the embrace.

"How's Roman?" Lark asked like she hadn't just violated him. "Will we see him tonight?"

"Unlikely."

"Not the right answer," she said, gaining all focus. "If that man is loose on the island—"

"You'll be safe, I promise you."

"Yeah, it's not like he actually hurt us," Lark said, kind of affronted. "He's just… passionate."

"That's an excuse."

"He's a creative. All creative people are dramatic."

"Dramatic shouldn't be traumatic."

"Maybe we could visit him," Lark said, ignoring her to address Zane. "He might like that."

Alessia leaped to her friend's side. "Yeah!"

"No." And she couldn't be any clearer. "Mr. Dyce was just leaving; he wouldn't want us to be late for dinner."

"He could join us and—"

"No," she said, firm when her gaze touched his. "He has his own arrangements to make." Like for their departure. Ideally, their speedy departure. "Thank you for the apology, Mr. Dyce."

Alessia leaned in. "You know, if you and him were like—"

"Alessia, go pick a dress."

Her sister huffed but went to the bed with Lark.

"I'm not done with us," Zane murmured.

"Get the message. Go home. Have someone let us know when the plane will be departing… please."

And with that, she went to join her sister, giving him no choice but to go. The man didn't need her or her sister. Maybe he'd call this one a loss, she was chalking it up to experience. Alessia's safety was her purpose. For a minute, she'd forgotten that. Never again.

FOURTEEN

"YOU WERE RUDE," Alessia whispered to her.

They'd made it to their table for dinner. The problem was the two other people at it with them. She wouldn't cause a scene, but she really was ready for the conversation to change.

"It's not as simple as that."

"It is." Alessia just wouldn't take the hint. "That guy came to our room for you. Do you have any idea how many people would love to get five minutes of Zane Dyce's time? How many people would die if he knew their name?"

"Wealth and popularity don't account for everything," she said. "Though he is being kind enough to facilitate our early departure."

"An early…? Why would he do that? Did he ask us to leave? Why would he—"

"Because I asked him. It's not safe here, Alessia. You shouldn't be around men like Roman Lowe."

"Since when were you so judgmental? I don't want to leave."

"Leave?" Lark piped up from Alessia's other side. "Who's leaving?"

"We are," she said. "And anyone is welcome to join us."

"We're not leaving." Her sister was adamant. "I'm not leaving anyway; you can go wherever you want." Servers came over with the food providing a reprieve. Brief though it was. "I'm staying."

Why didn't her sister understand she was protecting her? "I came here to look out for you and look what happened. We're in a confined space with a man willing to exploit the environment. If I tell Mom—"

"Mom wanted me to come. She wants me to live my life."

"I want you to live your life too, but with options. Here you have no choice but to take crap like what happened last night. We have no escape option here, nowhere to go if things take a nosedive."

Again.

Alessia picked up her wine. "You can escape if you want, I don't want."

"It's a disease," Alana interjected. Had she been listening the whole time? "Addiction is a disease. It's not his fault."

Maybe. Maybe not.

"His addiction is none of my business, disease or otherwise. My sister's safety is my primary concern."

"Running away from him will send a message," Alana said. "You'll be telling him he's broken."

It could be argued he was, wasn't everyone broken in one way or another?

Lark leaned toward the center of the table. "Zane Dyce came to Alessia's room to apologize!"

Shit, how long had the woman been biting her tongue on that one?

"Oh my God," Alana said. "Do you think he'll

visit everyone?"

The sneaky look Alessia and Lark exchanged almost deserved an eye roll.

"No," she said uninterested in being the subject of gossip. "He and I have been working together while you've been on excursions with Roman."

"Last night Roman said you were perfect for each other," Lark said. "That you captivated Zane, is that true? Are you together?"

"No."

"So just sex then?"

"No! Not just sex, not just anything." How had this all turned around on her? "We had a friendship and now it's through."

"Because of what happened last night?"

God, these women were relentless.

"So you think he's broken too? That he's responsible for his cousin's actions?"

"Not the actions, but enabling him, yes," she said. What the Lowe and Dyce families decided to do for each other was their business. "There's no denying last night wouldn't have happened in another environment. Dyce gave Roman all the tools he needed to—"

"To what?"

"What the hell is with the inquisition? Aren't we going to eat?"

In silence, if she had her way. No one had even looked at their plates. Deciding to take the lead, the quicker she scarfed the food, the sooner she could get away from the table. Maybe Alessia would be more reasonable alone without her posse.

The last thing she wanted to do was deprive her sister of this once-in-a-lifetime opportunity. But what exactly did looking after her mean if she let Alessia spend time with a potential abuser?

"I've never known anyone who slept with a

billionaire before."

It was like she wasn't even there. Or she was there, screaming into the void, and no one could hear her. Drama was fuel for these women, and they knew exactly how to use it to its full potential.

"You don't think about it do you? Weren't you terrified?" Alana asked. "He's probably had sex with the hottest women on the planet."

Alessia's shoulders went back. "My sister is hot."

"Yeah, but, not like supermodel hot. Look at Sway, she's just… on another plane."

"You think she slept with Zane?" Lark asked on a gasp. "Maybe that's why Roman was so upset last night! He found out his cousin had sex with the love of his life."

Wow, it was just… wow. Did people really live their lives this way?

"If Sway and Zane got together, she wouldn't marry Deacon."

"No. You think she's heartbroken? That Zane broke her heart?"

"And she's using Deacon to make him jealous? They've been together like ten minutes, they're not really going to get married, are they?"

"Maybe," Lark picked up Alana's thread. "Maybe she wants them to object."

"At the wedding?"

Excitement grew to a frenzy. "Yeah! Like a big church full of people and—"

"Okay," she said, putting down her fork. "Can you hear—"

"Oh my God, they might fight!" Alana should write movies… teen movies. "Roman rushes in to declare his love and there's Zane already there with her! Stealing her from Deacon!"

"This woman is popular," she muttered, understanding they were in their own little world.

"Do you think she's coming here? Will they ask her to come here?"

"Maybe she is already here. We haven't seen Roman, have we? Maybe she came when she heard about last night."

"Oh for God's sake." And that was the moment the three others chose to focus on her. "If any reasonable woman heard her ex-boyfriend got trashed and terrified a group of innocent women, the last thing she'd do was get on a plane."

"You don't understand," Alessia said. "She loves him."

"If she loves him, why is she engaged to this Deacon guy?"

"They went out like a million years ago."

"Then she should marry him and live happily ever after. She and Roman can go about their lives separately and never see each other ever again." Alana snorted while Lark blinked in surprise, both set their incredulous stares on her sister. "What?"

"Deacon is Logan's lead guitarist."

And she could only shake her head and shrug. "Okay, and—"

"Logan," Alessia said like she was an idiot. "Logan Lowe! Roman's brother."

"Oh." Okay, then maybe... "Are they close? Do they hang out? I don't see your co-workers... ever."

"It's hardly the same thing," Alessia said.

"Yeah, they hang out. They're in the same places all the time. Roman lives in LA. Everyone in LA hangs out in Crimson—"

"Oh my God, do you think they'll fight?" Alana was big on men getting physical. "They'll be there, drinking—"

"If it's a big club, they don't have to see each other."

All three women groaned.

"Thea," Alessia whined. "Don't you know anything?"

"Apparently not."

"Crimson LA has a VIP area for—"

"Very important people?" she asked, sort of joking, only no one laughed.

"Who is Zairn Lomond closest to?" Alana asked, pondering. "Who would he bar?"

"You think he would bar someone?"

"If he doesn't want a fight in his club, he'll have to exile someone."

"But if he bars Deacon, he'd have to bar Logan, right?"

"Yes, oh, and, hey, remember that time Roxie got it on with Logan? Like a year ago, in London. Do you remember that? The pictures were all over the internet!"

"Oh, yeah!"

"So Zairn's probably desperate for an excuse to bar Logan."

"For putting his hands on Roxie, yes!"

"And he wouldn't bar Roman, that would like half his numbers."

The women swooned. "He is incredibly popular."

Though she had no goddamn idea why.

"Is it popularity or people looking to cash in?" she asked. "Hangers-on have always been a feature in celebrity life."

Alana snorted again. "Like you'd know."

"Don't bully my sister."

Alessia's affront was appreciated but unnecessary.

She laid a hand on her forearm. "The last thing we want is fighting in here. She's right, I don't know much about celebrity life."

"If Thea knows Zane…" Lark said, drawing out the suspense. "Maybe she could ask him."

"Ask him what?" she questioned only to then shake her head. "I don't think I'll see him again before we leave."

She'd asked him to send someone to tell them when to be ready. Hopefully, he read between her deliberate lines and wouldn't show up himself.

Alessia finally took note of her food and began to eat. "I don't know why you think I'll be safer without you here."

"Alessia—"

"We came here for thirty days and I want to see it through. Yes, last night was… intense…"

"Alessia—"

"But no one was hurt. And you can't blame Zane either. He came as soon as he heard what was going down." True. "He didn't abandon anyone or wrestle people to the ground. No one was hurt. He showed up, defused the situation, and got everyone back to their rooms safe."

Not personally, but okay.

"Yeah," Lark said. "If you think about it, he was kind of a hero."

"A hero?"

"Yeah, swooping in to save the day. When you showed and he was worried about you, he didn't want you to get hurt."

"He wouldn't want anyone to get hurt."

"You think he doesn't care about people?" Alana asked. "That he's like some cynical, afraid to be sued heartless money-monger who thinks he's superior to—"

"He's not superior to anyone," she said and sighed. "Are you sure you want to stay? Completely sure?"

"One hundred percent," Alessia said and linked

their hands. "It's the right thing to do."

Was it?

Alessia and her friends may not be the most concise, but justice weighed their side. Zane hadn't caused the upset and he had tried to limit it. Like she'd said, when she got scared, she got mad. If her sister wasn't leaving the island, she wouldn't either. Now all she had to do was find Zane.

FIFTEEN

HE WASN'T AT the corporate suite.

After breakfast and a swim to clear her head, she'd said goodbye to Alessia and her friends at the spa. Honi was outside, waiting, and drove her to the corporate suite at her request. Except it was abandoned.

Maybe Zane didn't want to come across her. She couldn't object if that was the case. After all, wasn't that the same damn reason she'd avoided the building the previous day? He must've taken what she said to heart. Or it pissed him off and he never wanted to see her face again.

If he didn't stay at the resort, which he wouldn't, he must have his own house on the island. Stood to reason, right? Why buy an island and build a resort only to deny yourself the opportunity to enjoy it in peace?

With a sort of dread circling in her belly, she went back to Honi and the cart.

"Will you take me to the main house, please?" she asked.

Honi did a double take, but a gradual smile curled

his lips. "The main house?"

"Yes, I won't stay… I know it's probably out of bounds for guests." Maybe she could leave a message somewhere. "I would never invade his—"

"No," Honi said and got them going. "You don't have to explain, Miss Florin."

Because he could see right through her or he'd been given special instructions on what to do if she made extravagant requests? Maybe he'd drive her right off the end of the island. She'd always considered Honi a luxury, a resort-provided kindness who ensured she got to the right place in a safe and timely manner.

Now she wondered if he wasn't some kind of spy, or maybe a guard with instructions to take her down if the need arose.

They didn't drive back toward the hotel, which was something. Maybe. They passed the airstrip and the employee block, as well as the private beach she and Zane spent their evenings on. The road kept on going and going, past a fenced area and a gate. Without signs, she didn't know what either were protecting. Foliage from each side of the road thickened as they drove up a gradient. Not much, just enough that it felt different from the other end of the island.

In the final bend, the foliage thinned and right in front of them were two grand wood paneled gates flanked by endless natural stone walls. Honi stopped, but it took her a second to see the intercom. Actually, it took him nodding at it for her to figure out she needed to press the button. A single bleep was the response and the button lit up.

Did security have a hut somewhere? She couldn't see it. Yeah, it was kind of intimidating. No wonder Zane hadn't brought her there on their dates, she had so many questions. Though, apparently, her subconscious just answered its own questions without bothering to request them from her lips. She reasoned away this and that because, come on, who believed they were going to work with a billionaire every day?

"Yeah?" a female voice yapped all of a sudden. "Forget your keys? What's the password? Hmm… think maybe the power's going to my head."

"Uh…" What was she to…? A female. Zane's female? "I'm looking for, uh… Zane, Mr. Dyce."

A pause. "Looking for him for what?"

Reasonable question, though she hadn't expected to answer it to his staff, or with Honi right beside her.

"I just need to tell him something and there are no phones here. Cellphones, I mean." There was obviously an internal system, though it wasn't like she had his number. "Could you just tell him Thea dropped by and—"

Another beep. No more words, just a beep and the light disappeared. Okay, great, so much for leaving a message.

She didn't expect a gap to form between the gates or for it to continue widening. Even watching it took a second to… Oh, shit, the gates were opening, for her, for… Honi drove through when there was just enough space like they were in some kind of hurry. No. No hurry. Uh… she couldn't straighten out her thoughts. A message, she was supposed to leave a message, or see him, not see this… woman. A woman in his house, God, was she in an episode of Cheaters?

The smooth golden stone beneath the wheels wound around trees and lush greenery. When it opened out, the house was… wow… Right at the tip of the island, she couldn't see beyond the building, but with the ocean on three sides, she guessed the view would be incredible.

When Honi stopped the cart, she swallowed. Her

driver wasn't going in, no… coward. Okay, so in fairness, he never joined her in the corporate suite, why should that change now? Because safety existed with him, didn't he get that? Whatever lay ahead was… unknown. And they were all alone, on a private island… where a body may never be found.

"Your timing couldn't be better!" A woman strolled from the open doorway into the covered portico. "Do you like Sex on the Beach?"

"Uh… excuse me?"

The woman raised a pitcher. "We have a lot to talk about, beautiful."

Honi smiled and nudged her on. No going back now. She dipped one foot onto the pathway and then the other, slithering, somewhat begrudgingly, from the seat onto her feet.

"We… we do?"

"Mm hmm," the woman said, sunglasses and floppy hat topping off her dazzling smile, twinkling even in the shade. "And they're not here. Come on. Come. Come."

The stranger spun on the spot, not rushed, just determined as she shook her hair down her back, disappearing inside.

Okay, had she been expected? Who was the woman and where was Zane? Surely if this was his girlfriend…

The only way to find out was to go inside and do what the woman said.

A sweet smell enticed her to traverse the portico and cross the threshold. Light. The whole place was filled with light. Glass panels far above the double, maybe triple, height space, embraced the sky. Stairs curved on either side up to a second-floor balcony. Incredible.

"This way!" the woman up ahead declared, descending a few stairs.

Still dazed, she hurried after the hostess and stopped on the huge semi-circular terrace jutting out from the building behind, just like she thought, the view was…

"Wow."

"Breathtaking, isn't it?" the woman asked, seating herself on a double-wide lounger, curling her legs up at her side while pouring from her pitcher into two fruit rimmed glasses. "I thought our island was amazing but this…" The woman put down the pitcher and picked up the two glasses to hold one out to her. "It's a step beyond, right?" Her smile spread. "Dyce didn't say you were twitchy. Come sit down, I don't bite… not you anyway. My beau would get jealous. Though for the show alone, he might buy me another ruby."

Still sort of staggered, she went to take the glass. Be polite, courteous, listen, smile… What the hell was going on? Maybe this was where she should explain herself, yeah, this would be the time for that, but—fuck, what was that on her hand? A ring?

"Tha—wow—"

"Right?" the woman said, waggling her fingers to show off the huge ruby, then turning her hand to admire it herself. "A sign of wealth to some, passion to others." She sucked in a breath and gestured at the lounger parallel to hers. "Come and sit down, Thea."

After a few stuttering steps, she sat. "You know my name?"

"Of course I do," the stranger said, blowing something from the back of her hand. "Dyce never shuts up about you."

"I—he doesn't?"

"No," the hostess said, extending her legs as she rested against the back of the lounger. "Okay, so that's not strictly true—I never shut up about you. Dyce is all, 'don't harass her,' 'leave her alone,' blah, blah, blah. It's my duty to know my girls, what's so difficult to understand about that? How will we take over the world if we're not tight? He doesn't get it. He's a man. Some might say your guy's the most intelligent in our group…" The stranger angled a little toward her to whisper from the corner of her lips. "Maybe the second most intelligent, but we don't tell Rourke that." She corrected her posture. "Yet, somehow, he doesn't get that women aren't wired like men. Our men think they run the world, but what would they be without us?"

And she was… none the wiser.

"I'm sorry, I…" Was it guilt or embarrassment quaking and spiking her gut? She didn't get it. Something was happening, clearly, this woman got it, but they weren't on the same page. Were they even following the same book? "I don't know who you are."

The woman's head swiveled ninety degrees, then tilted with a little attitude. Oh, God, had she insulted the hostess? Getting kicked out would be one thing, maybe the best possible outcome she could expect.

Could be she'd breathed out too soon, the end of the island was right there, how easy would it be for the stranger to give her a swift kick and say sayonara? In that eventuality, she'd probably never see Zane again. Ha, idiot, the guy? Her first thought was the guy? That would be the least of her worries.

The last thing she expected was for the woman to laugh out loud. Bold and proud, that laugh wasn't offended at all.

"Oh my God, I love you," the beauty said, putting down her glass. She swung around to set her heels on the stone and extend a straight arm. "Roxanna Kyst-Lomond…" She hummed. "I'm trying it out, what do you think?"

"Think of…?"

She shook the woman's hand, still off-balance.

Maybe it was a good thing Mrs. Kyst-Lomond didn't let go.

"The hyphenate."

"Oh. It's… nice."

"Roxanna Lomond sounds kind of weird, doesn't it? Boring. Maybe I'm just not used to it. But if everywhere I go people call me Mrs. Kyst-Lomond, it sounds like an accusation. Like we're back in high school. Yeah, I kissed him, a bunch of times and in a bunch of places, most of which you can't see… when he's clothed. Which he rarely is when we're alone… Okay, so that part's not high school, we're talking triple-X there."

"I don't…"

"Maybe it's 'cause it sounds like I define myself by him. Like the only thing people will know me for is who I make out with at bedtime." The woman, Mrs. Kyst-Lomond's, smile grew to a grin. "You're absolutely none the wiser, are you?"

"I'm sorry, I don't—"

"It's okay. It's okay. Dyce said you had no idea who he was either. Any doubts about that are gone now. You don't watch much TV, do you? Read the gossip mags? Follow celebrity-watch blogs?" Her loose head shook. "You're like the cherry on our sundae…" Her jaw shifted out of place and back in. "I wonder who you have heard of… Did you know Roman?"

"Lowe?" It was something of a relief to catch a whisper of the thread of a conversation that whipped around in the invisible wind, teasing her with proximity only to then snatch it away. "I knew he was—that he is an actor. I'd heard the name. I don't think I could tell you anything he's been in though."

"If things don't work out with Dyce, I'm giving you K2's number… Not that it would do you any good because he's never reachable on the phone. Maybe his coordinates. Yeah, I'll give you his coordinates, the last known ones anyway, and we'll parachute you in."

Okay, was this a prank? Was Zane somewhere laughing at her confusion? Was it payback? She was… stumped.

"K2?"

"Oh, if you don't know Zane Dyce, you'll never know Kinloch. Fun fact, I won a contest once."

Whiplash to—what?

"You… won a contest?"

Was this the same conversation or had they moved on to something else? Talk about dynamic.

"Your sister won a contest, right?" Mrs. Kyst-Lomond said. "That's how you ended up here?"

"I ended up here because my mother didn't want my sister coming alone. Alessia's the baby."

"Protecting the people you care about is important."

"Mrs. Kyst-Lomond—"

"See…" she said, spinning again to lounge on the lounger. "It sounds like you're accusing me of something."

"Accusing you of—no, why—"

"Oh, I know, I couldn't have more permission if I paid the man. If anyone's allowed to kiss Lomond, it's me, times a million. The things I put up with for that dude…"

"Your husband?"

"You ever been married?"

"No."

"You know, marriage… It's this weird construct we accept the world over, yet it's… I don't know. People like Jane, my closest, sweetest Jane, for women like her weddings and marriage are a life goal. She's dreamed her whole life of the dress and the man. Me? I never thought about it much. Not until my ex did the whole down on one knee thing. God, I ran and ran and ran… At lightning speed. Poor Porter. Then there's Z, who didn't even bother to propose, he just opened the door, and I walked on through. There's wrong and then there's right. Porter was a good guy, he is a good guy, and I thought we fit but…" She sighed. "Sorry, enough about me, tell me about you, Thea Florin. Sister to Alessia Florin, fan of Roman Lowe… right?"

Cool condensation trickled down the glass, dampening her fingertips. It slipped, just a little, until she tightened her hold again.

"Yeah, that's about it."

"Never married. Kids?" She shook her head. "You're some kind of mentor, right? You'd have a blast with Roux. I'll give you her number, doesn't matter if you know her, she'll pay you more money than you've ever seen in your life."

"Pay me for what?"

"To work with her, and to exploit her husband, her favorite hobby."

"Mrs. Kyst-Lomond—"

"Just call me Roxie, Thea. We're girls now. Do you like seafood?"

"Yes, I… yes."

"Good because we're getting a spread for dinner. Everyone will be here. They have to be, it's a sort of intervention. I feel for Struan, but what's a guy to do, you know?"

"Mrs—Roxie…" She put down the glass then put her hands out almost like she was stabilizing herself with an invisible force. "I have no idea what's going on right now."

Roxie's broad smile glittered again. "That's because you haven't drunk anything. Sex on the Beach, trust me, it's the preference of a good friend of mine. She's pregnant right now, so we drink in honor of her."

"We do?"

"Yep. And don't worry, it's mostly juice," Roxie said, raising her own glass to the sky. "We drink to Lilya Kearns, soon to be, Lilya Kintyre—no hyphenate for her, very important—and then…" Roxie's arm lowered toward her, glass hanging in midair between the loungers, waiting… She grabbed hers up and touched it to Roxie's, then drank because the hostess did. Roxie smacked her lips. "I'll tell you anything you want to know."

"What do I…? I don't know what I want to know."

"Okay, let's start with this: you ever hear of a show called *Talk at Sunset*?"

And that was it, the brakes came off—if they'd ever been on—and Roxie really did tell her everything. All about how her relationship started after winning a TV contest. About her fiancé, who, it turned out, owned all of those Crimson clubs Alessia raved about. She probably should've figured that out.

She believed every word of the epic adventure. One that started in LA, Chicago really, and took Roxie to every quadrant of the globe. What a whirlwind. Hearing the details, it was no wonder Roxie was such an energetic person, she needed to be just to get through the day.

"Oh, wow, that's terrifying."

"That's exactly what Lilya said." Roxie topped off their glasses. They were onto their second pitcher… almost ready for their third. "We were already in the air, thank God."

And it was… inspirational. "It sounds like you have an amazing support system."

"We support each other, yes. We're family and see each other through. People think the money means private jets and luxury houses, yeah, that's true…" She gestured around with her glass without raising her head. "But it's not shallow, it's not the frivolous that matters.

The latitude means something, that's true opulence. It's why Casanova gave me Lola's Liberty. It's the freedom, the… never having to worry. If one of our people need something, if anyone we care about needs something… Hell, even if it's a complete stranger…"

"It's beyond seductive, I can't imagine it. Most people think they're doing okay covering the bills. There's a lot of us regular folk living in our own bubbles, focused on what's right in front of us."

"I get it. I was that girl, in my own bubble, focused two feet in front of me. Jane wasn't, she's always been the type to give her last, she's always been the way she is. I'm not sure I can call her a 'type' because she's just, the best of us, the best of humanity."

"Being with Knox must give her more options though, more resources to work with."

"Hence the whole wedding thing. Jane needs to be needed; Knox is a work in progress."

Yeah, and that was the opposite of what the world might think.

She swallowed some more cocktail. "Men always think they're complete."

"Oh and men like ours, the rich overachievers, they get the award for thinking they know everything. Even if it's not close to their field, they always have something to say. They always know best."

She'd put money on Roxie being no shrinking violet, no matter who was in the room. Zairn, Roxie's other half, would have his hands full if he tried to quiet or dismiss her, on any subject.

"Zane's not—"

"No, you're right, he's not as pushy as some. I'd say that's because he's confident in his intelligence. I'd also say he grew up with Rourke and the rest of the guys and didn't care so much about shouting the loudest. Sometimes it's the quiet ones you've got to watch. And his brilliance, it speaks for itself. The thing is, our guys don't compete, not really. They're proud of each other; they want to raise each other up."

"I can't imagine them all together, if they're as, large as you make out."

It was hard to imagine such an accomplished group respecting each other without conversation turning into a rabble. Just watching those at the top of her department often gave her a headache. Roxie's people, Zane's people, were about twenty grades higher, there wasn't anyone above them in the chain of command.

"You better get used to them being together. When something goes down, we congregate fast. Best advice is to take any chance you can to hang out with the girls. The guys keep themselves entertained and if we need something, or someone needs to know something, we use our own network. It's a brave man who'd say no to his woman. Even if they'd take it, like Jane might, the rest of us will speak up for her. Not that Knox would deny her anything, Jane's his world, as such an incredible woman should be."

"You're lucky. To have that kind of support."

"It's not just my support. These aren't my guys, their women are my friends, we're our own ecosystem. Us women stick together." She smiled and rolled her head, lowering her sunglasses to the end of her nose to peek at her. "You're part of that now, my dear."

"A part of…"

"Don't pretend you don't know," Roxie said, full of delight and mischief. "You've got him, baby."

"Got him?"

"By the balls," Roxie said. "Just how they love it."

"You don't mean… No, Zane and I, we're not, I—we never—"

"We don't define our relationships by sex, if that's what you're talking about," Roxie said. "Not until after we've surrendered to it, the love, not the sex. You did a number on him though, that whole Roman thing, man, was he pissed."

"Zane was pissed?"

"Yeah, damn right. He didn't just give up the island for nothing. All through Roman's time in rehab, Magnus tried to persuade Dyce to let Roman use it. His reputation was trashed, seriously trashed, and he needed something big to pull him out. This is only a step on the path, was supposed to be a step on the path."

"I don't understand."

"People, women, might like the man, but they might not enter a contest just to have dinner with him or meet him at some hotel." Didn't that sound seedy. "But a tropical island, a private tropical island, all expenses paid, all-inclusive. I bet some people entered for that more than Roman."

Not if what she'd seen in the dining room every morning was accurate.

"And he gave in?"

"Family's important to Dyce. And I shouldn't say it, but Roman's probably his least favorite cousin. He did it for Struan, and maybe too soon."

"Lola!"

Roxie's back arched as she rose to sit up and call into the house. "We're out front!" Roxie put her glass down. "If he asks, you've been here the whole time."

Now she was confused again. "I've been…?"

"With me the whole time."

"Oh… kay."

Was he likely to ask? Whoever he was? What crime were they concealing?

"Welcome to the rabbit hole, Thea," Roxie said, wearing a proud grin. "Keep your hands and arms inside the vehicle at all times."

SIXTEEN

BEFORE SHE COULD ask any questions, or even attempt escape, a tall, dark-haired guy swaggered on out. He noticed her and raised his sunglasses to his head but kept on walking.

"Thea," he said. "Hello. Welcome."

"You say hello to the guest before you say hello to me?" Roxie asked but angled her chin to accept his kiss.

"It's the only way I can judge how much damage you've done."

"I haven't done damage," Roxie said, catching his hand. "I've been filling her in."

"On?"

"Everything, everyone, getting her up to speed on… the Roxiverse."

"Where did you get to?"

"What do you care? It's nothing to you, you know the stories. It was nice she showed up, given you abandoned me for golf." Roxie shifted to peek around him at her. "He abandoned me to go play golf with your guy. Golf!" She sank back to talk up at her man again.

"Do you know how long it's been since I was alone, Casanova? Like completely alone?"

"Probably a while."

"A *long* while. Think of the damage she prevented me from doing by keeping me entertained."

"Now that you mention it, I should ask, how much do psych ward vacations run for these days?"

"Joke, my love, enjoy yourself," Roxie said. "Won't make me forget you play golf."

"Golf?" she asked. "What's up with golf?"

Was there a reason Roxie kept reiterating that?

"Yeah, I know, how embarrassing. Our men are golfers." Roxie shivered. "I'm never admitting that again. Anyone asks, I'm pleading the Fifth."

"Rox, did you—Thea?" Zane paused for a moment before coming from inside the house to stand by his friend. "Are you okay?"

"I didn't damage her," Roxie said. "Why do people think I'm some sort of disaster zone?"

"You're a crisis event, Lola. Did you forget?"

"Ha-ha."

"I…" she started, hesitant to inject herself into their rapport. "I assume this is—"

"Right, yes, duh, sorry," Roxie said. "Thea Florin this is Zairn Lomond. Mr. Kyst-Lomond."

Zairn was deadpan. "Is that what we're doing now?"

Roxie beamed up at her partner. "What's so wrong with that? Shouldn't you be as obliged to take my name as I am to take yours?"

"What happened to no arguing on our honeymoon?"

Horror hit. "This is your honeymoon?" She turned to sit side-on, then pounced to her feet. "Oh, God, Roxie, I'm so sorry!"

"Don't be," Roxie said, using her link to Zairn to

pull herself onto her feet too. "It's only our rehearsal honeymoon, and I've had a blast of a day."

"No, not that." Thea couldn't stop herself from embracing the blonde. "I'm so sorry you married a man who'd choose golf with a buddy over sex with you on your honeymoon!"

When she pulled back, Roxie's amusement landed on the man next to them. "See what taste I have in friends? Thea gets it. Just like I said, I could never be with a man who plays golf."

"Except you are and it's hardly grounds for divorce."

Zairn was good at playing it straight even as the energy between the couple fizzed.

"It is in California," Roxie said, absolutely certain. "I've got an in with the DA."

"Droll," Zairn said. "Watch out you don't get arrested on your way to his office."

"Why would I? I won't go by way of Crimson."

"No breaking and entering planned?"

"I find it's better to be spontaneous," Roxie said, tossing her hair for effect. "Reduces the sentence if they find there's no premeditation."

"Just because they don't find it, doesn't mean it doesn't exist. I can help them out with that. And, FYI, if you go to prison, I'm having our babies without you."

"All of them?"

"All of them."

Roxie sneered. "You just can't wait to get your hands on that exchange student, can you?"

"I'll be living the life, baby. Might even get me more than one."

"Don't expect child support."

A hand slid onto her lower back, Zane's. Yeah, she'd been kind of blocking out his proximity.

"You okay?" he asked, guiding her away from the

couple still sparring.

"You have a beautiful house."

"Thank you," he said. "I haven't been staying here. Zairn and Roxie were supposed to have it to themselves."

Horrified, she tensed. "I'm sorry. I didn't mean to interrupt. Roxie didn't say anything. I didn't expect—"

"No, that wasn't aimed at you. With Roman's bullshit, all plans have gone to crap… Everyone's having dinner here tonight."

"I heard. Roxie's looking forward to it."

"She's a people person."

They stopped at the stone wall surrounding the terrace. The water beyond was so awe-inspiring, the sky, the glorious light, she couldn't take it all in. "You picked the perfect spot."

"To talk?"

She smiled. "For your terrace."

"Oh, yeah, that's Cam Collier for you—baby, did you come here for a reason? Is there something you need?"

"Right, sorry."

"Don't apologize."

"That's why I came here," she said, hoping he could read her contrition. "I came to apologize for yesterday and—Alessia doesn't want to leave."

"She doesn't have to, I want both of you to stay."

"I overreacted, or maybe I reacted in the right way, I just aimed that emotion at the wrong person. You can't be responsible for another man's actions. And I shouldn't have unloaded my fear and anger on you—"

"Thea," he said, sliding in closer, catching her hair in the breeze to tuck it behind her ear. "I'm exactly the person you should unload your emotions on."

"You didn't know your cousin was going to do

that. It wasn't your fault he—"

"Because your boyfriend is exactly the person you should share your feelings with. I want to know if you're scared, if you're angry, and I will always do everything in my power to right any wrongs."

"Boyfriend?"

"You know how I feel about you," he said, his hand skimming onto her waist to edge her closer. "I thought I blew the whole thing, but if you're telling me there's a chance."

And the bounce of her diaphragm lightened so much that the cascade of hope became relief.

Her hands opened against him. "You still want to…?"

"I still want to," he said, his palm continuing to her mid back to hold her against him.

"How do you know it's not, that I'm not…" Her lips parted as he stooped. "All about the money."

"Baby, if you forgive me…" he murmured. "I'll sign it all over to you."

"There's nothing to forgive. I was out of line. You should be the one refusing to forgive me."

"You're forgiven," he said. "Can I kiss you now?"

"Uh huh."

Tipping her head back, she welcomed the heat of his mouth closing over hers and the gentle sweep of his tongue as it—

"You guys want to have Sex on the Beach with us?" Roxie called out.

The moment broken, they smiled at each other before turning to their mischievous friend.

"You know exactly what you're doing, Kyst," Zane called. "Didn't I give you my house? Twice now?"

SEVENTEEN

"TWICE?" she asked as Roxie turned on the spot and sashayed away, Zairn in her wake.

"They stayed at mine in California for a while."

"I thought they lived in New York."

"Officially," he said. "They're kind of nomads. More so than the rest of us."

"Roxie is certainly full of energy. I can't imagine how Zairn keeps up."

"He gives as good as he gets. Now…" He wrenched her closer. "Enough about them, what about us?"

"What about us?"

"You want to go back to mine?"

"Yours? Isn't this—"

"I've been staying in a villa by the beach," he said. "Near where we first met."

"The light," she whispered. "You live in the light."

"I… guess," he said and snickered. "Don't worry, any other day of the week, this place is yours to explore. We can kick Roxie and Zairn out if it means—"

"No. Roxie's… overwhelming, but she's kind too. She told me about your friends. About your brother… and his wife."

"Roux is a step up in the sassy stakes from Roxie, but she aims it at Rourke. And he laps it up. You don't have to worry about her mouth turning on anyone else."

"I'd like to meet him, them, some time."

"Any time you want. You'll meet everyone eventually." That suggested more, suggested a future. "If you want, we can go back to our hammocks on the beach…"

"No, I should get back to Alessia, I left her in the spa with her friends hours ago."

"You should stay for dinner."

"No, I—"

"It's important," he said. "The plan is to talk about the Roman situation. And you have a unique perspective on that."

"It's not my business to—"

"Family doesn't have to be blood in this house. When there's a problem, we pull together the people we care about, the people we trust, and we hash it out as a group. Alessia's welcome to join us if—"

"No, that wouldn't help. She can't be objective. I'm not sure I could be either. And I'm not sure I'd trust myself around your cousin."

"Hey, if you want to lay it out for him, feel free. The rest of us are about as mad as you were, and with good reason."

"He abused your trust," she said. "He scared my sister, harassed that server, and betrayed a man I care about. It'll take a lot for me to volunteer to hang out with him any time soon."

"I never want to hang out with him. To say we tolerate him is generous."

"You did it for Struan, that's what Roxie said."

"A cousin I actually like," he said, easing her away from the wall. "There's time for a drink before the others show up."

She resisted. "Oh, I don't know. I've been having Sex on the Beach with Roxie all day." His lips quirked and she laughed. "You know what I mean."

"I'm jealous."

"She's very spoken for." When he walked, she went with him, pinned to his side with his arm holding her there. "She says the drink is a tribute to Lilya, us drinking the cocktail lets her live vicariously."

"Lilya's expecting with Kintyre. They're getting married in a few weeks." They crossed into the house. "I'll need a date."

"Plenty of women on the island who'd jump at the chance to escort you."

"Only one I'm asking."

She smiled up at him expecting to join Roxie and Zairn wherever they were. Instead of going further into the house, he went toward the front door only to lead her up the stairs.

"Where are we going?"

"There's a better view."

"Better?"

"You like to take it all in, I've noticed." How could he not when she went dashing around the beach and wading into the water any chance she got? "I think you'll like this."

From the second floor, they went into an enclosed staircase that curved upward too. And she couldn't deny being intrigued. Light from above lured them. Zane pressed something on the wall and a whirr from above signaled a glass panel sliding aside.

They went up, at the top, Zane held a hand out for hers, which she gave as she emerged and…

"Oh my God," she whispered, her breath stolen.

On the roof, she could turn any way, all around, and the world was laid out for her. The island, the sea, she could see it all, three-hundred and sixty degrees, back over the island toward the resort, the canopy of trees and…

"What do you think?"

Her heart raced. "I think it's amazing." Letting go of his hand, she went closer to the water, except… every way got her closer. She laughed. "Zane, this is incredible."

"Yeah, it still gets me too." Loungers, a couple of couches, a firepit, this wasn't just a walk on the roof, they could really hang out there. "Cam's good at utilizing space. Making the most of the artificial in a natural environment."

"It's impressive."

"Now you want to meet him too?"

When she whirled around, still beaming, exhilaration heated her more than the sun. "You live an amazing life."

He sauntered over. "I'm with an incredible woman. Do you want a drink?" She shook her head, sliding her hands up his body when he wrapped her in his arms. "We've got some time before dinner."

And she didn't want to waste it sipping drinks politely, making small talk. Not that small talk with him was ever…

"I feel like I'm on top of the world." Literally and figuratively. "Like we're the only two people left in existence."

"Then we've got nothing but time."

"Still…" she murmured. Her hands ascended until her fingers met his jaw. "We shouldn't waste it."

Drawing him down, her eyes sank shut and she breathed as his mouth touched hers. A kiss. One that was more profound than any that had come before. Was it possible to convey, to talk, to breathe, to kiss, to express how deep her need for him went?

For a glimmer, she'd severed their connection. There in that moment, their souls linked as she rose higher, pulling him down, begging to complete the link that drove her desire.

He backed them up and picked her up just long enough to sit on one of the loungers. Maybe he could read her mind. Maybe their bodies communicated without words. Each beat of her heart was echoed by his, their pulses providing a bassline for the deeper thump of desire that undulated her hips. Rubbing herself against him, the full weight of her body, pressed down, hard, trying its best to merge with the thick line of his want, trapped within fabric.

"Babe," he gasped under his breath, tipping his head back. "Slow it down."

"You want to slow it down?" Stroking his face, she tempted his mouth back to hers. "If this is too much—"

"No, baby, but we're not in any hurry."

Except she was, her need was in a hurry, the functions of her being would cease if he didn't respond, if he rejected her, if they were to part again without…

"We've been good." Her mouth brushed across hers. "So good, Drift. Will you make me beg?"

Grabbing her ass, he yanked her tight to him. "Never, baby. Anything you want is yours."

"Anything?" she asked, her lips curling to a smile as they touched his again. "Anything I want?"

"Mm hmm."

His hands stayed where they were as she pressured her weight on her knees to loosen the cord of his shorts. That proud smile on his face knew exactly where they were going. He could've walked her to it, manipulated her into thinking this was all her idea. Maybe. Except he'd proved himself, how he valued and respected her.

So as she curled her fingers around him, tightening, loosening, guiding him from his shorts and edging closer, she kissed his smile and rested her cheek against his face.

"Are you sure?" he asked, his fingers threading into her hair.

Oh, it was that restraint, that he could be so hard, so in need, yet still prioritize what was best for her over everything else.

Inhaling through her nose, her eyes closed, and she guided his cock into her, slow, in a tender move she wanted to memorize. This was it. Their first time. And damn, if felt too good.

"Mmm," she moaned, sliding lower, giving herself time to adjust and experience every second.

"Shit, baby." His whispered words got lost in her hair and his hands snatched her ass again.

The thread of his restraint had to be stretching. The strength of his grip wanted to pull her lower, wanted to force her down. His hips rose, not a lot, but in an automatic, instinctive need to fully occupy her.

She wanted it too, wanted him.

"Zane," she said, rising again the very moment she completed their union.

Down, and up, slow, breathing, she held his shoulders, and tipped her head, accepting each move of his mouth on her skin. His kiss goaded her, provoked her, stimulated that encompassing comfort of his acceptance.

He groaned as she sped up. Instinct of her own bred with impulse. The more she moved, the more she wanted. The faster, higher, lower, oh, shit. Her muscles burned, her hands gripped tighter and—

Snatching her waist in an explosion of movement, he put her on her back and hammered in, hard and fast.

"Yes," she whispered, though it was more of a gasp. "Zane…"

"Baby," he groaned against her, his body working itself in hers, firing, heating, stirring hormones to a boil beyond a simmer.

"Zane!" she called, her hips jolting upward, staying there as her muscles tightened. Everything in her cried in silent harmony to bathe in bliss forever. "Zane…" His name again, and he kept going, shifting enough to meet her eye. "You're… oh!"

Another orgasm burst, and her next cry got locked in her burning throat. Had she been—had they been? Was it—

"The…"

His own throat barely let out the first syllable of her name before it became a growl that eventually stilled him. Then breath was all there was to hear, to feel. Together, panting, pulses still racing, their gazes lounged in each other as endorphins dwindled.

"Zane," she managed to whisper and her fingertips met his cheekbone, just lightly.

A smile creased his dimples. "You really liked the view, huh?"

She laughed but clung onto him when he tried to move. "I like this view. You… there…"

He dipped quick to kiss her forehead. "It's one you'll be seeing so often, you'll get bored of it."

"Never."

Letting him go, she pushed down her dress as he tied his shorts again, and they adjusted to lie on the lounger together, her held to his side.

Turning her face to his chest, she glowed against his sure heartbeat. "How long do we have?"

"We can stay up here all night if you want. Gets colder after sunset, but we can—"

"Until dinner, was what I meant," she said on a laugh. "What a disappointment though, just the night? What if I never want to leave here ever again?"

"Then I'll get someone to bring blankets."

"I really did just come here to apologize." Her hand moved up and down, stroking him, still trying to convince herself this was really real. "If you can believe it."

"Best apology I've ever had. By far."

She sighed and skimmed her hand across his ribs to pull herself against him. "Just a few minutes more."

"Baby, we really don't have to—"

"Your people come together." She sat up. "When there's a problem or a scene, that's how your group works."

"This is not really my group. Rourke and the guys wouldn't traipse all the way over here because Roman's an asshole. If they did that, we'd all have to live with the idiot."

She patted his chest. "If you ever think of telling me that being with you means living with Roman Lowe…"

He laughed. "I'd dump myself if I ever said that."

She bowed to steal a kiss. "Is there somewhere I can wash up before…?"

"Sure," he said, vaulting up with a frustrated exhale. "I suppose the world won't stop for us."

He extended a hand to pull her onto her feet. "Maybe later?"

"No," he said, holding her again. Though the rejection seemed—"Not maybe."

Oh, Zane Dyce. How had this happened? It didn't matter, she never needed it to happen again because… Shit, that was dangerous territory. She'd never gone ga-ga for a guy, but with Zane it was… What was it? Figuring that out while still drenched in the satisfaction of desire might be dangerous. For now, it was dinner with his people, those he cared about, in his life, with him.

She'd just keep her opinions to herself.

She could do that.

Easy… maybe not so much.

EIGHTEEN

WASHING UP MAY have led to a little more than expected. A little more that ended with them having to wash up all over again. Was it the sea air? The incredible home? Or was it the man who swept her up with his adoration?

They'd got there. Somehow. Still together. But at the bottom of the stairs, she stopped, holding him back from joining the voices rumbling from elsewhere.

"I should go back."

"Back where?" he asked.

"Alessia will be worried and—"

"She's eating with Alana, Lark, and some other girls. She knows you're safe." He tucked her hair back from her cheek. "I've posted security to keep her in their eye line. You don't have to worry about her."

Because he'd done it for her. Without asking. Was that an overstep or…?

"Thank you," she said, having learned her lesson about jumping to blame him for things that weren't his fault.

Okay, so maybe acting without her authority could be classed as his "fault," but it came from a place of love, well, affection anyway. Love would be getting carried away… though if she thought her sense was on solid ground, she'd be lying to herself.

"I said I'd make you happy and I meant it. Whatever you care about, I care about. Nothing will happen to Alessia. Not here or at home, anywhere. If you want security to stay with her for—"

"The rest of her life?" she asked, her lips quirking. "She might have something to say about that."

Though if the guys posted were hot, her little sister could get them into all kinds of trouble with her flirting.

"Unfortunately for her, it's your happiness that means most to me."

And, geez, the guy didn't let up for a second. She'd wanted him since they'd met… okay, so maybe not the exact moment they'd met—why did it feel with every step, she was slipping deeper into trouble? Not the bad kind of trouble, the kind of trouble that led to ideas of grandeur. Ideas of tomorrow, and the next day, and every one after that. She couldn't let herself think—no, be smart, sensible.

She tried to back away, but he kept hold of her hand. "Still, I shouldn't…"

"Shouldn't what?"

"This is a family thing and—"

"Roman won't be here. We talk about him, not to him at times like this."

She winced. "It's not that," not only that. "I'm a no one in your life, and the people in there don't know me. You're riding the sex high and maybe, you know, aren't thinking with the right head."

"You're not a no one in my life."

That wasn't a judgment on either of them, just an

observation from an outsider's point of view. The people in there could think she was insinuating herself into something that didn't involve her. And from their perspective, it didn't. Hadn't she herself said Roman's addiction was none of her business?

"You know what I mean. Your family may not want to speak freely with—"

"You met Roxie, right?" He smiled. "Think anyone holds back around her? She gets to the root of everything."

"Zane—"

"Thea," he said, pulling her to him. "Come and have dinner with me."

They'd eaten more than a dozen meals together. And did she really want to leave…?

With her single nod, he smiled and kissed her head.

Dinner.

Hands linked, she let him lead her through a vast living space into an even bigger kitchen, dining area. The two far walls were gone, open to another broad terrace. The layout registered fast, then it was the people at the long dining table in the kitchen, who stopped talking, that got her attention.

Okay. Four of them. That wasn't bad. Roxie smiled. Having a friend in the room was a comfort. Zairn was there too, not exactly known, but not a stranger either. Thank goodness she'd met them in stages.

"I don't have to tell you who this beautiful woman is," Zane declared.

So he had been talking about her? And it was just at that, she checked the guys and…

"I thought you said Roman wasn't going to be here."

He leaned in, kissing her hair before speaking above her ear. "Thea, meet Struan Lowe."

"Struan?"

"They're identical twins," Roxie said, full of glee. "It's so cool, right?"

Now that she mentioned it… Yes, the guy there had the same height as Roman, the same face, but his stature, the way he was put together… and there was something astute in those eyes. Okay, so she'd only been exposed to Roman for a short time, but already she didn't get the same impression from the guy over there, on the other side of their seafood bonanza.

Another cursory glance, but the other guy… She narrowed her eyes on him. Why was that face familiar? Ah, from Roman's meltdown in the dining room.

"And that is Struan's best friend, Tripp Breckenridge."

"Tripp is everyone's best friend," Roxie said, sidling away from her own guy to put an arm around the smoldering man nearest Struan.

Attractive, yes, she immediately got confidence, yet there was an ease about him too. So effortless. He was just there, and damn if he didn't know it. Rumpled shirt, finger-combed hair that curled around his ears, the man suckered her in just by standing there.

"Tripp Breckenridge…" she murmured.

It wasn't just the face, it was…

"You're Thom Redrick's ex." Hers wasn't the only jaw to fall at Tripp's deep, cool words. "How is he?"

"You…" Roxie backed off to look at him and then at Zairn. "Between the two of you, I think you know every person on the planet."

"How do you do that?" Dyce asked. "You didn't tell me she—"

"I never forget a face or a body," Tripp said, fixated on her. "They gave him the New York transfer, and you stayed put."

"Yes."

"And no one could quite figure out why—"

"Rigley and Klein."

"Ah," he said, his head going back. "That'll do it."

"I wanna know the gossip," Roxie said, creeping back to Tripp. "What happened at Rigley and Klein? Doesn't Lilya know someone there?"

Zairn caught the back of her neck to yank her against him. "One problem at a time, Lola."

"You think you can fix Richard Rigley?"

"No one can fix Richard Rigley," Zairn said. "Roman on the other hand…"

"You think he's fixable?" Zane asked, guiding her to the table. No one was sitting. It was a buffet. Plates, food, pitchers of cocktails. "Didn't we try that already?"

"No one in the world is more ready to wash their hands of Roman than me," Struan said, "but you know how this works, it's not just about him."

"It's not just about him?" she heard her voice. Sometimes keeping it in her head was impossible. "I'm sure he would disagree. Your brother seems like the type who believes everything is about him."

"Oh, I know a lot of those guys," Roxie said, her head bobbing. "And I have to say, she's right. That's why he thinks he can get away with bullshit like the other night."

"So what's left? We've put him through rehab," Zane said. "You want to do that again?"

"He can't live the rest of his life in rehab," Zairn said.

Was that an absolute?

"This is a setback," Struan said. "What the fuck was Deacon thinking?"

"What was Logan thinking? Why didn't we get a heads-up?"

"He can only give us a heads-up if he knows," Struan told his cousin. "Hit him as hard as it hit us."

"Are they in love? For real?" Roxie asked, picking food for a plate. "Deacon and this Sway? Deacon always struck me as a 'keep his options open' kind of guy."

"He's also a, 'don't think things through' kind of guy," Struan added. "Sway's got a way of screwing with a guy's head."

"Let's not touch that one with a ten-foot pole," Roxie said, yet carried on anyway. "Does that mean you've been screwed by her too?"

"Sway's a complicated woman," Tripp said.

"Wow…" Roxie's eyes met hers. "I haven't slept with her, have you?"

"No!" she said quickly but followed it with a short laugh.

"I think we're the last two on the planet."

"I feel wronged."

"Me too," Roxie declared. "Where's she at? We should get over there now, before she gets married. Maybe we can be her engagement gift."

"She and Deacon went out before she and Roman got together," Zairn said, probably used to getting his woman back on track. "This could be a rebound thing. A comfort lay."

"We've all had those." Tripp drank before finishing, "Never proposed to one though."

Struan laughed, startling them all. "If you were the first Breckenridge brother to go down, it would be a sign of the apocalypse coming."

"I will get married first, just to collect on the bet."

"What's it running at now?" Zairn asked. "Breck's odds were going up, last I checked."

"Since he and Sequoia broke up."

"Again?"

"Who keeps track?"

"No one is keeping track of this conversation," Zane interjected. "Has everyone eaten, should we start with that?"

Nothing on the buffet was touched, except what Roxie had on her plate, and what she popped past her lips.

"We were waiting for you," Roxie said around what was in her mouth and Zairn nudged her. "What? They're here, aren't they?"

"She has a thing for shrimp," Zairn said still looking at his girl.

"Everyone stock up, we'll go outside sit, eat, and figure this out."

People picked up plates to fill with food, and side-whispered conversations started.

Her whispers went to Zane. "Why isn't your brother here?"

"Because he'd only gloat," he said, smiling. "Roman is my mom's nephew, not related to Rourke. He gets a pass because the blood is mine."

"Ah… and you said he's married already?"

After a beat, she turned her head to smile at him.

He laughed. "Yes, unfortunately, off the market."

"Who's off the market?" Roxie asked, picking up a nearby pitcher. "I'm always open to offers."

"Rourke," Dyce answered the first question.

"You want some punch, honey?"

She waved a palm. "I probably had enough alcohol today."

"These are virgin," Roxie said. "Unlike anyone at this table." She poured into highball glasses. "You wouldn't want to get with Rourke anyway, honey. He's extraordinarily high maintenance. I don't know how

Roux does it. She's in incredible shape, I can only imagine she needs to be to keep up such stamina."

"Dyce," Zairn said and walked outside to the kitchen terrace.

Her guy rested a hand on her waist. "You okay?"

"Yes, go."

"Go," Roxie said, putting a glass in his hand. "Take your food and keep the guys busy."

Though he probably didn't know quite what that meant, because she didn't, Dyce went out onto the terrace after his friend. Struan and Tripp weren't far behind.

Four strong, virile men, good-looking, successful…

"How many women do you think Zairn has slept with?"

"I don't know," Roxie said, completely unfazed, licking punch from the side of her hand. "I think he stopped counting somewhere in the four-figure range."

She whipped around. "Really? You think…?"

"It's possible the number reaches into five figures. Some of his twenties were a bit of a blur. Why? You want to work out a timeshare?"

Roxie took a little interpreting, but when you got it, her sense of humor was spot on.

"No," she said on a whispered laugh. "I was just thinking the qualities of those four combined would probably cover every want on any woman's list."

"If you could pick and choose, sure. If we could piecemeal Mr. Perfect together. We wouldn't want Struan's baggage." Baggage? "We might get lost in Tripp's family. Dyce has the money and the intellect. Z has charm a-plenty."

"It's never bothered you? That he's been with so many women?"

"I care less about who he slept with then, and

more about who he sleeps with now. She's important to me. I care very much about her pleasure."

Mm, no doubt.

"Why are men eligible bachelors and women dried-up spinsters?"

"Because…" Roxie said, handing her a glass, then gesturing to start walking. "We haven't changed the rules yet. We're getting there, one bachelor at a time."

Another laugh and then they were with the men. Plates and glasses had been put down, but none of the men were sitting. Zairn pulled out Roxie's chair just a second before Dyce pulled out hers. There might be drama and arrogance on the island, sure, but there was chivalry and charisma too.

"Okay," Roxie said. "We eat, and then we solve the Roman problem."

Good luck to them all. If it was that easy, they wouldn't be in their current predicament.

NINETEEN

"IT'S NOT ENOUGH to lock him up," Struan said. "He has to want it."

"We've had this conversation before," Zane said.

Zairn exhaled. "Many, many times."

"They can't all be Riv success stories," Tripp said. "You ready to give up on him?"

"Are Breckenridges capable of abandoning anyone in need?" Roxie asked on a smile.

"Privately, maybe, but, you know, Mom gets everywhere. She hears everything."

Roxie laughed. "Got to love a man still afraid of his momma."

"Maybe if Roman was afraid of anything, we wouldn't be in this fucking mess."

These men weren't responsible for another man's actions. Yet the way they sat, each relaxed in their chair, enjoying their drinks in the moonlight, they weren't the most optimistic bunch.

"It's not just about the addiction," she said because someone had to come at it from another angle.

"Yes, that's a disease, that needs treatment, but was he on pills the other night? Is this a true relapse?"

"Roman takes whatever he can get his hands on," Zairn said.

Struan nodded. "Yeah, he shouldn't be drinking either."

"He says he can control it."

"He says a lot of things." Struan held a weight on his shoulders that didn't belong to him, that shouldn't belong to him. "He doesn't understand moderation. If he could stop at one…"

Imagine living your whole life in the shadow of another. Of someone who looks exactly like you. Watching them live their life with complete disregard for anyone else. She could almost feel his guilt, his regret. Roman wouldn't be the only one judged for his actions, Struan had to walk down the street wearing the same face. People wouldn't give him a break, they'd assume he was his irresponsible brother.

"Did you get along as children?" she asked, curious about the man they hadn't talked about. "You and your brother?"

"Roman gets along with anyone who puts him first."

"And you did?"

"He's spent a lot of time with therapists telling him all the things he missed out on."

Except it seemed to her, Roman got a lot more than most. "He went into acting and Logan's this crazy big rockstar…"

Struan's lips curled, for the first time that night, apparently enjoying the conversation. "So why didn't I launch myself into fame and fortune?"

"It's not the first time you've heard the question."

Of course it wasn't.

His eyes drifted to his cousin. "First time today, that's something."

Though she'd only known him, known of him, for a couple of hours, she wouldn't say he was the shy, retiring type. Quieter maybe than Tripp, definitely quieter than Roxie, he didn't strike her as meek or passive. Maybe seeing him with Roman would—

Sound carried and everyone piqued. From elsewhere in the house, what was—

"Suck my balls!" someone screamed, okay, Roman screamed.

The voice was familiar now, for all the wrong reasons.

"Oh, well, there's an invitation," Roxie said, putting down her drink and uncrossing her legs to sit straight. "Rock, paper, scissors? Tripp, it could fall to you as the only single, non-blood relative at the table."

Zairn's hand slid onto her shoulder to draw her back in the seat. "Settle down, Lola."

"Who said I was single?" Tripp asked.

"Certainly none of the dozen or so women you're stringing along back home, Priest," Roxie said, sharing a smile with Tripp.

"Only a dozen?" Zairn murmured under his breath. "You're slacking, Junior."

"Is he drunk?" she asked of their uninvited guest.

Zane squeezed her knee. Unfortunately, they were the only two sitting with their backs to the kitchen. To see what was going on, they had to twist, which would give Roman the audience he sought.

True enough, less than a minute later, he appeared at the other side of the kitchen, swaggering toward them.

"Oh, ye, of little faith," he projected his voice like he was on stage.

"Ro, what—"

"I got the gig," Roman declared to his brother. "You said I wouldn't get it—"

"I didn't say you wouldn't get it," Struan said, swinging his glass toward his lips. "I said you'd fuck it up."

"Seems inevitable," Roxie murmured.

It wasn't loud but was enough to gain Roman's focus. "You know, you're fucking hot."

And true to herself, Roxie didn't falter. "I do know that."

"The blonde hair, the tits—"

"Are real," Roxie said, pushing her shoulders back. "Not that you'll ever get a chance to find out."

As he approached, her focus returned to the table. He stopped just behind her, prickling the hair at the back of her neck.

"Baby, it would blow your mind."

Roxie just drew her unimpressed eyes away from him. "At least something would get blown."

Tension increased with each second that passed. Maybe it was her proximity to him that heightened it, Roxie didn't seem perturbed.

"You fucking little bitch," he spat. "Don't you—"

"Thank you, Ro," Zairn said, rising to his feet. Roxie's chin rose with him, watching his ascent. "I've been waiting a long fucking time for you to give me an excuse—"

"Z," Struan said, standing up fast with Dyce not far behind.

Tripp snickered and folded his arm. "Dinner and a show. Who needs Broadway?"

"You know he's a prick," Dyce said, rounding her and the table to get closer to Zairn while Struan blocked the other side. "He's not worth your time. You don't want to do this now, not now."

"Let him at it," Tripp said. "No better fucking place. We'll lose his body in the ocean. Struan will cover our asses a while."

Roman wasn't done with the insults. "What the fuck is a Breckenridge doing at our table anyway?"

"Our table?" Zane asked, incredulous.

Roxie took Zairn's hand and stood up, pressing herself against him, her fingers tempting his jaw until he looked down at her. The couple needed their moment of privacy, it felt wrong to gawk. And she didn't need to wait long for another break out.

"You're so fucking superior—"

"Is that why you came here, Ro?" Struan asked, stepping up to get his brother's attention. "To insult everyone? We were all fine before you appeared uninvited."

"You think I don't know what's going on here? You in your little huddles, judging everyone else, so far up your own asses—"

"I think we learned that one from you," Tripp said. "You want to make something of this? We'll go down to the beach right now, you and me. Talk it out."

Yeah, talking would be secondary on that agenda.

"Tripp—"

"Nah, Struan, how many times have you handed him his ass and he still doesn't get the message? He wants a fight, I'll take a turn at bat."

"Tripp," Roxie whispered.

His eyes stayed on Roman. "Like you said, Rox Out, single without blood."

"That wasn't what I meant."

"Come on, this is what he does," Tripp said completely impervious. "Shouts the odds, thinks if he swears enough, he'll scare everyone off. I have six older brothers." He scoffed. "This guy's a fucking amateur. We want to talk who has the most experience here? I'll fight him 'til the fucking sun rises. Let him embarrass himself, why not?"

Roman opened his arms, backing off a couple of steps at the same time Zane's hand slid onto her shoulder.

"You're all just fucking jealous. Think I'm all done? You thought I was washed out?"

"No, we thought you were coked up."

"Roman!"

That unexpected bark came a breath before an older man appeared storming across the kitchen. With some extra weight around his belly, he wasn't old, old, maybe in his fifties, but he carried a hell of a bluster.

"Magnus, fuck off out of here," Roman said without turning around. "I told you I was coming to tell them."

"And I told you we need to talk strategy," Magnus said, stopping at his side. "This role will put you back on top, get your face out there again, wipe out some of the bullshit from the past."

The past being a couple of nights ago? From what she'd seen, Roman wasn't the most stable even if he was sober. Though she hadn't got a definitive answer on his level of intoxication.

"What is it?" she asked. "The role?"

"Lead in an action show," Struan answered.

"Yeah," Roman crowed. "Lead, baby, it's all about me." Like the guy needed to say that out loud. Their pleasant night had been disrupted by his ego and there was little chance of them getting it back. "I call the shots."

"The press are getting here day after tomorrow."

"Excuse me?" Zane asked. "The press?"

"And there goes our privacy," Roxie said, sliding both arms around Zairn to hold herself against him.

His fingers combed into her hair. "If you want to

get out of here, we can be gone in a couple of hours."

When Roxie's eyes opened, they landed on her.

"Zairn—"

"No," Roxie said. "We can stay. I won't abandon my girl… I may even call reinforcements."

"He's signing the paperwork next week, meeting in Honolulu."

"So you invite the press into everyone's privacy, but keep the high-hats out of reach?"

"They won't want to travel further than necessary," Zairn said, his voice growly. Roman had insulted Roxie, it wasn't a surprise Zairn wasn't amused. If it wasn't for the woman literally holding onto him, he may not be so calm. "It's already a long jaunt from LA."

"You can't leave the island to sign anything in Honolulu," Struan said. "What about your adoring fans? The contest winners. You've already neglected them." Which could be a story in itself. Maybe. What did she know about the world's appetite for scandal? "And we don't want the press talking to them."

"It doesn't matter, the contest women have all signed NDAs," Magnus said. "We'll remind them of that before the media get here."

"Is it smart to do the press before the paperwork is signed?"

"Who said the press were allowed to come here?" Zane said. "I don't want those hoards on my island."

"It's like three people," Magnus said. "They're covering the comeback and will follow his progress through to filming season one." What a lot of fun… for someone else. "We already have the social influencer people here, what's another couple of bodies matter? Besides, we'll keep them apart from everything else. Maybe do a little gladhanding as a sidepiece, but we want it to be about Roman and him getting in shape to take on this grueling role."

"Him getting in shape," Tripp said on another snicker and as his attention went to Struan, so did everyone else's.

Struan himself didn't flinch. "You want to think about this, whether it's smart to take on something this big right now, Ro."

"What the fuck do you know?" Roman strolled right on up to the table to snatch up a glass of punch, her glass, but it wasn't like she was going back to it.

He gulped it down, then sneered at it.

"Yeah, sorry," Roxie said with sarcasm, not contrition. "Some people know how to have a good time without libation. Must be a turn up for you."

"You want to learn to keep your mouth shut."

"I don't," Roxie said. "Though if we're passing out advice, I'd tell you to get sober, lose a few pounds, and maybe even appreciate the people around you who give you everything."

"What do you know?" Roman snapped.

"Plenty." Roxie's arms dropped and she turned to lean back on Zairn. "And I also know you got this role by the grace of God and you're destined to fuck it up no matter what you think now."

"You—"

"Let's not get antagonistic," Magnus said, patting Roman's back. "Let's sit down together and work this out. There's got to be a solution that suits everyone. How about we take the winners with us to Honolulu? They won't pass up a chance at a night on the town with Roman, will they?"

No, but maybe they should.

"Is it safe?" she asked.

"We always make sure Roman's..." Magnus trailed off to glance around. "Who are you?"

All that had gone down so far and he was only

just noticing her presence?

"No one."

"Not no one," Zane was quick to follow up.

"I'm connected to one of your adoring fans," she said. "So I have a vested interest in keeping those women safe. I'm not sure I'd trust Roman to hold my purse, let alone protect my sister. He must attract all kinds of negative attention."

And she didn't want Alessia anywhere near it. People might think fame was cool, but she viewed it from a different angle and saw its dangers, not its virtues.

"We'll keep her safe," Roxie said. "We'll go along. Chaperone."

"Is there a Crimson in Honolulu?"

"Not yet," Roxie said. "But Rouge have clubs and bars all over."

"Who says I want to go to your shithole places?"

"Who said you were invited?"

"Okay," Zane said, sliding in front of her. "This is going nowhere."

"It's going plenty somewhere," Magnus said. "We chill, get a schedule for show prep going, the press shows up, do their interviews, see what they want, then Roman does O'ahu. It'll be fun."

For who? Though spending time in Honolulu might be fun, she couldn't think of anyone she'd least rather do it with. Roman Lowe was not a glittering star, grateful for his fans, she wasn't even sure he was a good person. From what she'd seen so far, the needle didn't swing in his favor.

That said, she wouldn't leave Alessia to his mercy. If there was going to be a trip, she'd be on the plane, next to the sister who adored the illusion of this man. Honestly, there should be some repercussions for selling the world such a bill of goods. This wasn't a man worthy of being idolized. After his actions on the island alone, he'd be better locked up.

Although a sense of expectation hung in the air, like maybe there was more drama to come, she couldn't sit there all night.

"I should get going." She stood up, finally, everyone else was already on their feet. Zane didn't see her as a no one, but it was obvious why the others would. "Thank you for dinner."

Roxie came around to kiss her cheek and give her a hug. "You can stay, if you want to stay. There's plenty of room here."

"No, I want to get back to my sister." She smiled at the men, the ones she'd had dinner with, the others she avoided. "It was nice to meet you all."

Zane put an arm around her and she didn't mind leaning on him as they made their way through the house to the front door.

He opened a closet and produced a light jacket. "Here, put this on. I don't want you to get cold."

"I'll be fine," she said, but threaded her arms into the sleeves anyway. "And you don't have to escort me, I can make my way back—"

"Are you kidding? You're my excuse to get the hell out of this madhouse."

"It's your house," she said.

As he opened the door, she slipped through it.

"It's Roxie's house right now, and the mad thing suits her."

"Do you think Zairn is still angry?"

"Yes," he said, helping her into the cart.

No equivocation or hesitation.

"Would he hurt him?"

Zane came around to his side to start them moving. "Zairn Lomond has a long memory and a lot of friends. Roman forgets that too often." Sliding closer, she held his arm when his hand went to her knee. "I'm sorry about tonight."

"Sorry, why?" she asked as they drove through the main gate. "It wasn't your fault."

Though it was clear why he'd think she might believe that. "I said I was sorry for the other night, but I will keep saying it. I know now you weren't responsible for what happened. You were with me, you had no idea he'd—"

"People enable him, you're right about that. He has squads of flunkies running around cleaning up his messes. He's used to doing what he wants, when he wants. I was only persuaded to let him even come here—"

"Because you thought his volatility was in his past."

"And because I naïvely thought he'd be easier to control here. We think we control things, control him, but he always finds a way to screw things up for everyone else while he comes up smelling like roses."

Lights warmed the road ahead, with more distance between them than regular streetlights, their color was warmer too. Funny the things she hadn't considered, yet Zane deemed important. Lighting the road made everything safer and gave her a sense of security.

"I had no idea he had an identical twin."

"It's not a secret, but it's not declared on the loudspeaker either." Which meant superfans, and probably Alessia, would know. "Struan does all Roman's stunt work, body doubles, you know any of the dangerous things Roman would have to be sober and sensible for."

Ah! Hence Tripp's amused outrage over the suggestion Roman would have to get in shape for the role.

"I feel sorry for him," she admitted, her head

sinking against him. "It must feel like his only value is what he can do for his brother."

"Struan's always been okay. He takes things in stride, doesn't overthink them. He's smarter than Roman, more honest, more honorable, but, yeah, we talk about it sometimes."

"Talk about it?"

"Where will he be in five years? In ten? In twenty? His life, his daily purpose, is to be whatever Roman needs him to be. He works with him, lives with him, covers his ass on an hourly basis. If it wasn't for Struan, Roman wouldn't have any kind of career."

"You'd never know it from the way they interact. Roman shows no gratitude."

"Gratitude is something Roman was born without. Struan's been doing this his whole life. Might say he doesn't know any different."

Sibling relationships could be complicated. Sometimes there was competition or one was valued and encouraged more than another. Love might seem like a given, but it had to be earned, right along with respect.

They'd expended too much airtime on Roman Lowe, more than he should be due.

"Tripp's interesting. Six older brothers?"

"And he's not the youngest," he said. "How does he know your ex?"

"I don't know. As far as I know, we've never met before. Maybe he met Thom."

Though why that would lead to Tripp knowing her, she had no idea. Especially when he said he never forgot a face. Didn't that suggest they had met?

"I'll call Thom when we get back to civilization."

"Hey, now I never said that." His smiling tone met her hair in a kiss. "I don't want you rekindling anything."

"He lives in New York now. We made our

choices." Though what did that say for them? Zane's lack of response betrayed he had to be thinking the same thing. "Do you live here full-time? You said you have a house in LA?"

"We're not in LA," he said. "We're in Northern California."

"We?"

"Rourke and me. We own a compound that houses both DT and Mosaic, his company. We live and work there." California. It wasn't forever away. It was better than Australia or Europe… or Mars. "I can stay anywhere, Wanderer. Live anywhere, work anywhere—"

"We shouldn't talk about this," she said, grateful they were closing in on the lights of the resort.

"Baby—"

"No, sex head, remember?" She sat up straight to put a little distance between them. "It's been an intense night, an intense few days."

Though he stopped by the service door they usually used, his reluctance came in overshooting it, just a little, then grabbing her thigh before she could leap out.

"Will you think about it?"

Their eyes met and she couldn't come up with anything. Think about it? She'd done nothing but think about it that day. A holiday romance could be frivolous. But she'd met his friends, people he considered family. She'd been in his house, made love on his roof. They weren't frivolous anymore, if they ever had been.

Yes, it was like a dream, some wild fantasy that could never be reality, yet she'd lived it. And it wasn't an illusion. It wasn't a temporary vacation affair. This was his life. His family.

She swallowed and leaned in, holding his jaw to steady herself as she kissed him goodnight.

Think about it?

She slipped out of the cart and back into the

hotel without another word. Her purpose was supposed to be protecting her sister, yet in that moment, she needed the grounding of her sibling. Alessia was real. Her touchstone to real life. Maybe getting back into sister mode for a while would be a hard reset and she'd start thinking clearly again… or she could just be sunk with no hope life-as-she'd-known-it would survive.

TWENTY

UNFORTUNATELY, her sister had other ideas.

"A suite?"

"Yeah," Alessia said, dashing around tossing things into the suitcase open on her bed. "For me, Alana, and Lark. Our security guys know every corner, we'll be protected there."

She wanted to ask protected from what, except she'd been the one harping on about safety regardless of their location. Changing that tune now would be hypocritical.

"And they just gave it to you?"

"We asked, 'cause we thought you wouldn't be back." Alessia stopped to look at her, a line forming between her brows. "Why are you back? Did you break up?"

"I was worried about you. This is supposed to be—"

"Don't worry so much." Alessia disappeared into the bathroom. "Everything is taken care of!" She reappeared embracing toiletries and cosmetics against her chest until she dumped them haphazardly in the case and flipped over the lid to zip it. "Was Zane Dyce an asshole?"

"No," she said, a little at sea. "He's kind and generous."

"I'll say." Her shoulders rose, squeezing in tight, as glee grew on her face. "This has been the most amazing vacation ever." The good did outweigh the bad. Alessia had a way of reminding her to cling to optimism. "Do you think he'd let us ever come back?"

"Zane? I'm sure if—"

"Are you going to marry him?" Alarm bolted through her. Danger approaching. Her sister carried on regardless. "If you marry him and have babies, we'll be here all the time, right? We could just live here, like I said before."

With a spa and twenty-four-hour room service, her sister might be happy for a while. Though without the bustle of the city, she might go stir-crazy.

"You're supposed to be grounding me," she admitted. "Reminding me not to get carried away."

Alessia came rushing over to hug her. "What's so wrong with getting carried away? He's a good guy, Thea, I know it."

And that might be reassuring if Alessia didn't think the same thing about Roman Lowe. What did that say for her sister's ability to judge true character?

Not that she thought Zane wasn't a good person. He was. The best of people, like Roxie's Jane. She had no doubts on that score.

"He is a good person, and if you want to move into the suite—"

"Thank you," Alessia declared, dragging her case off the bed onto the floor. "This has been the most incredible vacation ever." She came over for another hug. "It's like a dream come true!"

A dream come true. Alessia rolled her luggage to the door. The moment she opened it, a guy leaned in to take the case for her. And then they were gone.

She exhaled.

Okay, bedtime. Alessia would be okay. Friends. Security. And it didn't hurt that Roman Lowe was at the other end of the island, far, far away from her sister.

Before bed, she wanted a shower. A long shower, full of steam and refreshing heat. That would reset her. Then she could crawl into bed and close her eyes. The next day maybe she'd get back to work, find herself an even keel in routine.

More than an hour later, staring through the shadows to the ceiling, listening to the waves lap at the shore, she wasn't asleep.

Refreshed and reset she may be. Her head rolled to study the vacant pillow. They'd never slept together, not in the literal sense. And it wasn't like Alessia snored or anything, and she lived alone, so why did it feel like something was missing?

Maybe the steam had been too much. Lying there wasn't getting her anywhere. Sitting up, she slipped her legs from the cover and stood up. It wouldn't hurt to walk, would it? There was no one around. It was dark out. Only the moonlight would join her on the sand.

Grabbing a crochet cover-up from the closet, she didn't bother with footwear and went out the sliding door. Inhaling the cleansing air of the sea, it enveloped her with such warmth and clarity that the temperature didn't matter.

As she walked toward the water, she scrunched her feet, sinking them into the cool grains bathed by the ocean.

Alessia might be her reason for being there. The contest. The vacation and all that entailed. But it didn't feel like that, obligation didn't weigh on her there as it did at home. In her usual life, she'd never imagine taking time off each day to spend afternoons with debonaire billionaires. Something was different there, something in her, that had nothing to do with the environment.

It did help though, the vastness of forever skewed her perspective. Except the view was still obscured, it hadn't quite come into focus yet. She was supposed to be seeing something, a future maybe, a change, her life path was coming toward a fork, maybe an intersection that would present more than one route. The only one who could decide which to take was her. Did she want to live a life with a singular purpose? To get up each day just to show at the office? What was she building? What was she creating? What was… she?

Distance didn't register, not until the light caught the corner of her eye. The light she'd seen on her first night there. Did he leave it on all night? Glancing around, she couldn't see any sign of him on the beach or in the water. Not that she'd seen a glimpse of him that first night either. Maybe he was swimming, but it was kind of late for that, wasn't it?

Did he go out swimming alone every night? A barb of anger tightened her frown. How could he do something so stupid? What if he got into trouble and needed help?

Exhaling, her head dropped. It wasn't her place to tell him how to live his life or to make his choices. And she was jumping to conclusions anyway. That could've been a one-off. Her direction switched without much thought. Leaving the water, she traversed the width of the beach. Trees hung on either side with a little greenery providing some privacy. Some, but not much. A stone path took her to the wooden deck and the glass was open, pushed back to present a bedroom, his bedroom she could only guess. Light hung between it and the next section of the house. She didn't look. From there, she could see his bed, the open closet door. This was his privacy. This was her invading his personal space.

"Zane?" she called, not loud, but enough he should hear her over the waves and the swaying leaves.

It was only an invasion if she didn't declare herself. Though she knocked on the glass, it wasn't much of a sound, so she stepped inside.

What was she even doing there?

Whatever it was, the welcome relief of his scent lured her deeper. Definitely his room. Her fingertips touched the top of his headboard over the canopy net. That was where he slept. And suddenly things felt different, she felt different and closed her eyes.

Zane. He was the difference. The catalyst for her reassessment of her life, of her being.

"Thea?" Whipping around fast, her mouth opened but any hint of a response died at the sight of him. In board shorts, hair wet, his gorgeous form glistened with the sea she'd been inhaling not so long ago. "You okay, baby?"

"I couldn't sleep without you." The instinctual response was the truest she'd ever spoken. That was it. Dumb as it was, he was the thing missing from her soul. "I'm sorry, I shouldn't have—"

"Shh," he said and closed the space between them.

Scooping his hands around her jaw, he elevated her mouth, silencing it with his.

Salt merged between their damp lips, that was the ocean, them and the foreverness that surrounded them. All that she needed to be was enclosed in that kiss. What he was, they weren't supposed to apologize, they were supposed to be eternal.

He reached beyond her without breaking their kiss and swept the net aside. She assumed anyway because it wasn't there when he walked her backward and took her hips to guide her down to the bed.

She helped him rid her of the cover-up and as she slipped down the straps of her nightdress to wriggle out of it, he shoved out of his shorts and came down onto the bed with her, easing her up until her head was nestled between the pillows.

Her fingertips trailed down his body as his mouth spoiled hers again. No questions, no judgment, he'd accepted her there, accepted everything about her.

Just as her tongue got used to its companion, assuming it would be there forever, it slipped free.

"Zane," she whispered, prepared to beg. But he didn't reply, his mouth traced its way down hers until he guided her leg over his shoulder. "Oh, Drift, you don't have to—"

The slide of his tongue quieted her again. Oh, that man. This man. Her man? Oh, God, please. Right then, under the talent of his mouth rousing and awakening her, she couldn't think anything more than how much she wanted it to be true, how much she wanted him to be hers.

"Hmm," he purred against her then pushed his tongue into her and out, up through her folds.

"Zane," she gasped, her knees pulling higher.

Weight on her belly held her there, a deep pressure of need, of desire. That same anchor rocked her hips against the waves of pleasure sparking and clenching beneath his intimate kiss.

"Sweet Thea." The vibration of his mouth against her clit rushed her to the edge, so the moment his tongue caressed it, she called out, pushing into the stability of him keeping her steady.

Her chest rose and fell, each pant followed the other. Oxygen eluded her. The sparkles of satisfaction before her eyes, and in her heart, sought refuge. One they found in him when he appeared above her again.

"Thank you," she managed to whisper.

He kissed her. "Any time, baby. I didn't want to sleep without you either." Honestly? Maybe. She smiled anyway because truth or not, his welcome meant the world. "I'm going to take a quick shower and then I'll be back, okay?" She nodded. "Don't go anywhere."

How could she go anywhere when everything she needed existed right there. He slipped out of the canopy and disappeared into the closet. The shower went on… Hmm, she'd already enjoyed her own cleansing steam in her room, but she could sneak in there, see if maybe Zane wanted his own delight.

Her heart rate was still climbing down, and by the time she felt stable enough to even think about moving, he swept the curtain aside and dropped down next to her with a kiss.

"Alessia's in a suite with her friends," she said, running her fingers into his damp hair. "She's having the time of her life. Thank you."

"It's the company that makes the difference." Lying down, he pulled her against him. "You should move in here."

Her lips curled. "Just like that?"

It was hardly forever, but he barely seemed to give it a second of consideration.

"If your sister is with her friends, you're better here. We can go to work together every morning."

She laughed. "When we spend lunchtimes talking, we never get back to work. How much work will be done if we have breakfast together?"

"Hmm…" His fingertips tickled down her arm. "I thought all the sex would be a greater obstacle but, you're right, maybe it is the food's fault."

On another laugh, she closed her eyes. "If I get fired, I'm staying here forever."

"I'll call your boss then, tell her what you really

think of her. What time's it in Missouri?"

"I don't think you'd have to tell her anything," she said, lifting her head enough to brush her cheek back and forth against him. "If the Great Zane Dyce—"

"I'm not the Great anything."

Pushing higher, she met his eye. "I disagree." Boosting a little more, she kissed him. "It's kind of becoming my catchphrase but…"

Concern met his expression. "But…?"

"I have to apologize to you again."

After an inhale of laughter, he sighed. "No more apologies, please. You have nothing to be sorry for." He tucked her hair back from her face. "You never have to be sorry."

"I blew you off earlier." Nice as it was to say there was no need, she wouldn't settle until it was out there. "You said you can live and work anywhere."

"I did."

"And I guess an alarm went off in my head."

"An alarm?"

"It's not that I don't want to talk about the future or that I don't want us to have one…" She squinted. "That was what you were talking about, right?"

Another laugh. "Yes."

"Good, okay." She puffed out a breath and sat up. "We live like two thousand miles apart. And that's if you're in California. It's probably twice that if we're talking about here."

"Distance doesn't matter."

"Exactly," she said, laying both hands on his chest to keep him still when he shifted. "I'd like to…" And this was the crescendo moment, that had to be why her pulse kicked up again. "Maybe see where this can go." It took a few seconds, but he did smile. Wasn't exactly an exuberant response. Huh, maybe she'd overplayed the hand. "If… you want to…"

And if he didn't, she was the fool who'd just embarrassed herself by stalking him to his bed and declaring her commitment. Crazy person. She'd be shuttled off the island probably as soon as the sun rose.

"Thea—"

"Do you think I'm a money-grubbing slut?"

His lips thinned. "Do you want money?"

"No!"

"Then how can you be a money-grubbing slut?" He wasn't making this easy on her. Linking their hands, he sat up with her. "I'm okay if you're a slut, because I'm one. Or I will be with you. As long as we're talking about being exclusive sluts."

His twist of amusement relaxed her.

"And they say romance is dead."

He laughed and drove his fingers into her hair. "Wanderer, I want to see where this goes too. This doesn't end with the island, we'll figure it out when the time comes."

Plans for real life back on the continent were a world away. For the time being, this was their domain, and it gave her everything she needed… everything she desired.

TWENTY-ONE

SO THEY DID get to the corporate suite, but only because she snuck out while he was on a call.

Being with him, being his, it was a dream, so normal and natural while at the same time the most exhilarating period of her life. Sinking into him, losing herself in them, might be tempting, but losing her job to lie in bed with her super-hot guy might be more than a little stupid.

She didn't see a whole lot of Alessia, but Roman was keeping his distance, or so she'd been told. Four days and nights went by. No, there wasn't a whole helluva lot of work done, but she made progress, which was something. Or so she told herself.

That night they were having dinner on the beach. Not alone. A cookout on the largest beach beckoned all. Equidistant between the corporate suite and the resort hotel, they hadn't visited there before though Zane said it was one of the most popular spots.

Zane parked up and led her to a table set up on the isolated deck at the top of the beach, separate from the masses and the bonfire on the sand.

"I'm going to say hello to Alessia," she said, resting a hand on his arm to boost up and kiss his cheek.

Stairs at the side of the curved deck led onto the sand. A security guard stood there, and there was one at the gap they'd entered by at the back. Zane probably had to be careful about who got too close. If people were harassing him all night, he'd never get peace to eat.

With musicians in the sand and the scent of the grill merging with the sea salt, it was impossible not to feel festive.

Alessia was in a group of half a dozen, all crowded around her. Her sister wasn't shy, and it was just like her to find a team no matter the location. She touched her sister's arm to get her attention.

"Thea!" Drink in hand, she threw both arms around her to hug her tight. "I'm so happy you're here! Everyone, this is my sister, Thea!"

Okay, how many drinks had she imbibed? People knew her, she was the same her she'd been at the first dinner. Though, checking out the group, there may be a few more people close to her sister than there had been before.

"Are you drunk?" she asked, guiding her away from the others. "Should I be worried about you?"

Or people taking advantage.

Alessia's broad grin inspired enthusiasm all of its own. "No! This is the best time I've ever had in my whole life."

And if anyone could get high on life, it would be her sister. They got about twenty feet from the other partygoers, it was chillier further from the bonfire.

"How have you been? Are you still okay in the suite?"

Her sister leaned in closer. "Everyone's curious about you, you know."

"Curious about me? What do I have to do with anything?"

Alessia nodded beyond her. She turned to follow her line of sight to Zane, now talking to Tripp Breckenridge, at least he wasn't alone.

"You mean they're curious about Zane," she said, looking back to her sister. "There's nothing to be curious about. He's a man. An incredible, amazing man, but just a regular guy."

Alessia scoffed. "Zane Dyce is not a regular man. You know there's Dyce tech in every purse and pocket the whole world over. Anything worth having in the last twenty years was invented by him."

Which was weird, now that she thought about it. She saw him on laptops and with paperwork, she'd never seen him fiddle with any new device or anything.

"We don't talk about that."

"What do you talk about?"

She sighed. "Alessia."

Her sister laughed. "Okay, okay! Is Roman coming?"

"I have no idea."

Hopefully not, but that wouldn't be her sister's preference.

"Did you hear we're going to party in Honolulu?"

"Yes, I did."

"Of course you did," Alessia said and squealed. "We're going to party with Roman Lowe! Well, not you but—"

"I am, actually, coming."

Alarm lit Alessia. "You're breaking up with Zane?"

Sometimes her sister took the obvious too far. "We don't have to be on the same landmass to be together. I'm part of the contest group, right? Of course

I'll be there."

Hand on her arm, Alessia inched in, lowering her voice. "Have you seen him? Roman?"

"Since when?"

"He came out to see us yesterday, but he was really quiet. Everyone's worried this Sway thing has set back his recovery. We can't believe she would do this to him."

Oh, it was so difficult to keep her sanity sometimes. These women, these young women, idolized a man who didn't deserve their adoration. It wasn't their fault. Maybe it was a little naïve, but their interest came from a place of love… unfortunately.

She'd never met Sway, the woman could be an angel or a demon. More likely, Sway existed somewhere in between, as most people did. Whichever it was, she couldn't help but prickle. Why were Roman's negative choices being placed on another person? And a woman at that? Wasn't he responsible for his own actions? Wasn't everyone?

"Do you need anything?" Changing the subject was better than shattering her sister's illusions. They'd only disagree on the subject anyway. "You want to eat with us?"

Alessia's smile got saucy as she twirled a length of hair. "I want to eat that guy."

Another look back to Zane and Tripp.

"Tripp Breckenridge?" she said. "No, you don't."

"Is he an asshole? That's okay sometimes."

She laughed, shaking her head. "Oh, little sister, I love you so." She pulled her close to kiss her temple. "You can eat with us if you want, but just you, I don't want crowds harassing Zane all night."

"Is Tripp single?"

"No!" she said, taking her sister's hips to guide

her around until her back was to the deck. "He lives in New York."

"What does where he lives have to do with anything?" Alessia asked, trying to look back over her shoulder as they walked toward the bonfire again. "Tell him I think he's cute."

"Every woman thinks Tripp's cute. He accepts that as the default." That was certainly the impression she got from dinner the other night. "You'll start a riot if you get involved with him."

"Everyone thinks Zane is cute and no one hates you… not that they've told me anyway."

"They won't tell you they hate your sister."

"Hmm, good point." Alessia cheered when they stopped a few feet from her friends. "I'll come say hi later, when he's had a few drinks."

"Okay. I'll keep topping off his glass," she teased.

Her sister was beautiful, and she had a kind soul, any guy would be lucky to have her. Tripp might be a good guy, but she didn't want him and her sister hooking up, then forgetting each other existed.

In their final hug, Alessia tensed and squealed. "Oh my God, is that…?"

The hubbub grew in its excitement. Alessia vanished into her group. With so many important stories to share, it was nice her sister found kindred spirits.

Walking toward the deck before she got an eye on who riled the crowd: Zairn.

If these were the kind of people who loved celebrity, they'd have to know him. Chatting away with Tripp and Zane, he raised a hand in hello and that was all the encouragement the women needed. The swarm rushed toward the deck. The wave of them collided with her back just a breath before the guard edged aside to allow her through and no one else. The stairs were immediately blocked by more than one guard. A dozen guys were dotted around the fenced deck. Now she got why they were above and protected by a perimeter.

"Everything okay?" she asked when Zane put an arm around her.

"We were waiting for you."

He held out a seat for her and as she sat, so did the men.

"No Struan tonight?" she asked Tripp, then immediately wondered how that worked.

Not only was Struan's livelihood attached to his brother, he also had to be careful how he lived his own life. No one recognized him, instead, he'd be his brother in everyone's eyes whenever he went anywhere.

"Logan's plane lands in five minutes," Tripp said, doing the honors of ladling out punch for everyone from the bowl in the center of the table. "Figured I'd give the brothers their space."

"Logan… Logan Lowe? I didn't know he was coming."

"Someone has to field the ire."

Roman's ire. Idiot got way too much airtime in everyone's lives. Anyone in his periphery suddenly found their whole existence revolved around him.

"You have a lot of brothers," she said, accepting a glass. "You must know how it works."

"Yeah, sometimes it's better when there are no witnesses."

Everyone had their drinks, but it wasn't exactly the most relaxed of moments with a score of people clamoring for their attention. Not theirs, Zairn's and he was doing a great job of ig—

All of a sudden, he stood up. She had no idea why until, ah, Roxie came rushing past the guards at the deck and clacked across the deck in heels.

"Sorry, sorry, sorry," Roxie said, bowing to press her chest against Zairn, one of her knees bending to raise her foot high behind her. "I'm here now, did you miss me?"

"Always, Lola."

Together, they went to the rail to satisfy the crowd.

"Will they be okay?" she asked, unsure she'd want to be the focus of such fervor.

"They do this all the time," Zane said.

"There's a constant crowd outside Crimson Palace in New York," Tripp said. "Even when the Empress isn't in residence."

She smiled. "The Empress?"

"Zairn was always popular," Tripp said, examining the view of celebs and fans. "But since Roxie it's been…"

"Think she turned things around for a lot of people."

"You remember how much scrutiny he used to get?" Tripp asked, exhaling and slouching in his seat to address Zane. "The stress of it? Especially after Dayah."

"He handles it differently now," Zane said to Tripp and as a kind of explanation to her. "Now even when the press is hounding him for screwing around or their breakup thing… he's lighter."

"He knows it was bullshit," Tripp said. "Anyone who knows him knows it's bullshit."

God, she hoped that was true. "Why would the press think he's screwing around?" How heartbreaking, it was difficult to imagine it of the man she'd met the other night. "Why did they break up?"

"They didn't." Zane and Tripp shared a smile. "Roxie is great at the theater, and Zairn's a fucking rock. They are the most… I've never known a couple so together, so solid."

"And this coming from the guy whose parents have been together thirty-something years."

Another exhale and a laugh from Tripp. "My folks have never known life without each other, adult life anyway. Zairn and Roxie…" All eyes drifted to the couple. "They know how to appreciate what they have, how to nurture it."

"Roxie's got an energy about her," Zane said. "And she has good instincts with the media."

"Also helps that she's got them eating out the palm of her hand."

"Thea…" The female voice attracted her attention and there was Roxie, dipping to kiss her cheek and steal the seat beside her. "Who's eating out of your hand? Zane?"

"Not me."

"You," Tripp said. "We're talking about your innate talent for bullshit."

Rather than be offended, Roxie smiled, watching her guy pour her drink. "It's a honed ability. And a necessary one." Zairn put her drink down and Roxie immediately took his hand. "Isn't it, Skippy?"

"Uh oh," Tripp said. "What did you do?" Why would he think…? "She only calls him Skippy when he's pissed her off."

Her confusion must've read on her face for him to explain like that.

"That's not true," Roxie said, pressing Zairn's curled fingers to her chest. "Sometimes I call him Skippy when he's just plain wrong."

"She's sticking her meddling nose in."

"I always stick my meddling nose in, Casanova," Roxie said. "And that's not why you're pissed." Zairn took his hand back and Roxie leaned closer to the table. "He's in a bad mood because Logan's coming and there are pictures on the internet of said rockstar's hands on my ass."

Oh, there were? Why would there even be

pictures of something like that?

"Did you used to date?"

"No," Roxie said. "We partied together in London once."

"You've partied with him more than once."

"London's the only one that counts. And let's not forget, you were in Vegas marrying Kesley at that same time."

Zairn groaned. "I did not marry her."

"Which worked out for me in the end."

"Lola's changing the subject. It's nothing to do with Logan, I don't give a damn about him. Even if I did, I know her girl's rules, so what is there to worry about?"

Rules? What rules?

"You get along with Porter." The next look Zairn landed on his woman wasn't appreciative. "What?" Roxie asked. "You traipse around all over the world with your ex and I don't get jealous. You're financially and emotionally supporting at least one other ex too. You've slept with every woman on the planet and I don't get jealous of them."

"I'm not jealous."

"Okay," she said, nodding at the others. "He's not jealous."

Zairn seemed close to the edge of his patience. "You know why I'm pissed."

"Yes, I do," Roxie declared, sitting up straight. "And I am trying to divert you from that by making it frivolous."

"Roxanna—"

"Mmm," Roxie said, sliding a hand up Zairn's arm. "Are we getting formal, Mr. Lomond? You want to take me home and punish me?"

"Why is he really pissed?" Tripp asked.

"Don't stir her up," Zane said, sliding a hand over hers, distracting her from the other couple. "Are you hungry?”

Dinner, right, yeah, that's why they were there. “I might be—yeah, I am.”

TWENTY-TWO

ZANE'S SMILE LEFT her and a server person she hadn't seen came scurrying over.

"You want to just bring us a spread of whatever, please."

"Yes, sir," the server said and hurried off.

"How's Alessia doing?"

"Oh, she's in her element," she said and switched to the relaxed Tripp. "She thinks you're cute, by the way."

His brows went up as his focus floated to the crowd, now back on the beach, doing their thing. Though with one eye on the famous couple, no doubt.

The Breckenridge seemed a little more focused. "Which one is she?"

"It doesn't matter to you because you're not going to screw Thea's sister," Roxie said, apparently moving on though Zairn still didn't seem that relaxed. "You could if you're going to fall in love with her, but I think you have a decade or two of screwing around left to go before you think about settling down."

"Nothing wrong with being polite."

Oh, that swagger, and the ease of him. It was quite an achievement that he could be both cocky and laid-back at the same time, while also seeming oblivious and switched on.

Roxie swirled her drink in its glass. "Only you could see a screw as a courtesy."

"Nah, your man did plenty of that in his day."

"And now he's all locked in," Roxie said. "Don't you want to be single for Honolulu?"

"Thought the guys weren't allowed to join your Honolulu party," Zairn said, only unwinding when Roxie put his hand on her thigh, high on her thigh, like, beneath-her-skirt-near-an-intimate-area high. "Didn't you say that?"

"Tripp doesn't count."

"Yeah, I don't count."

The server came over, six of them actually, and laid out meats, skewers, salads, different breads, beans, shrimp, peppers, so much that she didn't know where to begin.

"Why doesn't Tripp count?" Zane asked when the servers left.

"Because I'm always invited to the party," Tripp answered for himself, getting up in time with everyone else.

"Always?"

"Always. You want to know how many bachelorette parties I've attended?"

"As the stripper?" Roxie asked, popping something into her mouth.

"If the need arose, yeah."

"And maybe need wasn't the only thing rising?" Roxie teased, picking out food and putting some on Zairn's plate too. "How many bachelorettes have you screwed at the party?"

"He's not answering that one," Zane said, handing her a plate. "Not while I'm around, 'cause I'd only tell his mother."

"Mom doesn't mind the screwing."

"Says you," Roxie said. "I can't believe that of a woman so pure and kind of heart. You must break hers every time you ghost a woman."

"I don't ghost women. You can't comment, you hooked up with Z before I ever got a shot, so you'll never know."

"I'll never know what?"

"How well I treat women."

"No matter how well you treat them, I'd prefer you don't encourage my sister," she said, filling her plate. "She's not the most worldly of women."

"Translated?" Roxie assisted. "She'll believe you're really interested if you speak to her."

"I'm interested. I'm always interested. Not like I'm a player."

Roxie scoffed. "You're the definition of a player, Priest." The woman paused to land a smile on him. "You just happen to be impossibly adorable too, so we love you anyway."

"Your guy was a champion player."

Everyone found their chairs again.

"I take exception to that," Zairn said, gesturing to Zane. "Tell them about Cam in the day."

"In the day? How about every day," Zane said, squeezing her knee when she sat. "You want to talk effortless with women…"

"Cam who?"

"Collier," Roxie said and swayed over to bump shoulders with her. "Wait until I tell you about him and his life choices."

"His life choices?"

"Yeah, he—"

"Rox Out!"

The call stalled them and security parted to let someone join them. Someone like Logan Lowe.

"Rocks Off," Roxie called in return and stood up to go around the table and hug the newcomer.

From the corner of her eye, she tried to see if Zairn was okay, but the guy wasn't fazed at all. He wiped his hands on a napkin and stood up to shake the guy's hand as he went around the table.

Logan kissed Roxie's head, then held up his hands and backed off, smiling toward Zairn. "Not taking it too far, man."

"Oh, he's okay," Roxie said, returning to her seat, dragging it closer to Zairn's to rest against him. "He knows the rules with my girls."

The rules again. So if Zairn truly wasn't bothered about Logan being around, why was he pissed off when Roxie arrived?

"You been to the villa?" Zane asked. "Didn't think you'd head over here first."

"Could be I'm avoiding it," Logan said, slipping his hands in his pockets. "Is he fucked? Where's Struan?"

Zane nodded beyond him toward the bonfire. "Keeping a low profile."

"Right."

The next scream heralded a rash of others, then the crowd were at the deck edge again. Logan didn't flinch. Though why would he? If he was used to playing to crowds of thousands in arenas, a handful of women on a beach wouldn't register.

"Do you have a plan?"

"Damage control seems sort of beyond," Logan said. "Roman wants to be pissed, so he'll be pissed. No one will take his drama from him." And that was a pretty accurate sentiment from her point of view. "He wants everyone groveling, 'cause then he's the innocent party."

"Not so innocent." Everyone looked at her. "Sorry."

"No, you're right," Logan said, though his expression skewed a little, probably because she was a stranger. "He's got plenty demons of his own, a lot of skeletons in his closet."

That his entourage would conceal just to remain in his good books.

"So you plan to go there and, what?" Roxie asked. "Tell him to chill out? Did you have to fly all the way here for that?"

"Problem is keeping him sober," Tripp added and gestured. "Sit down, eat, if you're hanging out."

"Nah, man, I'm waiting for…"

When Logan's head rose, she followed his line of sight to see another man creep through the security guards. Roxie's gasp suggested this wasn't the best guest to have at the party.

"Are you fucking insane?" Zairn asked Logan.

"No, no," Zane said and stood.

Zairn was on his feet a moment later.

"Who is that?" she whispered to Roxie.

"Deacon," Roxie said, shifting her seat again to link their arms. "Sway's other man."

Oh, God, this was—okay so maybe the guy wanted to clear the air. Maybe he wanted to smack Roman in the face, and who were any of them to stand in the way of that.

Okay, yes, that was a little catty.

Still, she could understand why the men were reluctant.

"Is that the smartest idea?"

"Logan can't fix it, can he? Why should he apologize or explain his bandmate's actions?"

Zane came back, extending his hand for hers. "This could get messy."

"What does that mean?"

"We'll have to go with him to—"

"You fucking asshole!"

As Zane turned, Roxie and Tripp both leaped up. And there was Roman, smashing his way through the guards to come stomping up on the huddle of guys.

"Ro," Tripp said and tried to intercept him, but it was left to Logan to get in his way.

Zairn stayed by Deacon, and, she had to say, he didn't seem as stressed or worried as the others. It was all drama, yes, and maybe Roman deserved to have his heart broken and his ego checked.

So why was she concerned?

Alessia.

The women on the beach were still crowded by the deck rail. With the shouting and the cursing, there was a lot of support for Roman, which would just fuel his insanity.

"You fuck my woman? You fuck my girl and—"

"She was never your fucking girl," Deacon hollered back. "You're just the asshole who couldn't get it up when he fell on her in bed."

She cringed, and Roxie's head turned showing a similar expression.

"Deacon, we're not doing this now," Zane said, slipping an arm around her.

The guy didn't seem to hear it. Roman shoved at Tripp, who shoved right back, Logan got between them just as Roman threw a fist. It bounced off Logan, startling him enough to drop his guard. Roman lunged, Deacon pushed him away, they shoved and then Roman's arm came flailing out again.

Wasn't exactly the most finessed fight in the world.

"Is he high?" she asked Roxie when the woman got close.

"Probably."

"Are you okay?" Zane asked and put her hand in Roxie's. "I'll have security take the guests home."

The men were still pushing, trying to fight, trading insults, as Tripp and Logan fought to keep them apart. Zane marched off to talk to one of the guards. Zairn came sauntering over to pick up his glass.

Roxie smirked at him. "I don't see you breaking a sweat, sweetheart."

"Guy deserves it." Zairn wasn't shy in swinging his glass up to his lips. "You ladies want to take this party to the terrace?"

"Providing we can leave Roman behind."

"That's exactly the idea."

"Let me make sure my sister's okay first."

And it was as she turned her back that the glint of light on glass startled her. Not just any glass, a lens.

She whipped back around, showing Roxie her horror. "Is that the press? There in the trees?"

Roxie leaned to the side and she stepped out of the way to clear the view. "Yep. Dumbass. He invites them here, then gives them a show."

"There'll be a lot more damage control needed now," Zairn said. "So much for salvaging his career. Now everything will go to shit."

She met his eye. "He deserves that too."

Another shout, another swing, and this time Roman made contact. Tripp threw him back, a look on his face that suggested maybe his own restraint was slipping too.

The hubbub on the beach grew to a furor and that was when the screaming started.

Alessia.

Passing through Roxie and Zairn, the mass of bodies pushing and shoving on the sand seemed to have no beginning or end. Her sister was somewhere in there and that was her only driving force. At the bottom of the deck stairs, someone grabbed her arm. A security guy.

She immediately tried to yank it back. "Let me go."

"Miss Florin—"

"Let me go! I need to get my—"

"Thea!"

Alessia's voice brought her around and there she was, being almost carried away by two big guys in black. Security. Her guard didn't let go but did move with her as she hurried in her sister's wake. Two other security guys came close, so she lost sight of her. They kept on going up the beach and over the grass toward the carts.

A massive crash stopped all movement. Shouting. Screaming. Crying. Shit, what had…?

The deck rail was broken and there was Roman rolling around in the sand with Deacon.

"Oh my God!" Alessia screeched. "Oh my God!"

"Enough," she said.

The press had moved in closer, but Magnus was there, trying to get in their way. Good luck with that. What a shitshow and what an idiot.

"But Thea what if—"

"No," she said, spurred to act when the security guards huddled in close and kept on moving.

Bundled onto a cart with Alessia, she held her sister as they drove away. She'd come to the island to protect her sister and tonight, she'd done that.

What about Zane?

She'd just abandoned him. Alessia wasn't the only person there she cared about anymore. Zane, Roxie, even Zairn and Tripp, she didn't want any of them hurt. Security had protected her, protected Alessia. Would Zane order them to protect him just as carefully?

Damn, not that he didn't have enough going on,

but she wanted to see him, to speak to him, to demand he be there with her. The guy was trying to keep his family together, and she'd just walked away. Another apology hung in her future.

TWENTY-THREE

BACK IN ALESSIA'S SUITE, waiting was all they could do.

"What if they're hurt?" Alessia asked of her friends. "What if something happened?"

Maybe now her sister would understand why she worried on an almost daily basis. No one wanted people they cared about to be in potential danger. And, sheesh, Roman Lowe was constant potential danger.

"More bodies won't help."

"Bodies?" Alessia shrieked and thrust to her feet. "You think people are dead?"

"It's a figure of speech. Having more people around won't help."

Maybe it would've been better to say it that way in the first place.

Though her view had been brief, it didn't look like the deck itself collapsed. Luckily, only the side rail gave, not the front where the majority of—oh, who was she kidding? She had to be calm, to exude composure for her sister's sake but—her throat closed.

There was just no way to be sure of anything. Her assumptions could be right, but they'd left. God knew what happened after they'd gone. Would Roman and Deacon have stopped fighting? Did Zane, Tripp, and Zairn have to go down onto the sand? What about the crowd? Were they mobbed?

Uncertainty kept her adrenaline alive. Zane.

"Oh, Thea." Alessia rushed over to pull her into a hug. "I'm sure Zane is fine, he'll have it handled."

Any doubt about his safety wasn't appreciated. At the same time, she couldn't deny it was all that occupied her mind. She wasn't usually a worrier, okay, when it came to her sister, maybe she was a little sensitive, but Zane… Anxiety itched her skin. She needed to see him, hear him, he could be in pain, alone, and on the island they wouldn't have—

"I have to go," she said, pushing out of Alessia's arms. "I'm sorry, I know it's… I don't want to leave you on your own—"

A knock on the door interrupted. Alessia started to move, but she held her back. Yes, this might be her sister's suite, but if there was danger, she didn't want her sister facing it first.

Why would there be danger? What a ridiculous thought, they weren't running from a crazed serial killer. The only maniac on the loose was Roman and he had other things on his mind than chasing down errant fans. Being on edge meant any little thing could feel like a threat.

Another knock. A little more insistent.

"I'll get it."

Alessia squeezed her lips together in time with her flat hands coming together beneath her chin. Yeah, pray, they might need all the help they could get.

She opened the door just an inch, and thank God she did. It wasn't Zane, no, the man under the ball cap had a right of discretion.

"You know who I am?" he asked in a whisper. She just nodded. "Zane wants you at the house. Your sister's friends are on their way here with security."

"Was anyone hurt?"

"No one who didn't deserve to be. Will you come with me?"

"Yes, just give me a second to—"

"Be quick, I can't be out here when—"

"I know." She closed the door because Alessia could not see the person on the other side of it or all hell might break loose. "Your friends are on their way, okay?" Hurrying to her sister, she hugged her quick. "If you need anything, tell the front desk and they'll find me." She stopped, holding her sister's upper arms. "Are you okay?"

Alessia nodded. "I love you."

Wow, maybe the night had shaken her sister up. "I love you too."

They hugged quickly and she slipped out.

"Like cutting things close, don't you?"

Except she wasn't the one skulking around. Yet, despite a surge of annoyance, she couldn't hold onto it. All she could feel was sorry for the man.

He shoved open the service door, holding it for her to go out first. "Why did they send you, Struan?"

The rabble of female voices quaked from the opposite end of the corridor just before the door closed behind them. Thank goodness they'd be distracting each other rather than checking out the rear view of her chaperone. Superfans would be capable of recognizing him, supposedly him, from any angle.

"Because everyone else is tied up with the bullshit."

He led her to a cart and gestured for her to sit first. Weird that Struan should have such manners while his contrasting brother didn't. His *twin* brother. How did that even happen? It couldn't be nature, not if they were identical, but—

"Zane," she said, kicking her thoughts into line. "Is he okay?"

"I don't know much. I was out when Roman left. When I got back the phone was ringing, Rox told me everyone was gathering at the house and Zane wanted you picked up."

Probably because if the press had their own carts, they'd be whizzing after their marks. A quick stop at the resort to pick her up would raise more questions than she was happy to answer. The rods and reels had enough chum to feed on.

"Your brother showed. Sorry, your brothers showed up."

"Yeah, Logan was flying in to square things with Roman. How the hell did that turn into a bust up?"

"Because your brother brought Deacon." Though his double take registered in her peripheral vision, she kept her eyes ahead. "And your other brother, the one that looks like you, he showed with the damn press. Him and Deacon started throwing punches straight away. They didn't even try to talk."

"Damnit, what was Logan thinking?"

Now she did shift to take him in. "Yeah, 'cause it's Logan's fault." Another double take. "I understand that it was maybe stupid to bring Deacon along, but if the men are friends and he truly wanted to make peace…"

"This would be as good a place as any, if the press wasn't around."

"That was Roman's call too. Bringing the press here because of that new show. You know, you blame Logan and everyone else, when is someone going to tell Roman to act like a reasonable human being?"

He actually smiled. Smiled! The nerve!

"There's not a single person in Roman's inner circle who hasn't tried explaining that to him. Hell, I've been trying since we were in diapers and it hasn't got me anywhere. Did Sway show?"

"Not at the beach." Though God knew if she'd stowed away on the men's plane to join them. That would be the perfect extra layer to really enhance the insanity. "I don't see how her presence would make the situation any better."

"It wouldn't, but if Logan brought Deacon…"

"Aren't the two friends?"

"Yeah."

"If Deacon is marrying Sway, she'll be in Logan's life, to some degree I'd imagine. Maybe bringing Deacon wasn't the smartest choice, but I can understand Logan not wanting to choose between his friend and his brother."

"That's exactly the kind of thing Roman will expect."

"And what does that do for Logan's life? For his work? If he dumps Deacon, he's saying Roman controls everyone. That will only fuel his ego. I'm not surprised Sway doesn't want to be with him. No offense; a relationship with him must be utterly exhausting."

"I know you're trying to help—"

"This where you tell me I don't know what I'm talking about?"

"No. This is where I tell you you're preaching to the choir."

Good, that gave her a chance to probe. "So why do it? Why pander to him all the time? Bow down and prostrate. Is it the money? Is he that good to you? Do you love the Hollywood lifestyle that much?"

"You're close to your sister."

"I love her, and would do anything for her, but I

don't rely on her for an income. She has friends she goes to with her secrets, we live separate lives. The way I hear it, you're Roman's lackey twenty-four seven."

"After our mom died, our father hit the bottle, and that was about all we saw of him. Magnus, our uncle, he looked out for us, nurtured what was in Roman. Maybe it was too late by then, I don't know, but he's always struggled."

"He doesn't look like he's struggling," she said. "He looks like a man who enjoys pulling strings."

"I guess you could see it that way; he does like it when we jump to attention for him. We have a cousin tied up in her own sibling bail out. Theirs started before ours, I don't know, maybe that's where it came from. It's a family thing."

That was never an excuse. Man, was she judgmental tonight. Seeing Zane might deflate some of her pressurized distress.

She sighed. "You do know other people don't live like this. That not every life is filled with melodrama and hissy fits."

"I've heard tell."

That flash of a smile lowered her shoulders a little. "I feel sorry for you."

And his smile vanished to a frown. "Feel sorry for me?"

"I don't know what kind of man you are, if you're like your brother or not. But no one deserves to be an understudy in their own life. That's what you are, you know. How do you even have friendships and relationships of your own?"

"Most of my friends know the deal. Tripp's the guy I rely on most of the time, even though we live on opposite coasts."

"That's got to be tough."

"Roman travels a lot. Even when he's not

shooting, he prefers not to stay put. He likes parties, likes the attention." Something that didn't need to be stated. "And he likes New York. It's been a while, rehab put everything on pause."

"For him," she said. "What about you?"

They didn't wait for the intercom, the gates opened for them, and he drove on through.

"It was good to get some time to numb out, focus on my own shit. I'm not a flashy guy like Roman and Logan, their lives always seemed exhausting."

"It's a life you live too."

"On the periphery," he said. "It's not the same as being the one always constricted by demands."

"Doesn't your brother put demands on you? If you're his double, a lot of the work has to be yours."

They pulled to a stop by the portico. "I like the physical stuff and I always had more stamina than Roman for pushing through when things get tough. Working out helps me focus, I like getting lost in it. Roman was always more interested in… other things."

Like drugs and alcohol, maybe like women and wild adventures.

"If it wasn't for you—"

"See, I don't like that." He shifted to get a better angle for the conversation. "If it wasn't for me, yeah, maybe he wouldn't have got this far, maybe Hollywood would've written him off years ago, but what do I get from that? Who would get schadenfreude watching their own skin tank?"

More than a pretty face. Struan was more articulate than Roman, more patient, more genuine.

"I don't think you want Roman to fail, or anyone wants him to fail. His success is built on your hard work."

He shook his head slightly. "I don't want it. I never wanted—"

"I get that because I'd bet twins are a big deal, if

both of you got equal recognition—"

"I get to do what I love. I keep fit, face new challenges every day. I like what I do."

"And do you ever think that maybe success is part of the problem? Roman's been told his behavior is okay by those who clean up after him. Failing is an extreme end of the spectrum, but maybe if Hollywood wasn't always weighing him down, the media wasn't always hounding him, he could find peace in that? One that maybe helps him deal with his addictions without immediately launching back into the environment that caused the trouble in the first place."

His almost defensive position loosened as he narrowed his eyes on her. "Have you been talking to Rox?"

"Not about this," she said.

Lights flashed behind them.

Three other carts came trundling up with a dark SUV in back. She hadn't seen any actual vehicles on the island thus far, so that last one was a surprise.

Struan appeared at her side and he offered a hand to help her out. Though as soon as she saw Zane in one of the carts, she let go to rush over.

"Oh, baby, are you hurt?" she asked, searching up and down. "Were you injured?"

"No. Are you okay? Did you get hurt? Where's Alessia?"

"I left Alessia in her suite." The moment he was upright, she threw her arms around him. "Don't do that to me again. Please."

"I know, I'm sorry," he said, wrapping her in his arms, stooping to rest his mouth in her hair. "I told you I'd never endanger your family again and then—"

"I don't care about that. I don't! We talked about it." She held on tighter. "I'm so sorry I left you; I was so scared you got hurt."

"Wanderer, you had no choice," he said, sliding a hand into her hair to guide her gaze up. "Security was instructed to take you to safety. You and Alessia. You're the most important—"

"Fuck you!"

Spinning around, the other carts were empty, and people crowded around the SUV. All except Roxie and Zairn who wandered through the portico, her tucked under his arm. Somehow, they let it roll off.

Roman appeared from the SUV.

Magnus jumped out behind him. "We'll iron all this out and—"

Logan came around from behind one of the carts. Deacon was there too, but he didn't follow. Maybe the guy was getting the message.

"No," Roman declared, pointing at his brother. "I don't want you near me."

"You're being a little bitch."

"Your fucking asshole of a friend—"

"This is the bullshit," Struan called, quieting them. "Where the fuck does all this posturing get you?"

"Let's leave them to it."

TWENTY-FOUR

ZANE SLID AN ARM around her to guide her through the portico. They met Roxie and Zairn in the living room on this side of the kitchen. Zairn was at the bar.

"Are you both okay?" she asked.

Roxie gestured her over to pull her down on the couch. "Z is mixing drinks, we'll be fine with a little of his elixir."

"I didn't eat much."

"Oh, don't worry about getting crazy, my Casanova has seen everything."

And Zane?

Hubbub rose in volume from around the front door. Thankfully, it didn't come their way. It carried through the house, getting a little quieter before rising again outside at the front of the building. A sliding door was open, but they could only see the corner of the terrace.

"Guy loves a stage," she murmured.

"I know, right?" Roxie asked, her head swinging toward her fiancé. "Isn't this the part of the conversation where you remind me to cut him some slack?"

"Lola, it's taking all my restraint not to go out there and throw the damn guy into the ocean. Good riddance. I'll do the fucking time."

"He's usually not like this," Roxie said, threading their fingers together. "He's a very patient man."

"Has to be to survive being with you," Zane said, dropping onto the couch opposite theirs. On an exhale, his elbow met his knee, and his palm cupped his forehead. "This place is supposed to be a sanctuary."

Zairn brought drinks to her and Roxie. Whatever the drink, it was good.

"Gin and It," Roxie murmured and touched their glasses. "Good for every occasion."

Magnus came striding in. "Let's straighten this out."

Who exactly was he appealing to…? Magnus fixated on Zairn during his walk back to the bar, then switched to Zane.

"What is it you're waiting for?" Roxie asked.

"This is your cousin, Zane, you must want to help."

Zairn snickered and continued pouring.

"We are helping, Magnus," Zane said. "You invited the press. That wasn't us, that was you." Without the media's presence, this wouldn't be such a big deal. But they just had to show off, Roman just had to toot his own horn. Well done, guy, does that still seem like a smart move? "On top of that, there's no cell signal or Wi-Fi accessible by them. It's because of us…" Or more specifically Zane, "that right now, this is still under wraps."

"Excellent!" Roxie declared, raising her glass. "So long as they never leave here, the world will never know. Perfect solution."

The elder man seemed certain. "We can control

this. We can. We call in a couple of favors—"

"We?" Zairn asked and bit into an olive.

"Yeah," Zane said. "What is this *we*, Magnus? This isn't an us problem."

"He's your cousin."

"You said that already," Zairn said, retrieving a bottle of Scotch. "Just what do you think he's getting at?"

The men snickered, but it was Roxie who tapped her wrist. "He's talking about the Colliers."

"Yes!" Magnus leaped on that revelation like he would a life raft. "The Colliers. You have influence, you have pull—"

"Not we anymore? Because you know they'll never do this. Why would they waste professional capital on a lost cause?"

"He is not a lost cause," Magnus snapped at Zairn. Interesting choice of action given he wanted the man's help. Maybe he'd momentarily forgotten that because he quickly pulled back. "Roman needs help. He needs understanding—"

"Rehab and a psych workup," Zairn said. "We won't call the Colliers. We will send him to rehab."

Again. She sighed. It would only work if he wanted it. Hadn't they figured that out yet?

"If he goes back to rehab, he loses the role. This whole trip will have been for nothing. He's heartbroken, not high. His sobriety—"

"Collapsed on a private island away from all regular temptations. You really think he'll keep it together on the continent? Hell, the group is supposed to be leaving for Honolulu tomorrow, what do you think will happen there?"

"We should keep Deacon here."

"He won't want to be here," Roxie said. "Sway's in Honolulu."

"Shit," Zane exhaled. It sounded like maybe

Magnus did the same. "So it's a shitshow waiting to happen."

"He won't stay away from her."

"We can call," Zairn said. "Keep her concealed or fly her back to LA."

"She's in Honolulu waiting for Deacon."

"Doesn't that mean even if you miraculously fix whatever happened today with the press, there's just going to be a bigger, more public blowout tomorrow night?"

"Yes," Roxie said. "That's exactly what it means."

"No, it doesn't!"

"You've got to rein Roman in," Zairn said. "If he won't be handled, it's a losing battle."

"This role is everything."

And in that plea, she read Magnus's desperation too. People relied on Roman. Wasn't that Struan's point? A whole machine moved around the central cog of Roman Lowe. If only his nephew, his client, could see more than his indulgent excessive ego would allow.

"Who is best placed to make him see that?" she asked.

"Sway," Roxie said. "If their relationship was as real as he's making out, if there was that much love there."

"You want to arrange a meet between them?" Zane asked. "On purpose?"

Magnus exhaled. "Let me go talk to him, he'll have calmed down now."

The guy went outside and they all looked at each other for a few seconds. Zairn's set brow fixed on his fiancée.

"What?" Roxie asked, all innocence. "I'm not helping the guy. I just… say things out loud and they happen. It's details, babe."

"Getting Deacon out of his eye line would be a good start. Struan and Logan will have a better shot without him around."

"Why doesn't he know what's good for him?" she asked the room. "He must see that screwing this up is a death sentence for his career."

"Either he's an idiot," Roxie said, stroking the back of her hand still linked in Roxie's other. "Or he really loved her. If you love like that and lose it…" Next time her new friend's gaze met Zairn's, his was much softer, much deeper. "You can't find your balance without it."

"Okay," Zairn said, eating another olive before he spoke again. "You compare us to them one more time, I'm looking for the emergency hatch."

Giving that couple their moment, she searched Zane. "Why did he think the Colliers would help? That's the CollCom Colliers, right?"

"We're close to them."

"Their influence must only reach so far though. What about the contest winners? The staff who work here? Anyone could talk to anyone."

"The Colliers—"

Roxie stopped talking when Magnus came in again, this time with Roman and Struan.

"Are you considering it?" Magnus asked. "Asking for their help? Knox's bit of fluff, you're friends with her, right?"

Roxie's brows about shot off her head. "His bit of fluff?"

The moment Roxie set her feet on the floor to rise, Zairn materialized to curve an arm around her shoulders, holding her back against him.

"Easy, Lola. Whoa, girl," he murmured before switching his offense to match his fiancée's in addressing Magnus. "Knox is serious about Jane. You're lucky he's not here to hear what you just said."

"Oh, he'll know he said it," Roxie proclaimed. "Because I'll tell him. We won't tell Jane, of course, she's too kindhearted to deserve pain, but there's a good chance after I tell Knox he'll set out to ruin you and your stupid, little show."

"The tension's ratcheting up again," Struan said. "We just got him calmed down."

"I'll see her," Roman said, like it was some big concession. "Sway, in Honolulu."

And then what? All would be well?

"The press will likely be interviewing the staff and contest winners as we speak."

"It doesn't matter." Magnus's confidence was surprising. "They all signed NDAs."

Damn, she'd signed one too. Not that she planned to go searching for an outlet interested in the story, but it wasn't nice to be contractually silenced, protecting someone who wasn't gracious or appreciative of the discretion.

"What about the releases?" Struan asked, sparking dread in Magnus' eyes.

"Damn. Damn. Damn!"

"What about what releases?"

"Everyone had to sign a release," Struan said. "Allowing footage shot or pictures taken to be used for marketing, advertisement, etc. It gave us the right to use anything shot in any way we wanted."

"Oh, that's right." A glimmer from her first morning there flickered in her mind. "I didn't sign that."

Hope speared Magnus a few steps forward. "You didn't?"

"No," she said, shaking her head. "But does it matter? Won't they just blur me out?"

"I didn't sign a release," Roxie said, holding Zairn's forearm at her clavicle. "Neither did Casanova."

"Isn't this just a disgusting back-alley retreat," Zane said and exhaled. "If you want to stop them using that footage—"

"We threaten them with a lawsuit." Magnus's energy skyrocketed. "Tell them our richest, most influential sponsors, will not comply with the footage being aired."

That might be good for keeping Roman squeaky clean, but it did feel kind of underhanded.

"We won't sue them," Roxie said. "I don't care."

"You don't have to sue them," Magnus said, glee shimmering in his aura. "The threat will be enough. They know you're connected to the Colliers, everyone on the planet knows that." Uh, no, she hadn't. Was Hollywood and celebrity always so Machiavellian? "This is good. This is good. The threat will be enough!"

"I'm not threatening anyone." Roxie's care-o-meter was registering pretty low, she couldn't say hers was much different. "You overestimate how much we care about Roman's career."

"You care about the careers of others though," Struan said. "His staff, the crew on the show, this is a juggernaut, you know that, it's never about just one man's livelihood."

Roxie's head fell back on Zairn in almost surrender.

"Don't you have news to announce?" Magnus asked the couple. "Something we can tell the press to divert their attention to something else."

"No," Roxie said, unhooking Zairn's arm to sit and snatch her glass from the end table. "We're not doing that. Absolutely no way."

"Agreed." Zairn went back to the bar. "We won't be a part of whatever BS you feed them. We won't talk to them. Won't out this... farce. But we won't use our relationship to bolster your cause or disguise the truth, to raise up a man uninterested in raising up others."

Or even maintaining the status quo. Roman didn't know what was good for him, sure, but the expression "being one's own worst enemy" had never been truer than it was with him.

Zane looked frayed. Tired. He dropped against the back of the couch, eyes closed. And just like Roxie and Zairn did with each other on instinct, she prioritized her man over everything else.

She sipped her drink and handed it off to Roxie, then offered a one-armed hug.

"Are you leaving?" Roxie asked, drinking from her glass and giving hers to Zairn as he joined her on the couch.

"We've done all we can do here." She got up and went around the table to open both hands to Zane. "Will you take me home, please?"

Once there, she wouldn't let him leave again. They could talk, make love, whatever he wanted, but she would not let Roman's mess weigh on him any more than it already had. His kind heart brought everyone to that beautiful place, now he had to be worrying he'd damned them all.

TWENTY-FIVE

HONOLULU.

Gorgeous, glamorous, bustling. They'd spent little time in the city on their stopover on the way to Dyce's island. And although they arrived in the afternoon that day, their itinerary didn't allow much wiggle room for sightseeing.

Dinner was next, and she'd just got out of the shower when knocking on her door diverted her from the lotion bottle.

It would be Alessia. Everyone had been given their own room. Great for privacy, not so great for security. Wasn't it easier to keep everyone safe if the group were watching over each other too?

Tucking in her towel, she opened the door, smiling. Except, surprise, Roxie was the one waiting there.

"Rox," she said and backed off to let her in. "Where were you? We didn't see you on the plane."

"I flew in this morning, I had a thing."

The woman went over to the window to admire

the view, though hers couldn't be much different… unless they weren't in the same hotel.

"Are you eating dinner with us? I have to get changed."

Roxie circled her wrist above her shoulder in an absent wave. "Carry on, carry on."

She rushed back into the bathroom to finish with the lotion and switched out the towel for the complimentary robe.

"You look amazing," she said, dragging out her makeup case to dump it by the mirror. "Do you have a squad of people who—"

"If I want to," Roxie said on a laugh, spinning around to perch against the windowsill. "How was Dyce last night?"

Oh, unexpected. She paused in her makeup for a second before meeting Roxie's eye. "He takes it all on, you know? He's really this laid-back, easygoing guy, and this is high stress."

"You'd think the multibillion-dollar empire would get a guy used to that."

Although Roxie was teasing, she saw a flash of what she'd seen in Zane too. That guilt and concern couldn't be for Roman, surely.

"You can't be a stranger to stress either."

"I don't feel stress," Roxie said, folding her arms. "Not since Zairn, he deals with all that serious stuff, I just look pretty for him."

"There's something on your mind though." She tossed her eyeliner back into the case. "Is it about last night?"

Roxie sighed. "We're only here because I demanded Zairn take me on a rehearsal honeymoon."

"You feel guilty? You could never have foreseen—"

"It's not guilt…" Roxie didn't sound guilty, it

was more like subdued impatience. "He's a good guy, my guy. A lot of people don't think that, and the media sometimes has a skewed view, but he really does have a good heart."

"I believe you."

Everything she'd seen of him suggested that was true.

"And he loves his friends, just like I love my girls, we'd do anything for any of them. Be anywhere, support anywhere, love anywhere."

"Except Roman isn't his friend."

"No," Roxie said with a single head shake. "But he loves Dyce, and Rourke, he likes Struan, and Tripp damn well lives in Crimson Palace back in New York."

She smiled. "That's a great name."

"I know," Roxie said with a faux hair toss. "We're part of this network, this unseen something that draws us all together. The world doesn't see it, the people around who read about us and talk about us, they don't see that we're real people. Or how close we are."

"You're aspirational. They want to be you, live your lives, spend your money. And, you know, the way you've described your network to me, and when I hear you talk about it… it's aspirational too. Not a lot of people have unconditional love in their lives."

Boosting off the windowsill, Roxie's hands rose, palms toward the ceiling, fingers slightly curled. "I want to do more for him. Be more for him. He doesn't understand how he's just everything to everyone. All the time, he's there, no questions asked. He's run after me as I've run after my girls, he's always there. Always supporting me!"

She didn't get it. "And you'd rather he didn't?"

Her friend grew solemn. "He takes it all on. All of it. Everyone else's—and part of that's my fault and— God, Thea, it's like I can't love him enough."

"You adore him, that's obvious to anyone who sees you together."

In private anyway. If they fed the press stories, presenting themselves as chum to cover others upset, the public may see them in a different light. She'd only known the couple a short time, and already she aspired to be part of something so consuming.

"We don't doubt our love for each other, that would be insane after all we've been through, that's not what I mean."

"So what do you mean?"

Roxie thought about it for a second before talking. "Even if I give him my all, even if every person on this whole planet was to give him their all, it wouldn't be enough. I love him so damn much that he's in my DNA, he's all of me, every part of me, and fuck it hurts to love him with every atom. He deserves the universe."

Her friend wasn't sad or scared or angry, Roxie just couldn't hold it all in.

"I don't know if you've noticed," she said, subduing a smile. "But he feels the same way about you."

"I know." Roxie rolled her eyes and came over to pick up the eyeliner again. "The idiot. Close your eyes." She sat down and did as ask, allowing Roxie to do her makeup. "We just had an anniversary, maybe it's making me sentimental. I just want to tell the people I can tell that he's secretly divine."

"Noted," she said, touched by the woman's need to praise her man.

"You snuck Dyce away quick last night. Horny?"

The tease curved her lips for a flash. "We do have a lot of sex."

"Preach it, sister. These men are overachievers in all kinds of imaginative ways. Sometimes you have to release the parking brake and just let them at it."

She laughed. "I hear that." An exhale came while

watching Roxie pick out some shadow. "Last night was… I just couldn't see him like that anymore. He wants to help, he wants to fix things—"

"Another thing our men have in common. All of them are fixers. Even when we want to vent and—you know what, I'll let Jane have that discussion with you."

She closed her eyes and Roxie continued with the makeup. "Zane's tired. The island is supposed to be his sanctuary, a safe space away from the real world. You know, he doesn't really like Roman that much."

"No one likes Roman that much. No one who actually knows him."

And in talking it out, she garnered new understanding of Roxie's meaning about Zairn. "Like you said, Zane deserves the universe. I want to support him, to hold up, and care for him the way that he cares for me. Roman's a burden for him, he'd never say it, but that's what he is. I don't want to be a burden, I don't want him worrying about me, I want to take care of him."

"Sometimes we're the only ones they'll listen to."

"Zane and I haven't been together that long, but I'm not sure anyone else could've stolen him away like I did last night."

"We have to be the ones who say no. Set those boundaries for them when they can't set them themselves. Z's big on boundaries."

"I noticed Zane was frayed and didn't want him to feel that way. It's not fair all this, he's neglecting his own needs."

"We have to be more subtle in our care sometimes, you did good."

"But it's only temporary, sex is only a temporary distraction." Which Roman liked to shatter as often as possible. "Is it just me or does it feel like a no-win situation?"

"With Roman? More like a no-hope situation.

I'm all for people kicking their habits and starting anew. Addiction is a disease, yes, and people need support, they deserve respect and understanding…"

"Yeah, but with Roman…"

"I get the feeling he's just an ass. No amount of rehab will cure that."

"Was he drunk yesterday?"

"I don't know," Roxie said, blowing away excess powder. "I try not to get that close to him."

"If he thinks pills are the only problem… Do you know any doctors? Anyone who could give sound, educated advice on this?"

"I know someone who knows a lot of doctors," Roxie said. "Do you want to go above and beyond for Roman?"

Her eyes opened to Roxie's. A beat passed. Roman didn't deserve their mercy, he didn't deserve them using their connections and resources to protect and help him. If he wanted to embrace those things and change for real, great, maybe it would be a different issue. But he didn't; he wanted to drag everyone else down to his level.

"I feel sorry for Struan," she admitted. "He drove me to the house from the resort last night."

"And he asked you to feel sorry for him?"

"No! I felt sorry for him before that."

"Growing up with Roman couldn't have been easy," Roxie agreed, carrying on. "And growing up wearing his face…"

"But that's the thing, it's not his face. I mean it is, but… Struan's whole sense of identity is tied into Roman's. How does the guy know what he wants anymore? Like last night, you and Zairn came to," what was supposed to be, "the cookout. Tripp, me and Zane, we can relax and be ourselves. Imagine knowing—"

"Everyone wants to watch, and maybe pounce

on, you because they believe you're your brother."

"Does he date?"

Roxie drew back. "Are you interested?"

"Oh my God, no!" She laughed. "You're crazy, woman! It's curiosity…"

"Like a freakshow exhibit." Roxie's head relaxed to the side. "That's a good point, how does the man get laid? Does every woman think he's his brother? Maybe he's gay. Still, guys might think he's his brother too." She sucked in a breath through her teeth. "Only one way to solve this."

The brush went back into the bag and she handed over the mascara tube before flouncing to her purse at the window.

"What are you doing?"

Roxie dug around for a second and pulled something out, triumphant, a phone, only to immediately deflate. "Shit."

"What's wrong?"

"Nothing!" Roxie declared and dropped the phone back into her purse before floating to the phone by the bedside to pick up the receiver. "If anyone asks, you're having a torrid affair with Zairn."

The woman said the oddest things. And though her brows went up, Roxie didn't notice. Her friend was busy tapping digits. She paused, hit speaker, then hung up and sat on the bed. Ringing echoed between them.

"Who are we calling?"

Just having the option to call was a novelty. One she'd considered embracing for a brief spell, then remembered she was way behind in her project so didn't want to speak to her boss.

"This is an unknown number," a male voice interrupted the ringing. "Juni? May? Is that April?"

"Do you have a woman for every month of the year, Skippy?"

"And day of the week too," he said. "Tibbs will fit you in."

"Oh, I don't know about that. Don't you need a headshot? Naked pictures or…?"

"Ah, I'm not that picky, sweetheart. Have you seen the Empress?"

"Funny, funny, guy," Roxie said, twirling the phone cord around her finger. "You know what will be really funny? Watching you try to suck your own cock. Mm, yeah, I think I'll get the camera out for that one. Host a special edition of my stream."

"Wouldn't be the first time you've shared us with the world."

"What we are is not their business."

Silence descended. Not awkward or uncomfortable, profound, intimate.

"I love you, Scroogey."

"I know, Lola Bunny," he said and quickly changed tack. "Now what do you want?"

"Is Struan seeing anyone?" The quiet that followed stretched so long, even Roxie jerked. "Casanova?"

"This is how these things start, with questions like that one."

"These things?" Roxie scoffed. "What things? There are no things. I have no idea what you're talking about."

"Oh, yes, you do, Little Miss Meddler."

"I'm not meddling in anything. We were just wondering."

"We? Who's we? No, let me guess, you're with Thea."

She licked her lips when Roxie turned to gesture at the phone. "Hi, Zairn."

"See, you and your girls. Always you and your girls."

A gasp of excitement thrust Roxie's shoulders back. "Oh, oooh! This could be another threesome opportunity!"

"He's not gay," Zairn said. How did he know what Roxie meant? She could've meant the two of them and the hot, sculpted, stunt guy. Although, hold up, they'd had a threesome before? "And, yes, I am sure."

"Fun sucker," Roxie mumbled at the phone. "Does he use the Roman thing? Maybe it's not just money he gets out of the deal. Might help him pick up women."

"Could do," Zairn said. "Though he wouldn't. Struan? Not in a million years. Commit sexual fraud like that?"

"Ah, yes, of course, we have to call Gauge for advice on that."

"You know him and Rainie are together now. Happy. That's all forgotten."

Roxie bowed closer to the phone and tapped her temple. "Not all forgotten, it still lives in here."

"Uh," she said, rising. "He can't see you."

"Mm hmm," Zairn agreed, kind of smug. "You want to know why I can't see you?"

"Because I'm not naked and you don't like video calls unless my breasts are exposed?"

Zairn hmmed. "That, yes, and because I will bet every cent I have that your cellphone isn't charged."

She tsked, her head rolling on her shoulders. "Well that's not a surprise. No points, no prizes, Caller. You have met me before."

"I'm calling Astrid."

"You could do that, Skippy, but by the time she got here, I'd be somewhere else."

"Planes can go in all different directions, baby. The pilot just presses some buttons, and the stick moves—"

"Yes, thank you, my big, handsome, mansplaining billionaire. Like you know anything about flying a plane. We should invite Struan to New York for a while."

And Zairn accepted the conversation shift without missing a beat.

"Okay. Don't know how that will work with the show being shot in LA. He spends a lot of time in New York. He stays with Tripp when he's there."

Roxie slanted her way. "Which, translated, means he spends a lot of time living with us. Life at Crimson Palace is a never-ending slumber party."

"You complaining? You were just saying to invite the guy—"

"I think everyone should live with us always."

"Yeah, damn our friends for having their own lives."

"How does Struan get laid?" Roxie asked, just tossing the question in there like it was nothing.

Zairn's inhale was audible. "I guess the same way other guys get laid. You know when I give you one of our special, special hugs—"

"You don't hug me during sex, are you kidding? You're too busy getting your kicks."

"What else are you for, dear?"

"That special edition stream is looking more and more likely, Scroogey."

A quiet laugh warmed the line. "Look, it's no major secret Roman's a twin. They don't crow about it, but Struan doesn't remain in hiding like a monster in the attic or under the bed. It's been a few years since he and I were picking up women at the same time, but from memory…"

"From memory, what?" Roxie asked, barely giving the guy the time to draw breath.

"He tells them."

Simple three word answer. Spoken kind of like they were idiots and, uh, okay, maybe they were a little.

"If I was Roman, I'd be more likely to tell people I was Struan."

Roxie laughed. "Woman's got a point. I know which guy I'd rather ride."

"That's touching, Lola. We should write it in this year's Christmas card."

Roxie gasped, suddenly pouncing to the edge of the bed. "We'll send joint Christmas cards! Like the President and First Lady."

"Yeah, because they're the only other couple to send joint Christmas cards."

"You're snarky today, Casanova. Someone miss their early morning wakeup call?" Another knock on her door. "We've got to go, baby. We're popular over here. Love you!" Without giving him time to respond, she hung up. "Want me to answer the door?"

TWENTY-SIX

THE ANSWER TO THAT was a resounding no.

Anyone could be on the other side, but she wasn't worried, not about anything except how her sister would scream if Mrs. Kyst-Lomond answered.

One guest behind, she opened the door, and, yep, this time it was Alessia. Time ticked down to the inevitable… She braced. The moment Alessia passed the bathroom to take in the whole room, she stopped, her chin dropped and… she screamed. There was something to be said for consistency.

"Right, Alessia, be calm," she said, pressing her ear. "Alessia, this is Roxie, Roxie, Alessia."

Usually, she'd include someone's last name. Wasn't so easy to do this time, she wasn't sure where her new friend landed on the hyphenate.

Roxie set one hand on the bed behind her and offered the other to Alessia. "Charmed."

"Your guy's a biscuit."

"And I eat him every night," Roxie said, non-plussed.

"And you're beautiful, super beautiful…" Alessia went around to stand in front of Roxie. "The way you guys met, and the engagement announcement… I watch your stream all the time. Like *all* the time. I couldn't believe it when Jane and Knox got married so fast." Alessia plopped herself on the bed next to Roxie. "Does Toria hate him?"

"Knox? Depends on the day of the week."

"We never hear of them together. Like you and Jane are all over, you're best buds, but Toria… We weren't sure if she didn't like Zairn, but no, that's crazy, she's been in love with him forever."

"Alessia!"

"What?" her sister asked. "It's true."

"It is true," Roxie agreed. "Her and half the planet. If it wasn't for Jane and Toria, I wouldn't even know who he is."

"Does Knox get jealous? When Jane spends time with Zairn?"

"You know, I've never asked him."

Leaving her sister to the interrogation, because Roxie seemed completely at ease with it, she went into the bathroom to do her hair. Her makeup was flawless, Roxie was a woman with many talents.

When she got out again, dressed and ready, her sister was still talking.

"…it couldn't have been just normal, you know, like, there had to be something. Wasn't there something?"

"Okay, if you're done," she spoke over her sister. "We're due downstairs."

Alessia jumped up. "Oh my God, I was supposed to be in Lark's room like twenty minutes ago."

She ran a couple of steps, then stopped, her head going left to right between Roxie and the door.

"Same rules as the other night." She read her

sister's mind. "You can eat with us if you want, but only you. I do not want Roxie mobbed."

"Are we going to 'Ula 'Ula after dinner?"

"Sure are."

So everyone else knew where they were going, how did her sister know? Okay, so she hadn't asked, maybe that would be an obvious first step to achieving that goal.

"Will we be in the VIP area?"

"God, yes," Roxie said. "Z banned me from the main floor of every club on the planet."

Alessia laughed. "That's funny. You can get into like the most exclusive level of every club, bar, and hotel in the world, but you can't go where the regular folks go."

"Hmm," Roxie said, pondering. "When you put it like that…" She inhaled. "It's not that I can't go, I would, I can, it just gets…"

"Dangerous," she said, channeling Zairn.

It was obvious why Zairn wouldn't want the woman he loved in the crush of a thousand bodies, in a hot, dark, wet cavern drowned in heavy bass and deafening tunes.

"My birthday party was on the main floor in Crimson, LA."

"Where you got arrested?" Alessia asked.

No big deal to them, but, uh, a big deal to her.

Shit. "You got arrested?" Now the little back and forth with Zairn about jail had some context. "Why were you arrested?"

Roxie did another of her dismissive waves. "It was nothing. A million years ago. The first time anyway. The second time was…" She made a strained sound. "Yeah, that was a little more dicey. At least I was alone that time."

"You weren't alone the first time?"

"Oh my God," Alessia droned. "Sometimes you are so embarrassing! I bet even Mom knows more about Roxie's relationship than you do."

And that was a good thing? She didn't go around taking notes on other people's relationships. Apparently, though, she lived in a cave, had to if this was such common knowledge.

"It's okay." Roxie wasn't that bothered. "I don't know that much about her relationship either."

"No one does, she won't even talk about him." Her sister wasn't impressed, but quickly perked up again. "How did you have your party on the main floor? Were there like tickets? Did you do a contest? How did I miss that?"

"No, it was just people we knew. Z closed the club."

And her sister swooned. "Aww, that's so romantic."

"He's good like that. Does his best work with an audience."

"You are so lucky. He's so hot and rich and—"

"Alessia," she said, linking their hands. "You might want to stop drooling on her fiancé." Roxie just smiled. "We have dinner to get to."

Her sister was too excitable. "Is he here? In the hotel? Can I meet him?"

"No! You can't meet him," she answered before Roxie could. "He's not here, and what do you plan to say to him? 'Hi, you're so hot and rich.' How's he supposed to respond to that?"

"He gets it a lot actually," Roxie said with a slow head bob. "It's the first thing I say to him every morning."

Alessia laughed. "You're so funny! I love how fun you are!" She growled. "I don't want to leave my girls alone—"

"I'd be the same," Roxie said. "Go be with your friends. We'll have a bunch of chances to catch up."

Alessia gasped in excitement. "Oh my God, we will?"

"Sure! Your sister's with one of my guy's best friends. We'll be in each other's lives a long time."

Now Alessia squealed. Even children at Christmas weren't so excited. "Can I hug you?"

"Yes!" Roxie opened her arms to gesture her over. "Bring it in."

At least her sister asked, unlike Lark with Zane. Roxie smiled through. Her sister scurried out of the room fizzing with adrenaline. When she closed the door and dropped against it, she was exhausted like it was the end of the night, not the beginning.

"Do you get that everywhere?"

Roxie shrugged. "You get used to it and I'd never trade it for the alternative." Of being without Zairn. "I'm better at it than Casanova. Believe it or not, I have more patience for these things, and it's something I don't mind taking off his plate."

"You're his fixer too."

"Hopefully no one will have to be anyone's fixer tonight," Roxie said. "And on the one serious moment of the night I'll allow, remember this…"

"What?"

"Someone's always watching. Even when you think there's no one watching. Someone's always watching."

Whatever that meant. "Okay."

"Some people, not me, of course, but some people might have suggested in the past that I'm a magnet for these things, that I'm a…"

Roxie cleared her throat.

She laughed. "A crisis event?"

Wasn't that what Zairn called her?

The narrowing of Roxie's eyes was almost a growl. "Just be aware tonight. I don't want you sucked into the vortex. I don't know how patient Zane is."

Given how he was with Roman, the man deserved a medal.

"I'll be aware."

"Alessia's got a point," Roxie said, going to sweep up her purse as she put hers together. "You don't speak much about your relationship."

"Will I need a jacket?"

"Are you deflecting?"

"No," she said, slipping her feet in her shoes. She double checked her keycard was in her wallet and went to open the door. "What do you want to know?"

"Oh, now there's a dangerous question." Roxie paused on the threshold. "You won't need a jacket; you don't even need your wallet."

"I don't need my wallet?"

Closing the door, they went a few steps down the hallway, then Roxie twined their arms together. "Zane has taken care of everything. If he hadn't, Zairn would've. It's a learning curve, this kind of relationship, but you'll get there." They hit the elevator button and waited. "Unless you won't."

She didn't understand. "Unless I won't, what?"

"You and Zane," Roxie said, coming around in front of her. "Is it serious? Permanent or a holiday fling?" She held up both hands. "No judgment."

"We don't know what it is yet. We've agreed we want to make a go of it, see what comes out in the wash."

"So you'll stay in touch? When the island is in your rearview?"

She exhaled a laugh. "Alessia wants me to marry him and have babies so she can come to the island any time she wants."

"What other reason is there to tie yourself to a

guy?"

Even with the deadpan delivery, the humor was obvious. Roxie was quite the woman. Somehow completely shocking, and completely expected at the same time. Her new friend could pull off anything.

When the elevator doors pinged, Roxie turned. They opened to three guys inside. Tripp was the one in the middle. She expected the other two to go their own way, but when Tripp opened his arms, the guys only stepped back.

Roxie went in first and kissed each of Tripp's cheeks. "You're very dashing tonight."

"I'm always very dashing, Rox Out," Tripp said and laid a hand on her waist to lean in and kiss her cheeks too.

She hadn't quite got the hang of the mwah, mwah thing, but Roxie distracted her awkwardness.

"As I live and breathe," Roxie exclaimed, the elevator doors closing behind them. She immediately threw herself into the arms of the big guy in the corner. "You did say you wanted island detail."

"Wrong island, but I'm not complaining."

"Do you have guys down the stairs?" Roxie asked in a moment of seriousness that vanished as she turned to introduce them. "Thea Florin, this is Trevor… just Trevor. He's my head of security in Chicago. And that guy…" Roxie pointed past Tripp. "Is Schmidt, he's Tripp's security detail."

"My driver," Tripp corrected to be greeted with a few snickers. "Anyone's ass needs kicked, I kick it myself."

His bravado was false and totally hilarious. Whether he did kick asses or not, he'd make believe, in front of an audience at least, that he got his own hands dirty.

"I don't know Schmidt well enough to kiss him,"

Roxie said and tilted her head. "I could kiss you, Schmidt, do you want me to kiss you?" She frowned at Tripp. "What are the rules on that these days? Is it an abuse of my power?"

"To go making out with limo drivers? Do whatever you want, Rox Out, my parents will settle if he makes a claim."

Trevor laid a hand on Roxie's shoulder to murmur above her ear. "There are probably cameras in here."

That might've been meant as a warning, but a slow, sly smile piqued the corners of Roxie's lips as she prodded Tripp's ribs.

"Want to hit the emergency stop and have a fivesome, Priest?"

"You know I'm up for anything, but paying off your guy won't be so easy."

"Pfft! I'll just tell him Roman traumatized me and let him off his leash. Z's desperate to knock his teeth out. We'll make it all his fault."

"All for the drama?"

"You know it."

"Imagine the scandal," Tripp said. "Mom will forgive me providing one of you bring her a baby. Doesn't even have to be mine, just a kid she can spoil."

"Oh, well, way to ruin the party," Roxie grumped. "My guy will never forgive you if you ruin my figure before he can."

"Guess I can't argue with that." Tripp hooked his arms around each of the women when the doors opened. Their security guys stayed close and other men encircled them as they walked through the lobby. "What happens in Honolulu stays in Honolulu, ladies."

"What does that mean? What exactly is going to happen?"

"Nobody knows," he said, all ease. "But I invited

a few friends."

Roxie laughed. "Cue another caper. You know we needed you in LA. I always said I didn't need an entourage, but I might start taking you everywhere I go. I love a man who can't say no."

"Any time you call, I'll be there, Rox Out."

"These friends you invited," Roxie said like she knew the answer. "Are they all female?"

Tripp's already smug expression gained swagger when they hit the sidewalk and a limo door was opened for them. "Could be, Little Rox." They got in the limo and he immediately poured champagne. "Doesn't mean you can't have fun with them too because—"

"What happens in Honolulu stays in Honolulu?" both she and Roxie said together.

He handed each of them a flute. "See how in sync we all are? No cameras in here if you want to get frisky." Settling back, he pushed out his lower lip. "I can just watch, I don't even need to be an active participant."

She shared a smile with Roxie before their three glasses met in a toast. Honolulu. Exotic. Beautiful. Rich. Vibrant… and, she was finding out, maybe a little wild too.

TWENTY-SEVEN

TRIPP TOSSED HER onto the hotel bed.

She landed in a bounce. "Ow! Fuck!"

Crazy. Honestly, what the hell? How was this her life? It was her luck, yeah, but if everything had a meaning, what was fate telling her? Don't party. Don't dance. Don't have fun.

"Don't think I've ever heard you curse," he said. "My mom would like you."

"Hush, idiot," Roxie said, sitting with her to stroke her hair. "Don't you know how to be gentle with a woman? Go get us some ice."

Without arguing Tripp disappeared from the bedroom. This wasn't her room. She didn't know if it was Roxie's or Tripp's, just that it wasn't hers.

"You didn't have to come back with me."

"Of course I did," Roxie said, slipping off both of their shoes. "You sure you don't want to go to the hospital?"

"No, I don't. I really, really don't. It's just an ankle sprain, ice, elevation."

Roxie jumped into action, grabbing pillows to stack them. "Right, the RICE thing."

In a mutual wince, both women held their breath as Roxie eased her leg up to rest it on the stacked pillows.

"You should go back to the club. Have a good time."

"This is a good time," Roxie said and unzipped her dress while disappearing into the closet. "Do you want something else to wear? We can have a sleepover."

It was after midnight. Way after midnight as far as her internal clock could tell.

"You don't have to stay with me. I can go back to my—shit."

Pushing her fists into the bed, her attempt to move clenched her teeth.

Roxie came rushing out in a man's shirt, other fabric in hand. "Stop it! Stop it!" She set her hands on her hips. "You told me to leave Trevor with Alessia, but if you don't behave, I'll bring them both here." She softened. "Are you sure you don't want me to call your sister?"

"She's having the time of her life, no, I don't want to ruin anyone else's night."

"Dyce would—"

"No! Don't call him either. He'll worry and blame himself for not being here. No. I'll be fine in the morning. It's just a sprain. You and Tripp can go back to—"

"Tripp and I party for a living," Roxie said, crawling onto the bed to unzip her dress and help her lift her ass to take it off over her head. Better that way than to move her leg again. "Literally every single night. We live in a nightclub."

"You don't live in Honolulu, 'Ula 'Ula—"

"We can visit any time. Haven't you noticed Tripp barely has a job and I live in cocktail dresses? Zairn brought me here, to Dyce's island, with zero notice." Her friend threaded her arms into the sleeves of another shirt. "I just showed up at CollCom and next thing he knew, we were here."

"Can you call him?" she asked and it only just hit her. "How did you call him earlier? There's no cell service on the island. Does he have a sat phone?"

"Dyce is working on a new kind of sat phone. K2 says Dyce is just trying to ruin his fun, and he could be right. But we can't complain given how much pleasure he accommodates."

She couldn't get comfortable. "K2?"

"Dyce."

The door swung open.

Tripp entered, carrying a bucket of ice. "Usually when there are two women in my bed wearing my clothes…" He put the ice-bucket down and wandered to the bathroom. "It's more fun than this."

He reappeared with a couple of towels.

"I told Roxie you should go back to the club. And I don't have to stay in your bed, I can go back to—"

"Ah, enough, woman," he said, scooping some ice into a towel. "You know what will be less fun?"

He folded a towel to lay it over her leg then sat by her with the ice-filled towel to rest it on her ankle. Although she winced, she relaxed as soon as he did.

"What will be less fun?" she asked, raising her attention from the ice to the man frowning at it.

"When your guy finds out we didn't take you straight to the hospital."

"I don't need a hospital, it's a sprain. Alessia doesn't need to know, and it's not like you can drive me. Showing up in a limo is less than discreet."

"Is that what you're worried about?" Roxie pounced onto her knees. "Oh, honey, we can make a scene, sure, but we also know how to slip in unnoticed. You're in pain, and you've been drinking." Roxie sagged and appealed to Tripp. "The alcohol could be masking the pain. We should take her to the hospital."

No objection from him. "Okay."

"No!" she exclaimed, opening a hand to each of her friends. "I will be okay."

"Dyce will be mad."

"Then let him be mad at me, this is my call."

Maybe it wasn't fair to demand they comply, but she did not want Roxie showing up in the press with her and Tripp in some clandestine middle of the night hospital visit. Goodness only knew what story the media would cook up.

"Anyone hungry?"

"If you're not going back to the party, you can still drink, still dance and—"

"Nah," Tripp said, lying along the foot of the bed, still holding the ice towel on her ankle, propping his temple on a fist. "Roxie and I live in nightclubs."

The woman beside her laughed and hooked an arm around the pillow beneath her. "That's exactly what I said."

Beyond the bedroom, a door slammed. What was that? Rather, who was that?

"Did someone order room service?" she asked.

Would they walk right in? Surely staff were required to—

Zane. He stalled in the doorway for just a second, concern etched on his face.

"This is where we slip out," Roxie said.

Before her friend could leave the bed, Zane moved. "No, you stay. We're leaving."

"Told you he'd be mad," Roxie muttered.

As Zane came to her side of the bed, Zairn wandered in. "Always knew you'd end up in bed with him, Lola."

Tripp enjoyed that, but she didn't have the time to judge Roxie's reaction. Zane scooped both arms under her.

"What are you doing?" she asked as he lifted her.

Tripp leaped up and the ice scattered everywhere.

"Taking you to the hospital."

"I don't need to go to the hospital," she objected as he took her sideways out of the bedroom door, navigating with an awareness of her ankle that escaped Tripp. "Please just take me back to bed."

"I'll take you to bed after the x-rays."

"We don't need x-rays. It was stupid, I went over on my ankle and I fell down like two stairs. It was stupid, the stairway was dark and there were people. I wasn't paying attention, I…"

They'd got all the way from the room to the elevator. As the doors closed, she sighed and her head fell against him.

"You think I'll take risks with your health?" he asked and kissed her hair. "I don't care if you're mad at me, Wanderer. This is important. Your health is important."

"How did you get here so fast?" she asked, stroking the buttons of his shirt. "Why were you and Zairn—"

"We flew in to have dinner with a friend."

"A friend you're hiding from me and Roxie?"

Though… Roxie may have known because she hadn't hesitated to call Zairn either. If they'd been there for dinner, Zairn didn't need a sat phone to speak to his other half.

"We wanted to surprise you," he said, a hint of scorn in his tone. "You should've gone straight to the hospital. You should've called an ambulance. What would you have done if Tripp wasn't there?"

"I don't know. Roxie's resourceful, she'd have figured it out. She looked after me."

"And Alessia?"

"I don't want her to know, she's having fun and security are protecting her. She has your people and Roxie's. She knows to stay with the group."

Reiterating that didn't guarantee her sister would make the smartest choices. Especially with alcohol in her system. To those who didn't know her, Roxie may seem like a frivolous person. For those who'd heard her talk about the people in her life, it was obvious how much the woman cared. Roxie's security was handpicked, people Zairn had approved, and Roxie could vouch for. If Alessia did wander a little from safety, security would protect her.

Paying no heed to bystanders, Zane carried her through the lobby and into a waiting SUV. He put her on the seat, legs extended and closed the door. Hey, he didn't expect she'd—he got in the door opposite her feet, carefully raising both her legs as he did. The moment the door was closed, they drove off.

"You have to keep it elevated," he said, snagging a bag from the floor to snap an ice pack and lay it over her ankle.

That he didn't ask which she'd hurt was a bad sign. Just how swollen was it? She didn't want to look.

"I thought Tripp carrying me through the lobby might look bad," she said, resting her head on the back of the seat. One of his hands stayed on the ice pack while the other stroked her knee and up her thigh. "I was wearing more clothes then."

Not by much. If anything, the shirt may cover more than her spaghetti strap dress. He didn't respond, his concern was still there, still potent. Maybe it wasn't just concern, maybe he was angry.

"Drift, are you pissed?"

"No," he said, his attention snapping to her. "Why would you think I'm mad?"

"You're not talking to me."

"I'm worried about you." He squeezed her leg. "I need to know you're okay."

"It's only my ankle. The rest of me still works."

That loosened him up a little. When a smile lit his eyes, she could've just won a marathon for the joy it gave her.

"I know how you love the sand." His caress went from one leg to the other and back. She slid a little lower, giving him more intimate access. "The feel of it between your toes."

And for the first time that night, a little concern speared her too. "God, and if they give me some kind of cast—"

"Thought it was just a sprain," he said like he'd caught her out, one brow rising. "Whatever it is, baby, we have to get it checked."

"It'll be okay and—"

"Do you want to come back to the island?"

"Right now?" she asked. "If there's a flight…" The moment she said it, she shook her head. "You know what I mean. Yes, I want to come back. I've been gone less than a day and I miss it already."

"What if I take you back and your ankle's not fine? What if you fall or it gets worse?"

"Then you have an excuse to keep me in bed." And away went his smile. "I suppose I can always work from bed. Maybe I'll ask Roxie to help me pitch a tent on the beach by the corporate suite, then I can sleep and work right there by the waves."

"You could do that, but pitching a tent on sand takes skill. Roxie isn't the outdoorsy type."

"Hmm, yes, if only there was a strong, attractive man who could keep me so busy in his sheets that I don't have time to do anything other than him."

"No sex until we know what this is."

Even if her ankle was broken, it shouldn't… No, he was right, she'd said it was a sprain, it was a sprain. If she'd known a visit to the hospital was the only way to get back on the island, she may not have been as resistant. Okay, it was understandable he didn't want her to suffer or need help while they were far from any kind of official medical facility. Still, it might've been nice to live in the dream for a while.

"You are pissed."

"I'm not pissed," he said and picked up her hand to kiss her fingers. "I'm sorry, just when we got the call you were hurt and—I needed to be with you. If I'd got that call on the island…"

"But you didn't. Roxie and Tripp took care of me. I told them they didn't have to leave the club, that they should stay and have fun, or go back—"

"They live in nightclubs." She laughed. "What?" He was frowning again. "Cutting out on one night won't slow them down."

"That's pretty much what they said," she whispered on a sigh, her eyes growing heavy. "I've had a good time in Honolulu."

"You wouldn't mind visiting again?"

"I'd prefer it just be a stop on my road to somewhere else." Her eyelids rose. To her delight, his frown was gone. "I told Roxie we'll keep seeing each other."

"Well, babe, she lives in New York. Traveling to see her takes you further from me."

"I meant you and me," she said, sensing his tease. Though that wasn't something she'd considered. "Do you see her a lot?"

"Roxie? Here and there."

"I'll miss her."

"She won't go far, or she won't go far for long anyway. Any time she's not at a nightclub, she's usually on a plane to somewhere. Her and Roux, my brother's wife, they're sort of going into business together."

"Sort of?"

"Roux is Head of Operations for Huddle Hope, an offshoot project from Huddle, the social media platform. It will give greater access to support and therapies to those in need, for mental health issues, trauma, that kind of thing."

"Wow," she said, shifting, suddenly not so asleep. "That's a good cause."

"It is. Roxie spends a lot of time in California, and when they're not in LA, they're usually in my house."

"When you're not there, but if you were there—"

"We can invite them or not. Rourke's is on the other side of the lake with plenty of bedrooms, and we have employee apartments on the compound. They won't be short of somewhere to stay."

Crooking the knee of her uninjured leg, she stroked her instep across his thigh. "Think maybe I can come and see your house in California one day?"

"Any time, baby," he said, kissing her palm this time. "I'll be spending more time there now."

"Why now?"

He snickered. "Because the closer I can get to you, the better," he said. "Ever considered working remotely as a permanent option?"

"I don't think my boss would like me constantly off the radar and—"

"From California, baby. Trust me, we have the tech to put you right there in her office. And if it doesn't exist already, I'll create it."

"Show-off," she said, maybe feeling a little smug herself. That was her guy there, threatening to use his skills to keep her close. What woman wouldn't be flattered? "I might be persuaded." She sighed because reality was sometimes so inconvenient. "I have to get through this project first. I'm already behind and it's a big deal for the company. The whole idea is to impress our newest client and bring in new custom under the…"

"What?" he asked when she trailed off. "Tell me."

"Will there be sex after we find out what this is at the hospital?"

Another laugh. "Maybe, baby. I might be persuaded."

"Tripp and Roxie are a lot of fun."

"I'm happy you like them. Tripp's in LA a lot too."

"But can I tell you a secret?"

Though she teased, he was polite enough to lean in. "Yeah."

"I prefer being alone with you."

Alone or with people, anywhere with him. The club was fun, the company entertaining, but it felt so much better to know she wouldn't sleep alone that night. Just one night without him had seemed insurmountable. How would she cope when they had to become part-time lovers and live in different states? Would it work out between them? Could it?

TWENTY-EIGHT

NO ONE COMPLAINED or argued when the SUV drove to a secluded service entrance of the hospital. In fact, there was a nurse and a porter waiting for them with a wheelchair. Someone had called ahead, had money exchanged hands? Did she want to know?

They were led to a private room in a quiet corner of the hospital. Her x-rays were done, she'd been given pain meds, and at that moment, they waited for a doctor.

"Are you tired?" she asked, propped up on the only slightly reclined bed.

"No."

"If you're tired, you should go back to the hotel."

His hand hadn't left hers since they got there, not for anything other than the actual x-ray.

He kissed her fingers, though his lips rested against her knuckles anyway. "I'm not going back to the hotel."

"It's so stupid." She felt stupid. Her head dropped as her eyes closed. "All this nonsense because I—"

"What did we miss?"

Lifting her head to Roxie's interruption, Roxie, right there in the room with them, with Zairn, with Tripp, Struan, and Logan. When did the brothers become part of the equation?

"What are you doing here?" she asked as they came to crowd the bed. "Who's watching Roman?"

"How do you know he's not Roman?" Tripp asked, slipping his hands in his pockets.

"Because why would Roman give a crap I'm here?" she asked, though that did suggest Struan would have a reason and he didn't. One quick scan of the room revealed another obvious clue. "And Roxie's standing near him without spitting."

"It's not my spitting the other twin has to worry about," Roxie said and bumped Zairn with her hip. Her friend quickly turned on the sympathy and rushed over to scoop up her other hand. "How are you feeling, honey?"

"I'm fine," she said, making a point of looking at each face. Which was weird, with Logan especially, they didn't know each other and hadn't spent time together. "Thank you for your concern, but everyone should get some rest."

"Night is our natural habitat. We're all nocturnal. He's a rockstar," Roxie said, pointing at Logan, then switching the angle of her finger to Zairn. "He's a playboy. Retired." Next she gestured at Tripp. "He's playboy junior."

"I've had more women this year than your man," Tripp boasted.

Roxie sneered and shook her head. "Not by choice. Original is shackled to me and has had sex with at least twice as many in his head, I'm sure." The blonde nodded at Struan. "And that one actually cares about people. Weirdly. Given his bloodline."

"I have his bloodline," Logan said, though didn't really seem offended.

"Struan's also used to running after Roman in the dark, so, you know, we're all vampires here. All possibly except Dyce there, but you're sleeping with him, he's obligated to be here."

"No one should be obligated to be here. It's an ankle thing, it's not life-threatening, there's—"

When the door opened again, everyone turned. The doctor held up an x-ray sheet, though was startled, presumably, by the volume of people in the room. Yeah, he wasn't the only one.

"I didn't realize—"

"It's okay," Zane said and stood up. "What's the word?"

"There is a fracture."

Well, wham, he went from she was right to she was not so right in a single heartbeat.

"What does that mean? A cast?"

"Ms. Florin won't need a cast, but she will have to be fitted for a boot that must stay on at all times."

"All times?" she asked.

The doctor shrugged. "You can take it off for bathing."

"What about sex?"

The surprise of that hit the doctor, but the others in the room snickered, Roxie and Tripp anyway.

"Woman's got her priorities right," Tripp said in approval. "You've got her well trained, man."

"Women can like sex too," Roxie said. "Sometimes… it really depends on our mood." Yeah, and the alcohol content of their blood. "And how hard you're trying. Everyone loves a trier… providing they succeed. In bed is one place you don't get a second shot if you fail the first one." Her shoulders shifted. "Except in exceptional circumstances."

"What's exceptional?" Logan asked.

"Fake sucking," Roxie said like that meant something to someone.

"You know…" Tripp exaggerated his pondering. "That's one place men and women differ. We don't really care."

"Yes, I know that. I've met many of your kind," Roxie said. "Often one woman is interchangeable for another for your people."

"Playboys? What does that say for your guy?"

"Only that he can imagine anyone he wants. Providing I'm the one carrying his credit card, I don't care."

Logan laughed. "You're unique, Rox Out."

"Yep, and taken," she said, fixating on the doctor. "Are you going to answer the woman's question? It's very important at this stage of their relationship that they get to do it a lot. A helluva lot. Like loads and loads and—"

"Lola."

One warning word and Roxie silenced. "Sorry. The doctor can speak now."

"Oh, uh, yes, there shouldn't be any reason to refrain, if you're—just stay away from anything too acrobatic."

Hmm, another startling blow.

"Wow, acrobatic sex," Roxie said, pushing out an impressed lower lip. "There's a gym club I'd pay membership for."

"The actual act is fine," the doctor said with good humor, thank God. "I'd just avoid anything that puts excess stress on your ankle."

"So, Dyce, you're doing the work for the next few weeks."

"Shit," Zairn said, and it was only then the phone in his hand became relevant.

"What's wrong?" Roxie asked.

"I'll leave you to…" The doctor backed away. "Someone will be along in a while to fit you and give further instructions."

He slipped out, which was nice, he could've stayed to nosey in on whatever got Zairn's attention.

Zairn gave his phone to Tripp who swore under his breath.

"What did he do now?" Struan asked like he just knew his brother would be the culprit of whatever.

"Where's Deacon?" Roxie asked, accepting the phone when Tripp reached over the bed to hand it to her.

If this was a Roman problem, why were they avoiding the two brothers in the room? That answer came when Roxie turned the device to let her and Zane see what was on the screen. A message:

> There's been a fight. Sway's on her way to the hospital.

Oh no, that couldn't…

"All we know is there's been a fight," Tripp said.

"What else?" Struan asked, proving he was perceptive too.

"We don't know who was involved."

Zane kissed her hand and stood up, returning Zairn's phone to its owner while sliding his own from a pocket.

"I'll get Rourke to pull up the phone call."

Zairn pressed his screen and raised the phone to his ear. "Want to bet *Sunset Entertainment* gets there first?"

The TV went on while both Zairn and Zane made their calls. Roxie had the remote and tracked through a few channels to stop on the first that showed Sway.

A picture of the beautiful actress on the screen got everyone's attention. It quickly disappeared to a nighttime view of a bustling street. This city. Their city. A crowd of people, a hotel, their hotel, and an ambulance.

"Turn it up," Struan said.

Roxie clenched. "I don't want to."

Logan grabbed the remote and did it for her.

"…specifics are vague. The confrontation must've begun elsewhere because no one reports seeing anything volatile in the club."

"That's something," Roxie said, sitting on the bed. She scooted over to give her friend room to put her feet up too. "Rouge is in the clear, Hunt's it." Though still on the phone, Zairn's eyes met Roxie's. "What? I'm just saying…"

The TV people continued. "…shouting was heard by others in the hotel. Sway Sheridan and her entourage were seen entering the hotel around an hour ago. We haven't yet seen footage of their arrival, though that will be important in revealing who was with the popular starlet."

So popular that men were fighting over her. What did Sway think about it? Some women might be flattered, but her, if the situation came to blows, she couldn't imagine ever putting up with that from a partner.

"Police were called when the suite underneath Roman's reported shouting and what sounded like furniture being moved or thrown."

"Ouch."

"Hotel staff attempted to gain entry and were prevented from doing so."

"How could the hotel be prevented?" she asked. "Don't they have keys for every room?"

Roxie seemed to agree. "Logan, do you want me

to call Carolyn? What the hell am I talking about...?" Reaching over, she prodded Tripp. "Call your mom."

"You think she'll know anything about this? They're probably at breakfast right now. Bastian won't have details. How would he divine information from LA?"

"You could call and find out."

"Why? To piss him off? He doesn't get into every fracas at his hotels. If he did, the guy would never sleep."

"Might explain why he works so much," Zairn said, though the phone was still at his ear.

"The reason for that is Robyn," Tripp said. "Let's not all pretend we don't know that."

Was Zairn talking to someone? Who would he be talking to? Could anyone help? Would anyone know something? Zane was on the phone too, though he was turned into the corner, talking quietly. Someone was connected to him, maybe it was Zairn and they were hatching a plot.

Struan and Logan quickly got their own calls going until it was just her, Roxie, and Tripp on the bed, fixated on the TV.

When Zairn turned, she slanted closer to whisper to Roxie. "Who's he talking to?"

"He should be talking to Salad," she said. "But it'll be Ballard."

"Who's Ballard?"

"The only sane man in the whole operation. You should meet him, he's cute."

"According to the doctor, I'll struggle to hook up with my current boyfriend. I don't need a sidepiece."

"Isn't Alessia looking for a guy? Ballard literally is security, he'd protect her."

"If he's security, why isn't he here?"

"Casanova," Roxie suddenly called and he turned on the spot. "Ballard's already on a plane, right?" The guy did a backwards nod of confirmation and turned his back again. "He didn't travel with us because we were supposed to be on a deserted island." Roxie folded her arms. "I don't even know why I'm surprised. The riptide is never far away. It's all Tripp's fault; he lives for the drama."

"You don't look upset, tense, worried."

"Zairn does the stressing thing," Roxie said, slouching down the bed a little to rest her head on Thea's shoulder. "He'll wake me up when he wants sex." She scoffed. "Or not, he might just have sex with me anyway."

"He'd…"

"Hell, yeah," Roxie said. "I love it. Don't tell me you've never woken up with your guy already inside you. Maybe not with Dyce, he's too nice. Tell him all bets are off and give it a shot. You won't regret it. He sure won't."

Hadn't Zane proved himself? Trusting him wasn't difficult and he made it obvious that he cared. He didn't deserve any of this madness. All he wanted to do was sit on his island, bask in the sun, and drink brightly colored cocktails. Okay, so maybe that was her, but he'd do it with her. Them, alone, just like it used to be every afternoon and for dinner on the sand. They had to get back to that, to them. Was it possible? Maybe not now with her stupid fractured ankle.

Their eyes met. His were still filled with concern. For her? For the Roman situation? She smiled. What other comfort could she give? God, it was selfish that all she could think of was his bed, in his hut, right there on the beach, scent of the surf, sound of the waves… She exhaled. They'd get back there, hopefully sooner rather than later.

TWENTY-NINE

FEET ON THE FLOOR, she tried to balance and slowly lifted her fingertips from the mattress. She wobbled and grabbed for it again.

"Hey!" Zane came rushing in. "What are you doing?"

"It's a little weird. I can't work out if it's the boot making me unsteady or the alcohol." Catching his arm, she surrendered the bed to use him as her stabilizing force. "How is everyone?"

"I don't know why they…" With a slight head shake, he exhaled. "I'm sorry, Wanderer."

"For what?" she asked, again testing her balance.

Apologies were becoming the theme of their relationship.

"All the bullshit."

"It's not your fault." Another chorus they'd sung before. "This is your family. You can't change them. Do you need to stay here?"

"Stay? No, I'm wherever you need to be."

"Is Sway okay?" Hop, shimmy, she bounced back to sit on the edge of the bed. No need to keep squeezing the guy if they weren't going anywhere. "Roxie said she had a black eye."

One by one people had left her room. Struan first, no shock there. Tripp went after, to keep him in check, then Logan jumped to when shouting from the other end of the hall alerted them to Deacon's presence.

Zairn trooped out to back him up, while Roxie followed to "keep the pin in the Zairn grenade" as her friend put it. At her urging, when the nurse came in, Zane went to check what was going on. Roxie had returned to hear the spiel and only just managed to tell her about Sway before more shouting stole her away.

"There was some pushing and shoving, she got knocked over in the fray."

Or that was the story. Whether it was true? It was anyone's guess.

"That won't look good. The press will know both Roman and Deacon were here. Sway's hospital visit… It doesn't take a genius to make the connections." True or not, that wouldn't get in the way of a good story. "What does it mean for his show?"

"Alessia's back at the hotel." He swept her hair from her shoulder, ignoring the question, which would be no accident. "She and her friends, all the contest winners were brought back to the hotel."

"For their safety or to keep them quiet?"

"As long as they're safe," he said and then there was that frown again. "You don't think I care about covering up—"

"You do that too much here." She laced their fingers together. "The frowning thing. You haven't had enough sex today."

That tweaked the corner of his lips. God, she loved to see him relax. "That your sound medical judgment?"

"Definitely." Guiding his arm around her, she

sank against him, closing her eyes. "I'm so glad you were here tonight."

"Ready to go back to the hotel?"

"If Roman's here with Deacon and Sway, the danger isn't over yet."

"I'm here for what you want, not for them."

"What I want is to fall asleep in your bed, in your arms, just us. Can't the whole world be just us for a little while?"

"A long while. As long as you want."

"Were you planning to spend the night with me?"

"I didn't plan on crashing your fun, but if Roxie told me you'd gone to bed alone…"

She looked up. "You thought I'd go to bed with someone else?"

On a snicker, he touched her brow. "Wouldn't be the first time Roxie's woken up with one of her girls, with or without clothes.

She settled against him again. "She and Zairn are good people."

"Yeah, but we don't tell the media that."

"Your cousin is an asshole and you don't tell the media that either."

"Jet's waiting for us." Oh, the temptation. "We can be in the air in twenty minutes."

"Back to the island?"

"To wherever you want. It's lady's choice."

And of the million opportunities that afforded her, none of them measured up to the first.

"I want to go back to the island," she murmured, holding him tighter. "But Alessia's having a good time and I don't want to ruin—"

"Security will stay with her."

"It's not just security. There's her emotional state, her well-being. For some reason, she and her friends idolize your cousin. If they haven't seen what happened tonight already, they will, and they'll make excuses for him."

"And I thought my family was exhausting." Again, Roxie's voice. Her head stayed on Zane, but she rolled it to take in more of her friend. "You two ready to hit the road?"

"Magnus going crazy?" Zane asked.

Roxie lingered over licking her lips. "He makes his own messes."

"Roman? I know. Never cleans them up himself."

"We're having a summit at the hotel. Upstairs. Cars are on their way."

"The press outside?"

"Oh, you know it."

"We can jam their signals."

"Yeah, but we'd have to give them back access eventually," Roxie said. "It'll be getting light soon."

"Won't be the first all-nighter you've pulled, Kyst."

"Yeah, but Roxie's nocturnal. She'll need to get to bed soon."

"And that seems unlikely if your cousin has any say. Are you ready?"

"Rox, you go along, we'll make our own way."

"We'll join you in a minute," she said, contradicting her guy.

Without hesitation, Roxie slipped out, leaving them alone.

"Wanderer—"

"Did you mean it?"

"Mean what?"

Their eyes met. "When you said you want to see where this goes."

"Yes."

"You said it didn't end with the island."

"It doesn't—"

"So your family shit is going to be my family shit. You deal with Alessia and my obsessive preoccupation with her safety. If you meet my mom, you'll learn she worries about everything. If I asked you to meet my mom, would you meet her?"

"Yes."

And she smiled. "Thank you, that's my point. If we want to make a go of this, we're not making a go of getting what we want all the time. Unlimited possibilities, remember? Yes, maybe it's exhausting, but look what the chaos has brought us already." Catching his other hand, she brought both to her face. "Us."

"I can give you everything," he said. "I want you to be happy."

"Your acceptance makes me happy. You understanding that I'm more than just a good-time gal makes me happy. If we're together, we accept each other. We welcome each other into the family dramas and dramatic events. We trust each other to stick, even when we're exhausted. Do you want me like that? In every part of your life? Do you trust me to be with you, to help you, through it all?"

Taking over the caress of her face, his fingertips roused her flesh. "You don't give up easy, do you, Wanderer?"

"I don't want you to hide anything from me. I don't want us to hide anything from each other. Roxie says Zairn accepts her one hundred percent, and that there's nothing that could come between them. They're a team."

"Never thought there would come a day I'd be modeling my relationship on Zairn's."

"It's healthy, from all I've seen… They play with each other, sure, but they are solid. Roxie brings him all kinds of support, and that has nothing to do with money. She told me she almost wrecked it once."

"Nothing almost about it, Zairn made everyone erase and block her cellphone number."

That was hilarious. "What difference did that make? She never charges the thing."

"Whatever difference it made, it worked. I've known him a long time. A *long* time… I've never seen him happier, healthier, more secure. And this is a guy who has always been extremely secure."

"And they don't have to show each other happy faces all the time. They don't put up fronts or lie to each other. They don't shield each other when things get ugly."

"They protect each other," he said. "But you're right, they always share the truth. He'd tell her anything and has always told us to open ourselves to her completely."

"No bros before hoes?"

As his hands relaxed around the back of her neck, his eyes grew heavy. "If I called Roxie a ho right now, you'd probably kick my ass."

"Yeah, and I have a weapon." She bumped the boot against his leg. "Can we go back to the hotel? Support your family with—"

"Our family. You're as much a part of this as I am."

He helped her up, hooking an arm around her to keep her steady. The stoop couldn't be comfortable for him, but he did it anyway. Support came in many forms, and it wasn't always so literal. Whatever she'd let herself in for in joining his life, this was going full throttle.

THIRTY

"YOU NEVER LOVED me! You're a callous fucking bitch—"

"Is that helping?" Roxie interjected, and not for the first time. "This is supposed to be a chance for everyone to make peace. What is it you expect to happen? That by screaming abuse at Sway, she'll fall to her knees and beg you to take her back? Trust me, buddy, no woman is that desperate."

Magnus, perhaps foreseeing how this might progress, glided into the space between the groups. "Let's everyone take a breath, five minutes to cool off."

Little chance of that when Roman struggled to keep his mouth closed for five seconds.

In a hotel suite, sitting in the middle of a couch against Zane, neither of them had said much at all. Honestly? Pathetic though it was, Roman needed minders. He needed a damn lion tamer, bring out the chair and the whip, then maybe they'd stand a chance. In his arrogance, Roman may think he was performing for an audience. If they were dealing with a petulant child, they'd simply leave him to his sulk and ignore him until he came around. Thus removing the excuse of playing to the crowd.

But he wasn't a petulant child. Hard as it was to believe, he was a grown man. One with too much latitude to do harm if left to his own devices. The audience weren't captivated, they were stuck in captivity, forced to witness his hissy fit like they were locked in some kind of medieval torture.

"You're pissed, brother, we get it," Logan said. Was a rockstar a good choice for mediator? Sad state of affairs that he was more responsible and reasonable than his non-rockstar brother. Weren't rockstars supposed to be wild? "But if she's not with Deac, she'll be with someone else. You both said this was done. So what's the problem?"

"The problem is she picks a guy to wave in my face all the time!"

Roman had done a lot of pacing and big, melodramatic arm gestures as he huffed and puffed his way around the living room. All the doors were open to the balcony beyond. The air should be a nice release, the sun was rising, the sky brightening up… yet his presence stifled the room. Already she was growing to resent him and she'd only known him a short time. How did the others put up with him for so long?

"I can't listen to this anymore," Sway said, raising her arm in a full wave only to then stalk into another room and slam the door.

"Where does she think she's going?" Roman barked. "She can't do that! You can't do that! Get the fuck out here!"

Roxie hurried over, holding open both hands. "This is our cue."

"Our cue?" She took Roxie's hands and with Zane boosting her up, she found her feet. "Girl talk time."

Okay, Sway she'd known all of three minutes. They'd been in the suite for at least an hour, and no one had even introduced them, now they were supposed to counsel her on this grief? Hmm, could she be qualified? Money and fame aside, a broken heart was a broken heart, and every woman had been there. Plus, secret weapon? Roxie. That damn woman didn't know the meaning of out of her depth. No matter the occasion, Roxie could plant her feet on the bottom of any ocean and grow as tall as she needed to be. Mrs. Kyst-Lomond could handle anything.

That was the idea anyway.

The boot wasn't so bad. Yeah, so being lopsided was weird, with no shoe for the other foot, she needed to lean on someone to keep her balance. She'd get the hang of it.

With Roxie's help, they went after Sway, finding her seated on the edge of a bed, clinging to the mattress at either side of her thighs.

After entering, they closed the door, and the woman still didn't look up.

"It went to his head," she said, sounding absolutely exhausted. "He wasn't always like this. Losing it, the addiction, rehab... There comes a point in a relationship like ours when you have to say let's do it. When you have to say, 'I'll be there for you.'" Now she looked up. "He wasn't always like this."

In a few short steps, they got to a wingback chair by the nightstand. She sat there while Roxie went to sit by Sway on the bed.

"We're not here to judge," Roxie said, taking Sway's hand into her own lap. "Yeah, our first question might be why the hell would you hook up with a guy like that in the first place, but we all have our own dating disasters. Only the virgins get to judge us."

End with a joke. Roxie loosened Sway up enough to get a polite smile.

"I can't win, can I?"

"If you want to be with Deacon, be with him. You agreed to marry him."

"Deacon and I went out before…"

"Was there overlap?" Roxie asked and quickly followed up. "Again, no judgment, might be why Roman's so nuts about it though."

"If you've spent any time with Roman at all, you know he believes what he wants to believe. Whatever he thinks, I never cheated with Deacon. Never. I've never cheated with anyone." Sway sighed. "Unless you listen to the media."

"God, the press announces Zairn's cheating on me every week, it's like, 'pass the salt,' you know? It means nothing. I know better than most that what the world sees, and the inside truth are two completely different things. We say what we are is not their business, and we're not."

They could play to the media's penchant for scandal because their relationship was built on such strong and sure foundations. In breaking up with Roman, Sway had been out there on her own. Though she doubted that even during the relationship Roman did much listening and supporting.

"Agreed," she offered, hoping there might be some comfort in numbers. "You have to make decisions based on your feelings, based on what you want. Don't make them for the fans or to appease Roman's ego."

"Maybe I should just go. Be by myself. Disappear for a while."

"Whatever you want, we'll support."

Switching the angle of her body, Sway's discernment landed on Roxie almost like suspicion.

She laughed. "She really means that." Both

women glanced her way, but she stuck on Sway. "Roxie is that honest and that supportive."

"We don't even know each other."

"Until a week ago, Rox and I had never met. She sees people, accepts them, recognizes the good, and who deserves her support."

Drawing in a long breath, Sway slipped her hand free and stood up to wander to the window. "There's no talking to Roman. None. He doesn't listen. Even when he thinks he's listening, he's not listening."

"You wanted out for a while," Roxie said. "That's what you meant by the 'I'll be there for you' thing. When he's getting help, in rehab, you have to stick around when they're sick. You couldn't walk out when he promised to get help because if you did, he could use that as an excuse to slip back into old habits."

"And blame that on you."

Taking no responsibility for himself and his choices. What a surprise.

"Everyone tells you it's a disease." Sway held herself in her own embrace. "And it is, I mean there are physical symptoms, and withdrawal is hell, that's real." In the silence, neither she nor Roxie rushed her. Letting Sway express herself in her own time, her own way, was a matter of respect. One the woman hadn't been shown by her ex in the other room. "It's easy to be understanding when you don't live with it. There are support groups and doctors and all kinds of help and support available to the person with the addiction. And maybe it's indulgent, maybe it's selfish, but for those of us who tolerated it, who forgave over and over again, there's no support for us."

"It's not fair." Roxie's sincerity touched her. More than just a pretty smile or a witty tongue, Roxie's empathy was enviable too. "I can't imagine what it was like."

"You don't try to help," Sway said, propping herself on the window frame, gazing out. "At first, you ignore the signals, the red flags, you justify it to yourself. Oh, he likes to party, it's not a big deal. He's just having a good time. Then when you ask, they dismiss you, or ignore you. If you persist, the gaslighting starts and it's so…" Her eyes narrowed like she could see into her own past. "They laugh at you, put ideas in your head, until it becomes your problem. No one else cares, why do you? I'm just having a good time, baby. Don't see you bitching at anyone else about partying. Loosen up! Come on, get with it…"

"Did you talk to anyone about it?"

"Who do you talk to?" Sway asked with a brief glance their way. "People in your life might support you, but they can't help, they can't get involved, they have no pull with the addict. And they've never lived it, if you say anything, they might tell you to leave like it's nothing but…"

"It's never as simple as that."

"And with us, there was all the extra pressure. We looked so good together, the public loved us, it's great for the image—"

"Yeah, great for him. You gave him credibility."

"Not just me." Sway licked her lips. "If it wasn't for Struan, Roman would've been done a long time ago, probably dead a long time ago too. I lost count of the number of times Struan was slipped in as sub at the last minute, and it was his arm I held on the red carpet."

"His brother doesn't deserve that loyalty."

"But that's just it…" Rolling against the window frame until her shoulders rested on it, Sway's hands stroked down her forearms. "He does deserve it. Isn't that what we're told? It's a disease. That means if you complain, you're unsupportive. If you try to walk, you're a deserter. You wouldn't leave someone with cancer, why leave them with an addiction?"

"The person with cancer wants to get better. They go to doctors, get treatments. The addict doesn't get to throw the disease thing in your face, and cry victim, then pop another half dozen pills."

"You know he never once said it to me. He's never once admitted his addiction, not to me. He wouldn't. Always said he was stronger than that and could quit any time. I was never enough, of course, he had to give the fans what they wanted, the industry needed their star."

"And all the time you're drowning."

"It's worse than that. There's a remedy to drowning, you have the ability to at least try to save yourself. Living with an addict isn't like that. You're completely at the mercy of the drug, whatever that may be, pills, booze, whatever. And you're the only one who remembers it all. The addict gets to wake up with amnesia, to minimize what it was. They kiss you good morning and go about their day…"

"You're left alone with the trauma."

"Unless you've lived it…" Her attention drifted to the view again. "You want to make yourself small, to disappear. You can see it happening, hear it's happening, even before, the minute you knew… He had stashes, places he'd hide the medication, the bottles, around the house, it would appear and then I would know, or he'd get that look on his face… You learn to smell it, to feel when they're on something, even before it kicks in."

"Did you ever talk to anyone about it? You said people on your side had no influence, what about people on his side?"

"The thing is, everyone else can walk away. Magnus wouldn't see it. I knew that he did, but he didn't put words to it. Not exactly. It got to the point I only had to ring once and Magnus would know it was time to get

Roman out from wherever we were, the party, or the meeting, whatever. I let it ring once and Magnus swooped in to get Roman out before he made a mess; everything is dumped back at the LA mansion. Everything including me."

"You didn't have your own place?"

"It was my place." That startled them both. "One day he showed up and he never left. What do you say to someone like that? When he and his entourage show up with truckloads of his things, and then they're just… there. I brought it up with Magnus once, that I might move to New York, get a change of pace."

"What did he say?"

"At first his thing was Roman didn't want to, right?"

"No one asked him," Roxie said, picking up on that hint.

"Exactly. Then it became how it wouldn't look good to the media. If I owned a separate house, lived on the other side of the country…? What would people say?"

"And why should you leave? It's your house, your things, why give that up to him?"

"It might be yours and you might be there, but it doesn't belong to you. The addict takes over everything, the house, the air, the energy. So you find yourself a corner and you wait, quietly, hoping to God they don't come looking for you. Bed, you think will be your friend. You lie there, try to sleep while… And then he comes in. Doesn't matter if you're asleep or not, you fake it. Try to just breathe. Not that it matters, if he wants you awake, he wakes you up. Sleep doesn't slow him down."

"Don't think he's changed much."

"You just lie there, staring straight ahead. It doesn't matter, he'll yell if he wants to yell, no matter what you say. You gave up crying long ago, he got a kick out of that, says you're pretty when you cry…"

Sway was right, Roxie too, it was unimaginable. How could someone live under such oppression and in their own house? Their safe space was violated, their free will taken away. Just like the way Roman took over the island and commandeered everyone's separate reasons for being there, he grabbed what he wanted and held on. The cost for others didn't even feature in his thoughts. He was oblivious to his own insanity, to his own selfishness.

"There are people you can talk to now," Roxie said. "To get help for that trauma."

"Do you talk to Deacon about it?"

"No, God, no way. I would never—"

"You're protecting Roman?"

"I'm protecting Deacon. He'd get mad and want to—he's passionate. I've already caused so much friction in—"

"This isn't your fault."

"Thea's right, this isn't your fault. Don't feel that way. Don't ever feel that way. You talked about gaslighting, you're gaslighting yourself."

"Deacon was a comfort. I sold the house when Roman was in rehab." She scowled at herself. "What a coward. I sold the house and ran the minute he got out."

"You had reason."

"He was doing better in rehab. Clean. He couldn't understand how I'd stay with him as an addict and leave him when he was sober. Too much damage was done. I was still broken. He was fixed and I was…"

"You don't owe anyone anything," Roxie said. "Shit, it pisses me off, how guys can manipulate and—"

"He says he loves me and I never wanted to break his heart." If he had one. "I'm not sure he knows what love is."

She wasn't sure he did either. Not when it came

to loving anyone except himself. "He broke your heart. Broke your spirit. Did either of you ever acknowledge that?"

Sway's chin went down; tension weighed in the air. Not aggravating or hostile, the aura was more one of nostalgia tinged with regret.

Roxie got up to go give Sway a hug. "You shouldn't be going through this alone. Talk to someone. A professional. In confidence."

"Who could I talk to? Who wouldn't sell the story to the highest bidder?"

"Anyone who wanted to continue to practice."

"The media get these things, even without permission, they pay off a secretary or get someone to go into computer files. It gets out there."

"We'll find someone, we know people, have connections, if—"

"This isn't just my career or reputation. Some of the things I might say… it would impact more than just me if anyone knew the full truth." Fortifying herself, Sway pushed back her shoulders. "I'm okay, I won't fall apart. I just… thought I was over it, that it was over. I thought we were past it. But now, with this… It won't ever be over."

"You have to stop pandering to him."

"That's exactly what we did, what I did in ending the relationship," Sway said, raising her arms. "We broke up. That was it. I was done. It was over. But it was never over, it will never be over."

"How did—"

"He calls, he texts, I block my number, he gets it again somehow. He calls my agent, my publicist, he calls directors and actors I'm working with. It's everywhere. All the time. Emails. Calls. He shows up. I thought with him on the island I'd catch a break, but somehow, somehow he still gets through, he still makes my life all about him!"

"Come stay with us in New York." Roxie took Sway's hand. "Crimson Palace is a fortress. Tripp can tell you, he lives there too. You can have an apartment, or a suite if you're not worried about cooking or whatever. We're full-service there, we'll feed you, house you, protect you—"

"Why would you do that?"

"Why wouldn't I?" Roxie asked. "We have the means. And I have a side hustle you'd definitely be qualified to help with."

Sway looked to each of them. It wasn't on her, but she smiled anyway.

"I need to talk to Deacon," Sway said. "I think maybe you're right. I need to be on my own for a while… Can I just have a minute, please?"

"Sure." Roxie gave her another hug then came to help her to her feet. "Want to get breakfast with us?"

"Yes. I think that's exactly what I need… Providing we stop for a shoe."

"You're like Cinderella." Roxie laughed hooking an arm under hers. "Let's go get your prince."

Eating with people without drama, but people who could appreciate their bliss. Stability might be a step too far, given her wobbling stance and all. They needed to decompress and then get some sleep.

THIRTY-ONE

SLEEP THEY DID GET. Thankfully, Alessia returned from her night and crashed in her own room, so there were no questions or concerns to deal with there. Had she once thought her sister liked drama? Shit, that was nothing to what she'd seen recently.

She missed her little sister and needed to check in. After breakfast and sleeping for most of the day, she'd sent a message to her sister asking if they could meet for dinner.

"Are you sure you don't mind?" she asked, putting in one earring and then another.

Zane came over and hooked an arm around her as he bowed to kiss her. "I don't mind."

"I'd invite you to eat with us, but I don't know what she knows about last night and if she has questions…"

"You don't need to explain yourself. You're at complete liberty to have dinner with anyone you want, any time you want."

"You're going to Roxie's?"

His lips curled. "Zairn's, but yeah."

Ah, cause for pause. "So it's more his suite than hers?"

"She's having dinner downstairs with Tripp, Struan, and Sway."

"Doesn't make it less her suite," she said then thought… "Huh." Her hand landed on her hip, necklace in her fingertips. "You and Zairn are eating separately from the others?"

"You were invited to the other dinner; I told them you were eating with Alessia. Can't see them having a problem with you bringing your sister if you would rather go to—"

"But I'm not invited to your dinner?" Offense didn't drive her. Didn't he know being cryptic intrigued her? "Like you said, you're at liberty to eat with who you want when you want but…" A little probing wouldn't hurt, would it? "Roxie would tell me to remind you that I share your bed. I share my body with you. We're supposed to share—"

"You can have dinner with Zairn and me, if you want." Returning to her, he swept both arms around her. "We're eating with the guys, it's a Kintyre thing. The wedding's in two weeks and there's a bachelor party—"

"Say no more," she said and held up her necklace between them. "Help me put this on?"

He went behind her and she scooped her hair out of the way. Watching his reflection in the mirror as his concentration went on opening the clasp, she got a chance to just appreciate the view.

"Is he nervous?"

"Kintyre? About the bachelor party?"

"About getting married."

"Oh no," he said, fastening her necklace then resting his hands where her shoulders met her neck. "Marriage is Kintyre's thing. Not marriage.

Responsibility. He wanted the wedding more than Lilya did, and now they're having a kid…" She dropped her hair, liking how happy he appeared for his friend. "Kintyre was made for this."

"That's nice. It's nice to see a dream come true, even if it is for other people. Where's the bachelor party? Is it going to be crazy? Should I keep one eye on the news apps?"

"No, it's…"

He didn't carry on, so she turned to him. "What?"

"It's next week. Next Saturday." And the gravity of those words registered with the regret in his eyes. "The day before you leave the island."

She smiled. "Don't worry."

"I don't have to go—"

"Yes, you have to go. I demand that you go. He's one of your best friends. The memory of this will last all of you a lifetime. I'd never ask you to give that up. I'd never want you to give it up."

He gripped her waist. "Being with you is what I care about the most."

"And you will still be with me," she said and nudged him to tease. "Don't, for a second, think leaving me on your island makes you free and single out in the world. We said we were doing this."

"We are."

Stretching her arms straight, she draped them around his neck to pull him lower. "Yes, we are. So go and ogle the strippers with your buddies and slip those c-notes into her thong, but you call me before you go to bed. Alone."

Except if she was on the island, there wouldn't be a way to call.

"I'll leave you the sat phone." Like they'd shared the thought. "You could come with me."

"To your friend's bachelor party? Oh, yeah, I'd be real popular, right behind you."

"Roxie will be at Lilya's, it's the Sunday—"

"Oh, the boys get the Saturday, and the women have to party on a school night?"

"Lilya's choice, no one else's. She's more than six months pregnant. Doing great, but she doesn't know the meaning of slowing down. They've got some Huddle Hope meeting and—I don't know, it's Rox and Roux, no one ever really knows anything with those two."

"Do you know Lilya? Do you like her?"

"We've met. The time we've spent together, yeah, I'd say she's authentic, which hasn't always been Kintyre's style."

"Authentic? You mean she doesn't just want him for his money?"

"Lilya doesn't need it. Her family has money."

"Do they have a prenup?"

"Nope, not a chance, Kintyre learned his lesson with prenups. And it's different with Lilya than it was with Julietta. They're such different women. Kinda makes a guy wonder how he could go from one to the other."

"Everyone deserves a little latitude in love, don't they?"

"Oh, Julietta got more than latitude with him, she almost got the farm."

"Julietta…" she said, pondering the name before she hit on it. "You don't mean Ines-Kintyre. Your friend was married to—"

"Just Ines now." He kissed her quick. "The only thing Kintyre asked for was his name back."

"It must be difficult, breaking up so publicly."

"Not something he'll have to worry about again any time soon."

As he walked away, she propped herself on the

vanity. "You'd look cute with a baby."

"I think they want to keep him. And if they're looking to hand him over to anyone, Jane's at the front of the line."

"Jane? Knox's Jane."

He slid his arms into the sleeves of his jacket. "You and Roxie did cover a lot of ground. Not all her stories are one hundred percent true. Sometimes she… embellishes." Though the smile on his face felt more fraternal than accusatory. "I guess it's no surprise she'd start with Jane. She's protective of her."

"Roxie's protective of everyone. She has a good heart, and good intentions. She never means any harm. You should've heard her last night with Sway." Or more accurately that morning. "She'd give her last to anyone in need. I hope Zairn understands it's his responsibility to protect her."

"Oh he does. There's nothing he wouldn't do for her." Coming back, his hands slid onto her waist. "Just like there's nothing I wouldn't do for you."

They were leagues behind Roxie and Zairn when it came to spending time together and getting to know each other. A lot of the past, to some degree, had been covered during their lunch and dinner dates before the truth came out and her world exploded.

These last few days, the last couple of weeks, they'd been in each other's worlds every day. Sometimes certainty wasn't grounded in reality, sometimes it came from within, and people just had to trust it. Theirs wasn't like that, her certainty wasn't only rooted in their attraction, or what she wanted it to be, they'd lived it. She'd seen him in adversity, seen him face anger and upset, all that did was strengthen her need to be with him.

She spoke about Roxie being a good person and Zairn needing to understand he had a duty to protect her. That duty existed there too, between her and Zane. He'd promised to protect her, had prioritized her, but it wasn't just about her.

"Have you ever thought about it?"

"Protecting you?"

She laughed and rested her hands on his chest. "Kids."

If they were truly doing this, it was an important thing to know. What would their future be?

"Not seriously thought about it. Do you want to have children?"

A knock at the door interrupted the moment. Damnit, she should've known better than to start something they didn't have time to finish. No, they did have time, just not right then.

"That'll be Alessia."

Pulling him down for a kiss, she wiped the smudge of gloss from his lips and took his hand to lead him to the door. Lead him? Well, kinda… It wasn't exactly easy to be the driving force. She couldn't move fast, short steps were easier. As he had at many other points, Zane became her pillar of balance. She was still getting used to the rhythm of walking in her new footwear.

And, while struggling with that difficulty, she figured out why he'd insisted she invite Alessia to the suite to eat.

Eventually, they made it, and just as she thought, Alessia was on the threshold.

"Oh, hey!" Alessia said, bouncing on the spot. "Zane Dyce."

"Zane is fine," he said to her sister, then dipped to kiss her. "Call if you need anything, Wanderer."

She nodded and he slipped out as Alessia came in.

"He's not joining us?"

She closed the door. "He has his own thing

tonight."

"Is anyone else here?"

Her voice was further away than expected. In fact, her sister wasn't even in the room anymore.

"Less? Where did you—"

Alessia peeked out of the bedroom. "I just want to look around. I've never been in a suite this big before."

"There's more than one bedroom."

"Is this your bedroom?"

"Yes," she said, hobbling her way.

"Oh my God! What happened to your foot?"

Was she only just noticing the boot? Didn't go with her dress, it had to stick out as noticeable. Maybe all the trappings of glamour disguised it.

"It's a long story and not a big deal."

Going to her sister, she still didn't feel exactly steady, but that was normal… or so Zane said. Like he'd know, he'd never broken a bone in his life.

"It is a big deal! You're wearing a… thing. Oh my God!"

Taking Alessia's shoulder, she guided her onto the balcony. "Come out here with me."

The table was set under a parasol, but Alessia rushed to the edge and gasped at the view. "It's so beautiful!" She spun around and dropped against the glass barrier. "I can't believe you're with a billionaire. Have you told Mom?"

"No, I didn't call yet. Did you?"

Sitting down, she poured from the pitcher brought up earlier. A special insistence from Miss Roxie, apparently. Even when not present, she still played hostess. Maybe they owned the Grand Hotel chain too, she'd have to ask Zane.

"I was going to call, but, geez, who has time to shoot the breeze? Mom will have a million questions and words just don't do this place justice!" Tipping her head back, Alessia shook her hair over the edge. "Can we just live here forever? Ask Zane if we can move in permanently."

"Mom might miss you," she said. "Come and have a drink. The room service menu is here. Pick something. What do you want to eat?"

"It's been a whirlwind, don't you think?" Alessia came over to sweep up a drink and the menu but went back to the glass barrier. "It feels like we just got here, yet it's like we never lived anywhere else. How could anyone get a taste of this life and not want to keep it forever?" She gasped and flapped with the menu. "Did you hear what happened last night? Is that how you got your foot thing? Were you in the fight?"

No surprise that her sister wanted to gossip. It was a surprise those weren't the first words out of her mouth. Okay, maybe not asking whether she was in the fight, but about the fight in general.

"I wasn't in the fight," she said. "I was already at the hospital when that happened. And it wasn't even a fight."

Not that she'd got many specifics on exactly what it was. When it was a game of who shouts the loudest, the truth rarely prevailed.

Alessia jerked. "You went to the hospital and didn't call me?"

"Roxie came with me. I was fine and you were having fun." Straightening her leg, she gestured at the boot. "This isn't a big deal. I wear it for a few weeks and my ankle heals, that's it. Nothing more exciting than that. And nothing anyone could've done standing at my bedside. It was better for you to enjoy your night, the experience of being in this incredible place with your new friends."

"Didn't Zane come to the hospital with you?"

What a memory that was. "He carried me to the

hospital. So, yes, he did. Like I said, I was fine, my drama is boring. How was your night?"

"How was my night...?" Rushing over, Alessia dragged a chair closer and sat down, transfixed. "My night's irrelevant. My night's nothing to what went on here at the hotel. Not if all I've heard is true. Tell me what happened? Who hit Sway? Did she start it? Was she pitting them against each other?"

She never liked it when women demonized each other just for the sake of it. Especially in lieu of blaming a guy or in defense of him. It might be easy to do, and maybe she wouldn't have cared, when talking about an abstract figure, but Sway wasn't abstract in her world, not anymore.

"Why do you want to put it on her?" she asked, genuinely curious. Malice didn't exist in Alessia. Still the impulse of the reaction intrigued her. "Since we got here, when people talk about the relationship, they put its failure on her."

"You don't leave someone when they need you. He was at his lowest and she walked away. Who does that?"

A person pushed to the edge. A person beyond love filled by the trauma of all that suffocated them. Someone strangled by the yoke of dependency disguised as love.

"Did you ever think about what it was like for her? Roman went to rehab, got months to talk about his issues, medications, doctors, everything he needed, and all the understanding in the world. If he couldn't make her happy, there's no way she'd have made him happy. Just being together isn't enough. The substance of the relationship matters."

"Is that what she said to you?"

"No," she said and touched her sister's face.

In her naïveté, Alessia didn't mean harm. None

of Roman's fans would, not really. In life, private life, people only had to face those around them. In the stratosphere of fame, a planet full of people awaited, and sometimes wished for, scandal and failure.

"What did she say? She must've said something."

Handing over the words couldn't explain the grief that bled out of Sway when she'd talked. Witnessing that burden was not something that could be conveyed. Not by her. She didn't have the capacity, the skill.

If she couldn't share the details, she had to at least share the wisdom and sentiment gifted in Sway's confessional.

"I hope we never know life like that," she murmured to her sister. "Every minute of every day belonging to some substance, to the disease."

"If she didn't love him any more…"

"What? When was she supposed to leave? Would you fans have treated her better if she left while he was high? What would've happened to him if she wasn't there to hold together his career and reputation for him? While he was in the quicksand, she was supposed to bolt? Would you have forgiven her then?"

"I never thought about it."

"If she'd waited until he was in rehab, then what? He'd have an excuse to leave the program; would that be her fault too? He'd only left for love, right? The woman couldn't win, no matter what she did. Put yourself in her shoes. See them as people, see her as a person. How would you react if Sway was your friend and Roman wasn't a famous actor with millions of fans?"

That got her sister thinking, she could see the wheels turning behind her eyes. These were people, with real lives and real emotions. Sometimes the masses forgot that.

"It feels like they have… everything."

And her sister wasn't alone in that assumption.

"I want to be with Zane because of who he is, not what he has. Shouldn't all relationships be that way?"

"He loves her." Alessia stacked her hands over her heart. "He loves her so much, and when it's love like that—"

"Roman, like you know him, doesn't exist. He's a construct. And that's okay, you're allowed to believe it, everyone is. Love him, hate her, do what you need to do. Just don't expect me to feel the same or feed the gossip monster."

Shocked, Alessia sat back. "You really mean that."

"I really do." She picked up a glass to give Alessia. "Now drink this. It's important to Roxie. And tell me what you want to eat. I'm starving."

Without revealing the truth, she couldn't make her sister see. She also didn't want to share Sway's private moment. Being in Zane's world, and all that came with it, she'd need to practice discretion like she never had before.

Roxie was private. Zairn. Tripp. Sway. They might be new to her, but she had to treat them as precious. They'd opened themselves to her, she had to respect that trust, and guard it.

THIRTY-TWO

FOR MOST OF the day, she'd been searching the island for her things. Packing was no easy feat when her possessions were scattered in various locations around a whole island. One sandal proved particularly elusive, and it was a favorite too, she didn't want to lose it and ha! There it was, right…

On her hands and knees, she stretched to reach under the bed to retrieve it.

"The sun's gone down."

His voice brought her head up.

Zane stood in the open doorway. The terrace behind him was the one she'd stood on that first day, staring out into the ocean, wondering what might come next. She never could've imagined him.

Grabbing the bed with her elbows, she held up her shoe.

"I was looking for this," she said. "Found it."

He sauntered her way. "You've been avoiding me all day."

"I haven't been avoiding you," she said, holding

the shoe to her chest as he approached. "I have to get everything together. Not like I'll be back here any time soon."

"You'll be back here any time you want to be." He bent to take her arms and help her to her feet. She stood for just a beat, then sat on the bed. "I can stay."

"We talked about this." She hooked her fingers into the pocket of his shorts. "There's no point. I'm leaving too; our departure difference is only a matter of hours."

"Everything is only a matter of hours."

"Yes, okay," she said, tick-tocking her head side to side. "If you want to get particular about it."

"You can stay at the house."

"You told me that already."

He sat with her. "Roxie and Zairn are leaving with—"

"I know," she said, resting a hand on his thigh. "If I told you last night that I wanted to stay at the house, would you have let me?"

"Yes."

"And I didn't choose that, did I? I chose to stay in your hut."

Closing his fingers around hers, he raised them up to kiss her palm. "Doesn't feel right leaving you behind."

"I'm choosing to stay with my sister. And, yes, I know, you said she could come too, but she's having fun with her friends."

"She might have fun with your friends."

No doubt Alessia would love to spend time with Roxie and the others. In the last month, she'd met people and had experiences, she'd never have foreseen. The adventure was surreal to look back on. A lot of dinners under the stars, drinks and conversation into the wee hours. This was a dream she'd love to repeat some time.

"I need the time to work," she said, fake growling at him. "Someone distracted me so much, I'm way far behind where I should be. Anika will not be impressed with my presentation the way it is."

"I told you I could help with that."

"Yeah, except, see…" Sweeping her hair from her shoulder, he bowed to kiss her neck. "This is what happens when you offer to help." His hand slid up her thigh, under her dress, and the sandal fell from her fingers. That might've been how it got lost the first time, except… "Have you had sex on this bed before?"

"I didn't think about this bed once before I knew you'd slept in it."

Alessia was still staying in the suite with Lark and the others. This was their original room. No one would mind if they… He hooked an arm across her waist and dragged her back, somehow finding his way between her thighs at the same time.

"You don't have time for this."

Tell his body that because it wasn't getting the message. Untying her wrap dress, he kissed her cleavage and her breasts, enjoying her for what might be…

"I can't go," he murmured against her, pressing himself into her. "I have to stay with you."

"No, you don't." Capturing his head in both hands, she guided his eyes to hers. "We're not saying goodbye. This isn't over."

"It's not over." And he meant it, through and through. "I don't want this to be over, I won't let it be over. Thea, you have to know—"

"I know."

"I don't want you to think this was frivolous, that I do this all the time. Baby, I don't—"

"I know. Don't you think I know you?" Widening her smile, it was impossible not to adore him when he was so adamant. "And if you haven't already figured out that I'm crazy in love with you, then you're not as smart as your friends say you are." The flare of his surprise endeared rather than scared her. "You have one last chance."

"One last chance? To tell you—"

"No. To enjoy me here, with the waves behind us and the salt in the air."

"You're coming back here. You will be back."

Nothing was ever one hundred percent certain, especially in matters of the heart. The prospect, the dream of what they could be, that was an enticing view she wanted to come to life.

"Not soon enough," she said, wriggling and rising, enjoying his hard arousal. "You want to take that on the plane? Might need its own passport."

Slowly, he lowered himself to kiss her. His mouth, their lips, they'd spent so much time joined that they were almost a part of each other. They'd learned how to yield, when to beg, and when to demand. With time against them, they didn't have the option of enjoying one of their long makeout sessions that were, had been, the highlight of every day.

Her work might have suffered, but the rest of herself flourished. Time, love, always, they seemed real on the island, tangible, just within reach.

Their lips parted and he pushed into her, reminding her just how complete really felt. All of herself could feel him, every atom and cell cried out for him, drugged and bewildered by the need of him propelling into her faster and harder, whispering her name before his burst from her lips.

"What are you doing for Christmas?" he panted.

On an inhale, she stopped breathing, then exhaled a blast of laughter. "Why? Was that my gift?"

"That was the appetizer." He kissed her again then got up to fasten his shorts. "That was a serious question. We should spend Christmas together."

Sitting up, she wrapped her dress again to tie it. "It's October."

"Yeah, I figured it was too late to lock down Halloween and Thanksgiving, but we can do Christmas, can't we?"

"I'm usually with my mom and Alessia."

"We could do it here."

"Christmas?" His eager optimism was a wonder. Something, maybe saying goodbye, spurred him to grab for what he could. "Drift, I am no less yours today than I will be tomorrow and the next day. We're together. I love you."

"You two are sneaky." As Zane turned, the terrace came into view. Roxie, owner of the accusation, pounced across the threshold. "You been getting naughty? You know you can do that at the house too. Or you could but…" The blonde looked at Zane. "Zairn's out front."

With a broad smile, Roxie's hint was less than subtle.

"We were—"

"I'll bring her with me," Roxie said. "We can do tears and kisses at the airstrip. It's really important you talk to Zairn. Really, immediately talk to him."

"Mm, okay."

Zane was right to be suspicious but was polite enough to go.

Roxie's eyes roamed a little in the grace period Zane got to put distance between them. It would've been quicker for him to go out via the hallway and staff exit they'd used during their dates. Speed wasn't necessarily of the essence.

"Is something wrong?" she asked, dropping onto her elbows.

"Yes, something is very wrong." Kicking off her

shoes, Roxie sat on the end of the bed facing her, legs folded in front. "You should be coming with us."

"Not you too."

"I don't understand why you're not! You should be at the bachelorette party, at the very least come there with me."

"Thank you. You know I'm honored you'd ask—"

"I don't want you to be honored, I want you to come. You said you and Dyce weren't over."

"We're not over."

"Then you're part of the team, one of the girls. You have to be there."

"I don't know anyone and it's not right that I should—"

"You know me! Stick with me. Come with me. I'll tell you a secret if you come."

"What secret?"

Lounging forward, Roxie pushed both hands up the center of the bed. "It's a huge secret, ginormous, you won't even believe the epic hugeness of this secret. If Zairn knew I was going to tell you, oh, ho, would he be mad."

"So tell me." Wriggling further back, the weight of her boot just over the edge was getting uncomfortable. "What's the secret?"

Roxie zipped her lips and threw away the invisible key. "I can only tell you if you come to the bachelorette party."

"Why is it some big announcement?"

Roxie frowned. "Oh no. No, no. This is a secret to be kept. A secret known only by the chosen few."

Maybe her friend had learned something about her in the last few weeks. "You're trying to get me curious."

"You're already curious." Raising her hands to

flop them down, Roxie couldn't be more proud of herself. "So you'll come?"

"I can't! You know I can't."

"You keep saying you can't, I don't understand why that's your position."

"I'm due at work on Monday morning. Leaving here on Sunday is already cutting it close. My boss won't be impressed—"

"Zairn will call her."

"I made all kinds of promises about this project and how thorough I'd be. And instead I've spent the last month…"

"Being all kinds of thorough with Dyce." Roxie bounced a fist on her knee. "Oh, phooey, as Merci would say. You don't want to get fired, I get it. I was like this with Zairn, trying to figure out how to be with him and still maintain my own life."

"How did that go?"

"Oh, you know, I gave up absolutely everything and trailed around the world with him for the rest of my life."

A pause, then a laugh. "I will miss you, Roxie."

"There are worse ways to spend your life, you know, than spending it with him. I thought I'd give up my life and lose myself. It wasn't like that. We moved in together, my life changed, but so did his. It's what love does to you, it gives you a new perspective. Don't hesitate to rely on him, to trust him. He'll need you as much as you need him. It shouldn't embarrass you, it should lighten you."

"It does. He does. And my life here with him has been incredible. I can't wait to come back and do it all again."

"So what's stopping you?"

"I have to see through my commitments. This project isn't just my job, it ensures others have theirs too.

Even if I quit, then what? I have bills, I have—"

"He'll take care of everything."

"And we'll talk about that." Another snicker escaped. "We have time. You're as bad as him. This doesn't have to be overnight." Like the words meant something, Roxie's head tilted. "What?"

"We just don't have to make all the decisions right this minute…" she whispered on a wistful something.

"No, we don't."

Accepting it, Roxie filled her chest. "Okay. This is your relationship and it's not my place to fix it."

Not that she'd thought it was broken. Is that what Roxie and Zairn thought? That her relationship with Zane was broken?

"I don't want to hurry things. Nothing about us has been pressured, that shouldn't change now. And I came here for Alessia, to look after her. That's still my responsibility, she's my priority."

"And you want to get her home safely. I can understand that." Her friend raised a pointed finger. "There is one thing you should know. Like you said, no pressure, but I think you'd be an amazing addition to the Huddle Hope team. Roux is smart, she's dedicated, and this will be her legacy. Huddle Hope is more than a job or a company, it's her reason, her gift to the world. They don't plan to have kids, so she's on this train for life."

"This wouldn't have anything to do with the fact Zane and Rourke share a complex, would it?"

"That working for Huddle Hope would be a convenient choice for employment if you wanted to be with Zane permanently?" Though she rolled her head, she didn't confirm or deny. "They have employee apartments. Roux used to live in one, she probably still has it for nights Rourke pisses her off. No, actually, hmm, second thoughts, he'll have given it to someone else, otherwise he'd sleep there every night."

"He?" She laughed. "She'd kick him out of his own house?"

"Without a second's hesitation. And he'd go too. Or they'd die staring each other out. Really, any of those outcomes are plausible." On her knees, Roxie ascended the bed to hug her. "I'm going to miss you."

"All of you are acting as if we'll never see each other again."

"No, it's not that, we're just used to you now. We like you in the pack."

"Zane asked me to be his plus one. If my boss isn't a bitch about it, I'll see you next weekend."

Roxie gasped and hugged her tighter. "For the wedding? Oh my God, you'll meet everyone!"

And that concept was probably the most terrifying she'd faced for a while. She'd take Anika's wrath every day for a month if it meant avoiding being the only stranger in the room. Still, Zane would be with her, and her role on the day would be supporting him… Things wouldn't be weird between them in the real world after a week apart… would they?

No going back. They were together. Real world or fantasy, they were each other's other.

The only way to not be the stranger was to spend time with those close to him. If Zane's people were anything like Roxie, it wouldn't take long to become familiar. Yeah, the group had experience with each other, but this was the start of her journey with them, and it was one she planned to be on for a long time.

THIRTY-THREE

TALK ABOUT AN early start! They were in Honolulu by eight in the morning, and LA by five p.m. local. Some people were staying the night in California, others had connecting flights to catch. Alessia's tears were expected, she hated goodbyes, but it was nice she'd made friends she promised to keep. Whether they would or not was anyone's guess. Good intentions and all that.

By the time she got home, it was almost two a.m., that's in the morning. Oh-two hundred. Usually, she'd unpack. Not then. What a day. She hopped in the shower for less than three minutes, brushed her teeth, and crawled into bed.

Even as she relaxed, she missed him. Being in his bed, their bed on the island, felt weird without him, but at least they had memories and the scent of him was in the air. Her own bed came with none of that joy.

Had he been in LA when she passed through? In her and Alessia's hour between flights, she had a fleeting thought of calling him. Meeting up with him for mere minutes would only be torture; a reminder of what she missed, what she needed so badly.

Oh, sleep, sleep. This was sleep time. For sure she needed it. Needed to recalibrate for work in the morning. It already was the morning. Work was coming in fast. Too soon. Like a meteor hurtling toward her, or was she the meteor? Who even knew? Everything was too soon while so bone weary.

What was that...? The buzz of her phone vibrating in its dock was so alien, she almost didn't recognize it. Who'd be calling that late? No one who'd known about her being on the island or the time she got back. Who would know she'd just got home?

She sat up. Alessia or her mom.

"Hello?" she answered before her tongue was really ready to move.

"I got you something."

"Got me..." She frowned into the darkness. "Who is this?" A guy, that's who it was. Not her mother or her sister, it was... "Drift?"

"Good, you got me worried there for a second. How many other guys would be calling this late? It's not three yet, should I call back then to tell you something?"

"Something trivial?" she asked, recalling one of their early conversations. "Tell me anything, any time." Loosening, she lay down. "How did you know I was home?"

"I'm tracking your location."

Her lips curled as her eyes closed. "That's kinda hot."

Or Red Flag City, but, hey, optimism had treated her well of late.

"Wait 'til you see what else I can do," he said. "Your present's in the hall."

"Present?" Right, he'd got her something. "I don't have a hall, it's a bedroom, a bathroom..."

"On your doorstep then."

"Oh." Suddenly, she didn't mind standing up so much. Tiredness could wait. "Is it flowers?" Leaving the bedroom, she hobbled across the living room. "Candy? Who delivers this late? Pizza?"

She opened the door, gaze down, expecting a box or bouquet. Instead she spied his boots.

"Dyce," he said, hanging up the phone as her eyes ascended, absorbing his presence.

Her wonderful, excellent, amazing—

Throwing open the door, she jumped up, wrapping her arms around him. "Oh my God."

"Guess you're pleased to see me."

She heard the door close, so assumed they were inside. Who cared anymore? Oh, her Drift. Their mouths met and she tried to hook her leg up around him, but it was just too awkward with her boot.

Against her will, she relinquished the kiss to drag him through to her room. "How did you know I'd need you?"

"By always needing you myself. You are no less mine today than you were yesterday and the day before. We spent the night together there, why not here too?"

And, damn, she loved his logic. "God, I'm so tired, and so horny, I don't even know which to—how to—"

First thing came with him losing the jacket, the tee-shirt, his pants.

"Whoa, hey, hey," he said, capturing her hands at his fly. "Can I take my boots off first?"

"If it gets you naked sooner." She crawled onto the bed as he sat to unlace. Sliding her hands up his back, into his hair, she buried her face against him. "I have to go to work in the morning."

"I know."

"Not like work on the island. Actual work. With people who don't want to see me naked."

"Can't imagine there are any of those."

He stood and was nice enough to face her as he lost his pants. Wasn't much time to admire the view. He scooped her up, shoved the covers away and settled them both skin-to-skin.

"Will you stay?"

"Little late to ask that, isn't it? I'm naked, people will frown on me going outside."

Nobody with eyes in their head.

"Tomorrow. I have to go to work, but if you stay, we can have dinner. This might not be the most exciting city in the world but—"

"I'm staying, Wanderer," he said, pulling her up to kiss her head. "I'm not going anywhere."

And it was nice, so goddamn nice to just exist with him in that moment. So they were missing the surf and tropical fauna, but that didn't matter, it didn't mean anything.

They'd left the island with so much still to say, still to agree on and organize. There it felt like the real world didn't exist, that they had all the time in the world. Almost as soon as her feet hit Californian land, the naïveté of that struck her. Just agreeing to be together wasn't enough. Saying they'd make a go of it didn't shore up their security.

Had he felt it too? Had he wished they'd said more before parting ways? In his defense, he'd tried to put more concrete foundations in place. She'd been the resistor. Was it naïveté? Fear? Uncertainty? Whichever it was, or all of them, doubt no longer existed.

"Drift," she whispered, her breathing slowing down.

"Yeah, baby?"

"You can work from anywhere."

A beat and then he spoke with a smile. "I can work from anywhere."

So it wasn't a scream of passion or an exclamation of devotion. It didn't need to be. When he'd said that to her, she'd ducked the prospect, now she got it. He could work from anywhere. That wasn't just about work, it was about them. Their future.

A lot of guys—see: most—would expect the woman to give up and move her life. Zane hadn't gone there. It was a consideration, and this wouldn't be forever, but he was his own boss. While she needed to be here, appeasing hers, he'd be with her, at her side.

Unless…

Maybe she was reading too much into it. Maybe this wasn't a long-term situation. Could be he'd just showed to seduce her and leave again. Except he hadn't seduced her. No more than them just being together did. So that was her point in the almost statement. Zane could work from anywhere. And he'd chosen there, with her.

"My Wi-Fi sucks."

"Not for long."

Because he'd fix it. Would anything keep him away? These weren't barriers, these were realities. If she could break down every possible reason he might have for leaving her, maybe he'd stay. For a long time. Forever.

"I think we should spend Christmas together."

On a snicker, he said, "Me too."

They'd be okay. One day at a time. The wedding was at the weekend. Maybe he'd stay until then. If he didn't, at least she had an idea about the next time she'd see him. Every minute was him, every thought, every flicker of consciousness.

Halloween. Thanksgiving. He'd said his plans were already set. Alessia spent Halloween with her friends and—damnit, she had to stop. Exhaustion, jetlag, dread over returning to the office. The weights on her mind lightened when she lost herself in him. Lost herself. It didn't feel that way. Lost sounded negative and he was the opposite. Zane Dyce held her up, strengthened her. And, if she got through her day at the office, maybe she could return the favor in some way.

THIRTY-FOUR

LEAVING HIM WAS hard. Really hard. He'd been there—in sweats he'd retrieved from a duffel bag she didn't remember seeing on opening the door—wishing her a good day at the office. How good would it be knowing he was at home? Okay, so she might envy the furniture he sat on, but at least the prospect of him hung on her horizon. He'd be there. He'd promised to be there; they'd have dinner together. One of another string of many, she hoped.

On the island, he'd been home and they'd worked even though she'd technically been on vacation. There in her apartment, was he on vacation? Was that how he saw it? Not as glamorous or luxe as his island, but so long as he was there, that was all she needed. Hopefully, maybe, he'd feel the same way about her. They really had to talk, to look at their relationship seriously and figure it out… or give it up. The latter was definitely option B, maybe option Y or Z because it sure wasn't high on her list of desired outcomes.

Their offices were on the sixth floor of a building

in the center of town. From the outside, it all looked the same. Inside was another story. The elevator doors opened and she stepped out. Everything was different. The carpet on the floor, the paint on the walls and, huh, there was security standing by the door. Had they had their own security agents before?

A new hip-height flapping glass gate by the reception desk stood in the way of the back office. Running her employee-pass over the scanner light… klaxon. Louder than it needed to be too. Try again. What else could she do? Anika hadn't warned her about any new security system. On the third try, a pause with no klaxon gave hope and—an alarm blared in the air. On instinct, she ducked, like what the hell? Suddenly security was on her, two of them from somewhere, each with hold of an arm.

"What's your name?" the first guy asked.

The intrusive alarm changed pitch to something akin to a siren.

"Shouldn't we… turn that noise off?" she screamed over the sound just as it stopped. Huh. Okay. Clearing her throat, she tried to recover from yelling into the silent room. "Thea. My name is Thea Florin and I've worked here for—"

"Thea!" Anika's voice turned her on the spot. "She's okay. Let her through."

The guards did and Anika beeped her through from the other side.

"What's going on?" she asked on reaching her supervisor. "I knew we were getting a remodel but—"

"Oh, it's the stupid new security system. They installed it ten days ago and we just can't get the hang of it. IT say they're on it, but they've been saying that for a week, so…"

"Where do we—"

A lot of previously open plan space had been

shuttered up into smaller chunks. Still open plan, just with tall glass partitions. Could be for privacy, or fear of some crazy virus taking over the world. Given society today and its hangups, she'd pick door number one.

On coming to work, her main goal was to be seen by Anika to prove she'd shown up. Now that was done, goal two came into play: explain her less than high spec presentation. Would hooking up with a crazy-hot billionaire count as a good reason? An excuse? Maybe. *Reason* might be a stretch too far.

"We're in here."

We…?

Anika swung a right and they entered a boardroom, glass walls again, though all but the external view were opaque.

The dozen people around the table looked pleased to see her. Extra pleased, which was super weird.

"What's going on?"

"So the contract we won that was meant to pay for these upgrades…" Anika said, leaving her by the door to go to the table. "Yeah, it's maybe not as guaranteed as we thought."

"Oh my God, what happened to…?"

"He decided to throw it out for bids."

Shit. Who'd been stupid enough to…? "Revland did this? Started writing checks before the ink was on paper. That's insane! He told us it was a done deal. Doesn't that mean the deal is actually done? God, what an idiot." Maybe not something she'd have said allowed before her vacation, as the faces around the table suggested. "Sorry, that's not helpful, I'm still in vacation mode."

"Who were you calling an idiot on vacation?" Sandreen asked.

"You wouldn't believe me if I told you."

"We have to pivot, away from the specifics and

out to volumes. We have to show we can handle every project, not just this one. We want to take a holistic view. Talk in broad strokes. Future proofing."

"While still sounding it and now."

"Hip and groovy."

"Okay, the quickest way to do none of those things is to use those words. Enticing the younger generation is something most companies strive for. The difference here is we're upselling, all the time. If you want to be ready to teach the next big thing, you have to know what it is. A Plus is a telecommunications company, right?"

"Yeah."

"So what markets are they aiming for next? What's the next big thing on their agenda?"

"Holographics," Mitchum called out.

"Next as in next week, next month, next year, not in fifty years."

"No, they are, we're right on the cusp."

"Of holographic technology?" Sandreen sounded as convinced as her, which, hint, was not in the slightest. "Of us having that ability in our pocket?"

And, oh, inspiration. "One sec."

Dumping her purse and laptop to the table, she fished out her phone.

And Zane picked up on the second ring, not bad.

"How far away are we from having holographic abilities on our phones?"

"Won't be out for Christmas, I'll tell you that. If you want me to prioritize—"

"No," she said, internally rolling her eyes at him, though her lips reacted with a laugh. "What is next? If we wanted to concentrate on—"

"Solar technology," he said, "self-charging ability, as per Roxie's request. Chiplets, think smaller, more efficient. Graphene will help with that, as it's thinner and lighter than traditional materials. With increased demand of simultaneous processing, it's smaller, it's faster. Microfluidics will bring back tactile keyboards and SIM cards will soon be a thing of the past."

Grabbing a pen, she started writing on the back of a folder. "How soon?"

"You want things you'll get by next Christmas? Expect an increase in foldable phones. Pressure sensitive screens, improved voice interaction, oh, and uh, mixed reality will come down the line not too long after that. Are we interviewing for something?"

"Trying to impress a client."

"Want my business? You know how to impress me."

"Where's the challenge in that?" Flirting reminded her of their office in the sun. "We're not equipped for business like yours."

"You've been doing just fine so far."

"The business I handle alone, in private, doesn't count."

"I don't mind if we do it in public," he said, provoking another laugh. "Want me to come down there for lunch?"

"You know how it goes. If we eat together at lunchtime…"

"Yeah, but there are other people in your office. Puts a dampener on the seduction."

"All you have to do is show up and it's mission accomplished."

"Is that a yes? I'll bring something with me, or I'll take you out."

Being with him was always tempting. "We're having a slight security meltdown here at the minute, even I couldn't get in."

"A security meltdown?" Suddenly, he was

serious. "Are you in danger? Has a threat been made to—"

"No, Drift, be calm. They're trying to set up a new security system and it keeps freaking out for no reason."

"Which system?"

"Sorry?"

"Which system is it?"

"I have no earthly idea." Everyone was looking at her. "Uh, I've got to go."

"Every company worth anything has a Dysaic system. Is it a Dysaic system?"

"Is it a—I don't know." How would she know that? She lowered the phone to address Anika. "Is our new security system Dysaic?"

"Yes, why what does—"

"Yes," she said into the phone. "What does that—"

"Give me twenty minutes."

And the line cut off. Huh, okay. Twenty minutes for what?

"What did he say?" Anika asked like she'd known who was on the line. "Who were you talking to?"

Okay, so maybe she didn't.

"My boyfriend, he's into this tech stuff." Slight—not-so-slight—understatement. "Foldable phones, improved voice interaction, and we'll want to research miniaturization and self-charging."

"All of this is good." Anika nodded at the others until they got their laptops up and going. "See what you can find out. Look for anything we might use to impress the client. Slap it all together in a five-minute presentation. We'll piece together the highlights. Revland wants progress and to see something by the end of business."

Not asking much, was he?

"When is the meeting?" she asked. "With the client?"

"I don't know. I don't know. We'll find out more later."

And she'd been stressing Anika might be unimpressed with her work? The woman hadn't even looked at any of it. Okay, not something to stress about. Putting aside what had been to focus on what would be was much easier.

They worked for a while, she didn't know how long until her phone chimed. A message.

> I'm here. On my way up.

His way up? That was Zane. Wait, twenty minutes, had he meant…?

She leaped up. "Uh, I have to nip out for just a second."

Why would he come all the way there? Hurrying from the room, she didn't have a clue how to get him through security if her pass didn't work. He didn't need to be there, unless he meant…

She got to the reception the same second the elevator doors opened to reveal her guy in cargo board shorts and a rumpled shirt over a tee-shirt.

Pausing there, memory warmed her lips. "You look a little out of place without the ocean behind you."

"Reliving the good times," he said, bypassing security and the reception desk to head straight for the glass entrance.

If he expected her to beep him through… Without any contact or specific movement, the scanner beeped and let him through without hesitating for a beat. He didn't even do anything, he just… walked.

"How did you do that?" she asked when he stooped to kiss her.

"It's my system, babe."

"It's your—oh…" Now she got it. And that clarity brought her joy. "Will you fix it?"

"Shouldn't take long if it's correctly installed." He glanced back at the security gates. "This is not the newest model."

"Yeah, Mr. Revland never springs for the most up to date anything. He waits until the old models are on sale."

"Do you want the newest model?"

"No, we already won't be able to afford this. The deal that was supposed to be done apparently isn't, so it's panic stations. Everything I did on the island is useless, until we get the deal, I guess. Maybe it will be relevant after—"

"There!" Anika exclaimed. "There! He's there!"

Turning around, Anika had an arm outstretched, pointing to her guy. Their boss, Revland, stood right there by her side.

"Oh my—Mr. Dyce!"

"I just saw him beep through and everything. It's really him."

Really him who she hadn't recognized, but the rest of her office knew instantly.

"Where's your security hub?" he asked, draping an arm around her.

Fully comfortable in his ownership, Zane's nonchalance about the public displays of affection was a turn on. Huh, she was learning new things about herself.

"Mr. Dyce, we can—I can—it's an honor."

He squeezed her opposite arm. "Do you know where it is, Wanderer?"

"Up a floor," was the sum total of her knowledge on the subject.

"Your server room nearby?" he asked, scanning every nook and corner. "I'll increase your energy efficiency while I'm at it because this is just… offensive."

"Is this why you came to mine?" she teased. "To play with security and server rooms?"

"Anything to be under the same roof as you."

"Can we get you anything?" Revland asked.

The rest of her colleagues crowded and craned in doorways just to get a look. Guaranteed not every one of them would've recognized him. Word traveled fast. All it needed was one person to whisper his name. From there it would carry in roars through every wall and window.

"Just directions."

"We'd be honored if you'd allow us to assess your company, Dyce Technologies, new and ongoing training processes with—"

"Thea makes all those decisions," he said and pointed to a door. "This is a stairwell, right? I'll follow the tech and find it." He tipped up her chin to kiss her lips and lingered there a second. "Even with people watching." He winked. "Come find me for lunch."

"I'm avoiding stairs with my boot," she called out, as he went into the stairwell.

"Call me and I'll find you," he replied just as the door swung shut.

Revland and Anika stood there, fixated on her.

"What?"

"You make decisions about Dyce Technologies—"

"He was kidding." And that was enough to send Revland hurrying after Zane. Her boss would probably stalk him all day. "Don't we need to get back to work?"

"Let's talk for one second about him kissing you," Anika said in almost awe-struck disbelief. "You're dating Zane Dyce? You're dating a billionaire with— what the hell are you doing here?"

"Not what I'm supposed to be doing." She pointed toward their boardroom. "Should we get back to work?"

Getting everyone back on track shouldn't really be her job. It was a better one than spilling all to her gossip-hungry colleagues. Her guy was there, he'd do his thing. She'd never really understood it, but he was good at it and seemed to enjoy it, which was enough for her.

His happiness, her happiness, she couldn't find hers without knowing he held his. What did it mean when one person's joy came from just knowing their other half was whole? On the island, on the mainland, every part of her yearned to be close to him. They had to talk, they really did, but what was the rush when there was a chance that conversation would shatter both of their illusions? Forever? Maybe. Was she ready for that? Was he?

THIRTY-FIVE

"OH MY GOD!"

Alessia's exclamation brought her around in the kitchen. Not an unusual thing for her to say but given she hadn't known her sister was even in her apartment, yeah, it was a surprise.

"What's going on?" she asked, quickly washing her hands. "Did something happen?"

Alessia dumped her purse on the counter. "Yes, something happened."

"What?" A million potential disasters rushed her senses. "Is Mom okay?"

"Lark broke up with her boyfriend."

She deflated. "Really? That's not a something happened."

"It is! She told him how she really felt, sooo much tea. And did you hear about Roman?"

"No. Hear what?"

Instantly she regretted asking. The question just slid out in reflex to Alessia's query. This week had been sans Roman Lowe so far, and she'd have been happy for it to stay that way.

"He posted this video online…" Alessia rummaged around in her purse and produced her phone. "It's him, talking to the fans, talking to us. Showing us how much he cares. We mean something to him. He really puts himself out there, it's just beautiful."

Alessia turned the screen and there he was, as stated, close to the camera, not much background.

He started by clearing his throat. "This is a message you all deserve to hear; one I should've sent long ago. I'll never be able to explain every incident in my past or justify my actions. Some of the things I've done have been… despicable. That doesn't get me off the hook. I apologize, and I should've apologized many times already. Why did it take so long? I don't know; there's no justifiable answer to that. I was broken, in so many ways, unprepared for the trappings of fame, I guess you could say. Cliché, maybe, yeah, it went to my head. I took advantage of the faith and trust others put in me, *you* put in me. To anyone who ever watched a second of me on screen, to those who expected more, to those I've disappointed: I'm sorry. I hope you can forgive me and that we can move on… together. Thank you to those who have stuck by me, supported me, continued to follow me and my career even when it was a hot mess. You deserve better and I should've given you better. I'm sorry, to everyone, I hope you can all forgive me."

The image paused then cleared.

Alessia snatched her phone to her chest and sighed. "Isn't that amazing? He really put himself out there! He's vulnerable, just like the rest of us. Can you believe he did that?"

No, actually, she couldn't, though didn't get the chance to say it, which was probably just as well. Zane appeared from the bedroom sparing her the confession, that one anyway.

"Sorry, babe, I—" He stopped when Alessia whirled around, shock written all over her loose face. "Hi, Alessia."

"Oh my God," her sister said again, jaw still swinging. "Zane Dyce is here."

"Yeah, I noticed that."

"You ladies need a minute?"

"No," she said, gesturing at the stove. "You started with the sauce, finish before I ruin it."

Accepting the task, he passed Alessia to take over at the stove. She moved on to gathering flatware and napkins. Her boot was just part of her life now, though on it, she was less than graceful.

"Are you living together now?" Alessia asked, coming in close as she went to work setting the table. "Is this permanent?"

"I don't know," she said under her breath. "We don't know, it just is."

"Have you told Mom?"

"Less, don't make a big deal of it."

Alessia prodded her waist. "Not so bad bagging yourself a billionaire." Her sister whirled around and raised her voice. "You better plan to do right by my sister. It's so weird, seeing you here." Alessia bumped her with a hip. "It's like you brought some of the island back with you."

And if she could go back there now and let it swallow her whole, she would.

Her guy took Alessia's reaction in stride. "How have you been doing since you got back home?"

"My life is completely boring," Alessia said then squealed. "Oh! But Roman! Did you know about his video?"

"No."

Though he didn't look that surprised or question what she meant. Maybe he'd been enjoying the Roman-free zone too.

"That better be true. Thea, would he lie to me?"

"If he'd known, I'd have known." Though that wasn't necessarily true given Zane understood her opinion of his cousin. "Are you staying for dinner?"

"Not if I'm crashing your date."

He'd been there with her for the last two days. It still felt new and thrilling, more so with this domesticity. They complemented each other, she'd never been in a relationship that felt so natural, where routine and intimacy slotted into place without effort. Or she was kidding herself and seeing things that didn't exist, feeling things that didn't…

"You're more than welcome," Zane said, tossing the pasta and sauce. "We should get to know each other better."

That was a good sign, and one she welcomed.

"Why did you leave the island?" Alessia asked, seating herself as Thea went to get the wine. "You own it, why would you ever leave?"

"I had meetings," he said. "And your sister is a powerful lure. We have a wedding to attend this weekend too."

"A wedding? Whose wedding?"

"A friend of mine," he said. "His fiancée's expecting their first child."

"Is that why they're getting married?"

"I don't think Kintyre would appreciate it being put that way." He brought over the food, while she finished pouring their drinks. "He loves Lilya, very much. They hit it off straight—well, I guess I can't really say that."

"Say what?" Alessia asked, accepting her plate. "Oh, wait, Kintyre, you mean Julietta Ines-Kintyre, her ex-husband. Damn, he's hot."

"And taken," she said, sitting when Zane pushed

her chair in under her.

"I bet you have a lot of hot, rich friends."

He descended to his own place. "The number of those single dwindles by the day."

"Will Roxie be at the wedding?"

"Yep, and her best friend, Jane. My sister-in-law Roux. Merci, Rainie, plenty of women to keep her entertained. I'm not sure they've ever been together in one concentrated group."

That could lead to all kinds of shenanigans. Maybe she should carry cash, in case bail was needed. With Roxie in the midst that wasn't outside the realm of possibility. Nothing was outside the realm of possibility.

"You have such a cool life. Where do you stay when you're not on the island?" Alessia asked without giving him time to answer. "Is Roman there? I mean, is he going back? Things must be so difficult for him right now."

Her eyes met Zane's. This was maybe something they didn't want to get into.

"Don't you think Roman deserves his privacy?" she asked really just as a way to move the conversation along.

Typical Alessia didn't take the hint. "His video is so bold, so raw. It proves he cares about people." Mm hmm, yeah, she was keeping her lips sealed. "Hey!" Something struck Alessia that jolted her like a bee sting. "When you get married, will Roman be there? Will he be part of the wedding?"

Keep on eating. Don't even look Zane's way. Eyes down.

"In the wedding party?" he asked. "No."

At least he refrained from saying "not a chance." Just because they were talking weddings didn't mean he was referring to her. A sign, that's what she needed. Something unequivocal from fate, or Zane, and then she'd broach the subject herself… when they were alone.

Alessia flopped. "No? Why no? He'd be a great best man."

Zane laughed. "Ha, not a chance."

Okay, so there it was. In his defense, there weren't many options for answering that question. And she couldn't say she didn't feel the same way.

"I thought you'd be closer." Alessia didn't at all question the certainty. "You both live lives of expectation. People always want something from you. It can't be easy to be chasing yourself all the time."

The next big revelation. What would Dyce Technologies release next? It had to be secret, had to stay under wraps, yet all eyes and ears and grubby fingers wanted to pick through every word and communication in hopes of even a hint.

"We don't have a lot in common. I prefer to live my life away from the limelight."

"But you could, if you wanted to, be famous. Like Roxie and Zairn, they're famous for being them and having a good time. And they know the CollCom people, they said it there on *Talk at Sunset*. You could be famous like them."

"I don't want to be famous."

"And Kintyre, it's Zachary, right?" Zane nodded once. "He was famous for a while."

Like it was something easily shrugged off.

"His wife was famous, and he got caught in that trap." Zane kept eating. "He's not sorry to see the back of it."

"People are still interested. Because his wife, his ex-wife, she's having his baby, right?"

"It's not his baby."

Alessia angled her chin like she didn't believe it. "They said that, or Kesley Walsh said it, but she didn't say who the real father is. Most people still think it's his.

If it wasn't, why not just name the actual father and be done with it?"

"It's not their place to do it. That's between Julietta and the father of her child."

"Kesley said it was someone rich and influential. Is he a politician?" Alessia gasped. "Is it the President?"

Couldn't get much more influential than that.

"No," Zane said. "And that's as much as I'm saying."

"But you know, don't you? You know who the father is?"

"Yes." Thank God he was taking this with good humor. Someone more uptight might take offense or start a fight. "And no, I won't tell you."

"Aww," Alessia moaned in disappointment. "That would be a cool thing to know."

"What happened with Lark?" she asked, seizing the opportunity to divert the conversation. Zane smiled at her, right at her, was he grateful? So long as he wasn't pissed or put off by her nosey sister, she'd take what she could get. "You said she'd broken up with her boyfriend."

"Oh, well, yeah, she's got this crazy idea of—well, not exactly crazy, but it's, you know, she wants to find an adventure. Lark said her ex wasn't an adventure, she wasn't even with him because they were mad in love. They were just together. Like some couples get in a rut. If he wants her, he'll prove it, that's what I said."

"Some relationships aren't meant to be," Zane said.

"And if you're in one that's not, there's no point treading water."

"Exactly! You want to be open to other opportunities that might present themselves, other guys. Like on the island, if she'd wanted to get involved, like you did, she had this guy at home holding her back."

Involved like her? There were male staff on the island, and God, she hoped that's what her sister meant. If Lark meant Roman, she wasn't sure they could trust him not to take advantage of every willing woman. When left to his own devices, the guy just charged on in without thinking. Fool.

Though he wasn't the only one. There she was sitting with a man she adored, hoping he saw a tomorrow. Ask. That's all she had to do. This wasn't a passing whatever for her, they'd said they wanted to make a go of it. What did that mean? What did it really mean? Forever, or until they sated their interest? Was this sustainable? Which, of course, took her back to the same point: ask. They needed to have the conversation, someone had to bring it up. Someone needed to take the leap. Ask. Converse. Simple… right?

THIRTY-SIX

SHE AVOIDED IT. Like a coward, for the rest of the week, she let herself be with him, and just enjoyed it. They fell into a rhythm. Neither crowded the other, they had their own space. She wanted him to succeed, and many, many times, he told her he believed in her and whatever she wanted to do. So much that by the Friday, it almost felt like she could lift the whole company up herself. With his support, that might actually be possible.

"I think I have competition," she said.

Zane hung up his cellphone. "No," he said, picking up her hand to kiss her palm. "Sorry, Wanderer, that was rude."

"I didn't mean your phone call."

Though it had gone on for quite a while. Long enough that their chauffeur driven car got them to the airstrip. Not even just the strip, a private jet sat there waiting, like in the movies. He'd said they'd have a flight, and this wasn't close to how she'd imagined it.

The car door opened from the outside and Zane ushered her up the stairs into the sophisticated cream leather interior lined with dark woods and recessed lighting.

He helped her sit and she'd just done her seatbelt when the plane moved.

"You okay?" he asked, maybe noting the surprise in her eyes.

"I've just never… we sat down and then we were moving."

Someone could have control over a plane that way?

He checked his watch. "We're a little behind schedule, but we'll make it up in the air."

She licked her lips. "Are you sure this is okay?"

"What's okay? The plane? It's safe, Wanderer, I'd never—"

"The rehearsal dinner. Technically, I wasn't invited."

"You're my plus one, you are invited."

So just like that she'd have to face everyone in his life in one instantaneous dump of potential in-laws. Was it too soon to think like that? He'd done so well with her family, her sister, now she had to get it right too.

"Alessia's a good sister. A little naïve maybe sometimes, but she has a good heart."

He frowned. "Okay. Where did that come from?"

Nowhere she'd want to admit yet, so she brought the conversation back to them.

"And my competition?" she teased. "How did you get Revland to agree to giving me the afternoon off?"

"There are advantages to knowing a man's alarm codes and security system."

She laughed. "Ah, so it was blackmail."

"He didn't put up a fight." Few people probably did. "You work hard, you deserve this time off."

Though she had just come back from the island the previous weekend. "This time last week, I was on your island." With the time zone mayhem, she didn't want to work out if he'd been there too. "It seems like so long ago."

"You can be there any time you want," he said, resting a hand on her thigh. "You want to go back there after the wedding?"

"For a few hours?" The sand and the ocean would be worth the crazy heavy travel schedule required to get her back to work on Monday morning. "How did you really get Revland to cave?"

"Promised him a call with Mosaic CEO, Xavien Rourke."

"You set that up?"

"Not yet, but I will. Rourke's good at sussing people out and his wife is a mentor by trade. They'll have a lot to talk about." He quickly shifted. "I'm not leading the guy on. If you want me to divert any of our business to—"

"No, I appreciate it. I appreciate everything. This week's been amazing."

"And the month before it?" he said, his loose delight as confident as it should be.

Like it was in control, the conversation seemed to have picked its own moment.

"We haven't talked about this. What comes next. We haven't talked specifics."

"No," he agreed. "We haven't."

"Do you want to… talk… specifics?"

Before he could answer, the door behind them opened. Two men came through with two beauties behind them.

"Do a guy a favor and he doesn't even stop to say hello," the first guy said, slapping his hand to Zane's to shake.

"Thea, this is Xander Gauge and his better half Rainie Tait." The couple sat down across from them. "The other guy's Reid, he doesn't say much, which works best for us because Merci is much more fun."

Everyone said hello and the other pair took their seats on the opposite side.

Zane kissed her hand and slanted closer. "Okay?"

Meeting his friends in smaller doses was definitely better. She showed that by guiding his mouth to hers. People would get lost in the crush at the rehearsal dinner. How would she know who was important and who wasn't?

No, they still hadn't had the conversation, but, hell, this weekend was about his friends coming together in love. This was that couple's time. They'd find theirs when the moment was right.

THIRTY-SEVEN

AT THE HOTEL, they didn't meet anyone else. Didn't check in either. They went straight up to a ready and waiting suite. No word on their bags or special requests. Though there wasn't time to ask too many questions. The dinner would start in an hour and she wasn't that practiced at being glam in an instant.

Coming out of the closet in her dress, she stopped as he turned, framed by the window behind.

"Oh, wow," she whispered.

"I'll say," he said and came over to offer his hand. "You're breathtaking."

"I'm breathtaking?" She ignored the hand to put a few feet between them and appreciate the view again. "You're like, wow!" Sauntering over, she slid a hand up his chest. "Next time we're going formal, factor in a little extra time."

Height eluded her, with her boot, she could only wear flats, or, rather, flat. On her tiptoes, she waited for him to stoop to kiss her. They lingered a second until she dropped back.

"We could be a little late…"

Any other day, she'd take him up on that. "I'm meeting a lot of these people you consider family for the first time. What kind of impression would that give?"

"That you're dedicated to this relationship, and to seizing the moment." After another kiss, he linked their fingers. "Come meet everyone."

Yeah, it was the everyone part that scared her a little. She'd be fine. As a rule, she didn't avoid crowds, but this was important. These people were important to a man who meant the world to her. In the elevator, alone, waiting for the doors to close, this felt like a last chance.

"Zane, I have to—"

"Hold the door!" Zane hit the open button, but a woman squeezed in through the gap before it opened again. "Oh, hey!" The stranger grabbed Zane's lapels and yanked him down to kiss him hard. "You need to stop disappearing."

"Yeah, so I've been told," he said and stepped back to gesture at each of them. "This is—"

"I know who this is," the woman said looking down and then up. "The boot really gives the outfit zing." The doors began to slide closed again. "You should know, I'm considering having an affair with your boyfriend."

"Babycakes," a not so happy male called from outside.

"Just ignore him," the woman said, diverting Zane's hand from the button, so this time the doors closed. "He could use the exercise."

Zane's amusement bloomed. "You're going stag?"

"Now you have two dates," the woman said, taking his other hand to wrap his arm around her.

Oh-kay, this was awkward. Until Zane laughed.

"Before you scare off the woman I love,

introduce yourself, Roux."

Roux?

She quaked. "You're… you're his sister-in-law."

"Minus the Lowe part, yes. We're not related to that side of the family. Maybe we mix it up…" Roux let go of Zane to come around to her other side and link their arms. "Maybe she's the stud today."

Zane squeezed her hand. "And you were worried about your first impression?"

"We're sisters now, get your mind out the gutter," Roux said, then faltered. "Wait, if you're my brother and she's my sister… How in the hell is the world okay with incest by marriage. There's really got to be a better way. Better titles. Better labels."

His sister? "Roux," she said. "You're Roux, Rourke's—"

"I'm not Rourke's anything. He's my something, and damn lucky to be, which I make sure he never forgets." The doors slid open to reveal a guy already waiting for them in the lobby; he crooked a brow. Rourke? "You know I'd be pissed if that wasn't so impressive. How did you do that?"

Leaning in, he grabbed Roux and yanked her out of the elevator and into his body, hard. "The husband is always right."

"Not in this marriage." When he tried to come down for a kiss, Roux jerked back to avoid it. "I already have a date, sleaze."

Linking their arms again, Roux got to moving and Zane let go. He just smiled and gave her a wave when she looked back. Without protest, he and Rourke followed a couple of yards behind.

"Roux, I don't—"

"I'll introduce you to everyone important. You already know Roxie, so you're halfway there. We'll make sure you know every story, who to avoid, who to flirt with, and whose hands wander." She tightened her hold. "There are a few of them in this circle, and it's LA, the kissing thing gives them an in."

"Shouldn't I stay with Zane?"

"If you want," Roux said, leading her down some stairs at the other side of the lobby. "But the guys are boring when they're all together. And knowing their women gets you an in without the need to show cleavage. Okay, that probably wasn't fair to anyone other than my guy."

"I want to get to know people."

"Good, because I've heard you work in my field. Let me tell you, getting Huddle Hope up and running will take more than hard work, you need to believe in it, you need to dedicate yourself to it. Huddle Hope will be the difference so many people need in their lives."

They stopped at a stretch of glass panel doors. Light within and fragrant air beckoned. She couldn't see people yet, but there were definitely rumblings of conversation.

"It means a lot to you. Roxie told me that."

Roux smiled and touched her chin to raise it an inch. "And if you let me talk your ear off about it, it will mean something to you by the end of the night. You've got Roxie's approval, when you're one of her girls, you have a whole posse at your back, ready to stand up for you. You're one of us now, Thea."

One of them. Acceptance by a stranger, maybe not so unfamiliar, but definitely a little strange. If they could accept her on Zane's word, she'd accept them on it too. Clarity gave her relief. These weren't enemies or an obstacle to overcome. If they were Zane's family, they were hers too.

THIRTY-EIGHT

THE DINNER ERASED all her fears. Most of the night was spent with Roxie and the gang of women she called her girls. It didn't seem there was an entrance requirement or initiation. Roxie accepted everyone, helped everyone, and never hesitated to talk to, and accept, anyone.

Jane was maid of honor. Roxie was a bridesmaid. Apparently, given Roxie would be godmother to the baby Lilya carried, Jane got the top spot in the bridal party. Weddings meant more to her too, so it wasn't a big deal.

Hilarity came in the line of groomsmen, because there were more than a few, including her guy and Roux's. The latter woman sat next to her, holding her hand, swooning in time as the little flower girl and ring bearer came down the aisle. Jane was quick to gesture them over and help the little ones find their spots in the front row, next to their mother, Rylee, who she'd met the previous night.

She wasn't supposed to, no one probably was,

but she caught the wink Jane got from her guy, standing opposite. Love radiated from everywhere up there. No doubt some people were uncomfortable, maybe some questioned their own life choices.

Her gaze drifted down the line of groomsmen as the Wedding March began. Everyone was supposed to be watching the bride. Apparently, etiquette passed Zane by. His smile provoked hers; as his faded, something else took over his expression. She tried to figure it out, but they were distracted by Lilya progressing to Zachary Kintyre at the altar.

This was a hotel ballroom, not a church. Lilya's first marriage. Kintyre's second. The baby was a first for both of them. Witnessing them exchange vows and their deep sincerity, really showed how when life came together, there was a peace that came with it, a certainty. She'd known these people less than a day and already felt invested in their future. Would she be there to see it?

With all the couples she'd met, and stories she'd heard, there was a good chance of other weddings taking place or babies being born. And there was Zane, gorgeous in profile, watching his friend dive into this life choice, this decision to share his life with the mother of his soon-to-be child.

There would be parties, birthdays, anniversaries, receptions, and these people would come together again. Not "these," but "they." They would come together again. She'd stick through the hard times, not just the easy ones. It wasn't all island living and high-class hotels. They were people, all of them, and regardless of economic status, their hardships and choices were as valid as anyone else's.

And that was it.

Right there.

Choice.

Lilya and Zach decided to be together. To have a baby. To get married. To have a future. Together. Like Roxie and Zairn, Roux and Rourke. It wasn't happenstance, they didn't fall into these relationships. Each of them made a decision to stick with it, to fight for it, to make their love a priority.

And that was it. All she had to do was choose what she wanted her life to be. Did she want it to continue unchanged without Zane? No. She didn't. He was what she wanted.

After the amorous kiss, the music started again. The newlyweds departed down the aisle together, others crowded from their seats to follow.

Before Roux could move, she tightened her grip on her hand. "Did you mean it?"

"Mean what?" Roux asked.

"Last night, everything you said about—"

"Welcoming you to Huddle Hope? Absolutely! You can't get a recommendation better than Roxie's in my eyes."

"And if Zane doesn't—"

"Fuck him," Roux said, jutting up her own chin, prompting her to reciprocate with similar pride. "We're the power." A whistle brought Roux around and there was Rourke at the end of the row. "Did you just whistle at me?"

"To any bitches listening, I guess your ears are good."

"Tell you what else I'm good at?" Roux said, shuffling to the aisle, hand still locked in hers. "Signing divorce papers."

"Oh, ho," he said, tossing his head back as he laughed. "Christmas has come early this year."

"Not that it matters to you. Naughty boys get nothing."

Zane approached. Roux let go when Rourke

yanked her against him and backed up, separating them to nuzzle at his wife.

"They're full on," Zane said.

"It's love, right?"

The couple disappeared behind a curtain. She wasn't all that sure anyone wanted to know what happened back there.

"Are you okay?" her guy asked.

"Am I…?"

"There will be some pictures and then—"

"I don't want to go back."

"What?"

The words came from her mouth, yet she hadn't processed their full power. The confusion on his face matched the sound echoing in her ears. No, her mind was one hundred percent certain.

"I don't want to go back," she said, taking his hand. "I want to work with Roux, with Roxie, I want to build something with them, something that matters."

"The—"

"I am not rushing our relationship or expecting anything from us." Though she wanted to do just that. "Roux said I can stay in the employee apartments."

"Babe, my house is your house, everything that's mine is yours. This is what I want. I want you to live with me, for us to be together. I've been trying to bring it up… No, I haven't tried. It's been on my mind." Like it had been on hers. "This is a big decision; I want you to be sure. It's moving away from Alessia and your mom, away from your work—"

"My work is meaningless. When I look at what Roux and Roxie have built, everything you've built, you matter to this, and your group, you matter to each other. Think of the time I spent working on the island." Might have been frequent but wasn't half as hard as it should've been. "I took time away from us, and stressed that what I'd done wasn't good enough, and then what? Anika didn't even look at it, the project was pointless, it went nowhere. That might be no big deal any other day of the week, but that was time I took from you, from us. If I'd known how it would work out, I'd have locked myself away with you and never thought of work."

"If you work here, it will matter. This is a sensitive field and Roux is steadfast. She screws around with Rourke, but Huddle Hope is deeply personal to her."

"I know. She explained it to me. We've talked a little and…" The adrenaline felt right, she felt right, like nothing she'd done before in her life was even close to right compared to this. "She offered me a job and I'm going to take it."

That was it. Decision made. She'd have to call Alessia, pack up her apartment… Starting a new venture might be a daunting prospect, but she had support in Zane and wanted to be a support to Roux. In New York, Roxie had plenty of people around her. Roux was on her own with only her antagonistic husband. Lilya zipped back and forth; a lot of parts were in perpetual motion.

On the Dyce-Mosaic compound, Roux could hire help, but she could be more than just another employee. Huddle Hope was something real, Zane was right about that. Why wouldn't she want to be a part of something that could come to mean so much to so many?

"Are you certain?" He needed reassurance. Vehement, her eyes stayed on his when she nodded. "Forever wasn't out on the ocean, it didn't hide behind the horizon."

"It's right here. I see it now."

Another second passed then a grin burst his expression. "We've got a lot of work to do."

Pulling her hard against him, he hugged her tight, releasing just a second later to grab her head and land his mouth on hers.

Of all the reactions he might have had… She didn't think he'd be angry or upset, but this elation… Oh, God, fate was blessing her for something amazing she must've done in a past life.

One kiss and… forever.

She'd looked out on the ocean and wondered at all the possibilities. In response, it delivered her this incredible man, her incredible man. This was forever, everything about it was right. She needed to scrunch her toes in some sand and scream out her gratitude as soon as possible. But with him, Zane Dyce, her driftwood, anything was possible.

Read more from the Roxiverse in *Nothing to No One...*

Thank you for reading this tale!
If you can, please take the time to review.

~

Ask your local library for more Scarlett Finn novels!

~

For all things Scarlett Finn
check out:

www.scarlettfinn.com

Next in the
Roxiverse:

SCARLETT FINN